There You'll Find Me

Other Novels by Jenny B. Jones

Just Between You and Me

Save the Date

YOUNG ADULT NOVELS

The Charmed Life Series

So Not Happening
I'm So Sure
So Over My Head

There You'll Find Me

Jenny B. Jones

THOMAS NELSON
Since 1798

NASHVILLE   DALLAS   MEXICO CITY   RIO DE JANEIRO

Published in Nashville, Tennessee, by Thomas Nelson. Thomas Nelson is a registered trademark of Thomas Nelson, Inc.

Thomas Nelson, Inc., titles may be purchased in bulk for educational, business, fund-raising, or sales promotional use. For information, please e-mail SpecialMarkets@ThomasNelson.com.

Scripture quotations are taken from the King James Version of the Bible and the HOLMAN CHRISTIAN STANDARD BIBLE. © 1999, 2000, 2002, 2003 by Broadman and Holman Publishers. All rights reserved.

Publisher's Note: This novel is a work of fiction. Names, characters, places, and incidents are either products of the author's imagination or used fictitiously. All characters are fictional, and any similarity to people living or dead is purely coincidental.

Library of Congress Cataloging-in-Publication Data

Jones, Jenny B., 1975–
  There you'll find me / Jenny B. Jones.
    p. cm.
  Summary: Eighteen-year-old Finley, seeking God, quiet time to prepare for an audition at a prestigious music conservatory, and knowledge of the land her deceased brother loved, spends senior year in Ireland, where teen movie idol Beckett Rush, equally troubled, desires her company.
  ISBN 978-1-59554-540-4 (soft cover)
  [1. Celebrities—Fiction. 2. Actors and actresses—Fiction. 3. Grief--Fiction. 4. God—Fiction. 5. Foreign study—Fiction. 6. Diaries—Fiction. 7. Ireland--Fiction.] I. Title. II. Title: There you will find me.
  PZ7.J720313The 2011
  [Fic]—dc23   2011025477

Printed in the United States of America

13 14 QG 6 5 4 3 2

~~~~~~~~~~~~~~~~~~~~~~~~~~~

Like Finley, this year I unexpectedly lost a member of my family, my stepdad. He left us just a few months before he would've seen his dedication. I'm so grateful for his impact on my life. He taught me to appreciate food—a little too well. He was chili at the stove, food delivered to my door on deadline, Mark Twain quotes, house disaster calls at 3 a.m., one-liners, and intelligence. He would've walked through fire for me, then brought me back some clever souvenir. He was one of my biggest supporters and my friend. I loved him for the dad he didn't have to be. But was.

So I'll just pretend it's not too late, and he can read this. To quote John Mayer, "Say what you need to say."

This book is lovingly dedicated to Kent Hughes. Long ago you took on two kids when a new Labrador would've been easier. Thank you for all you've done for me, from fixing my toilet to encouraging my career. If I had to count each favor, it would be in the billions. And we both know if I count past a thousand, I get a little confused.

~~~~~~~~~~~~~~~~~~~~~~~~~~~

Look for yourself, and you will find in the long run only hatred, loneliness, despair, rage, ruin, and decay. But look for Christ, and you will find Him, and with Him everything else thrown in.

—C. S. Lewis, *Mere Christianity*

Prologue

Sometimes I think about when I was little, and my older brothers would take me out to fly kites.

"Give it some slack!" Will would yell.

It was almost painful to watch, that kite of mine.

Tethered to the string in my hand. Dancing in the sky all alone.

My breath caught in my throat, my pulse beating wild and crazy in my chest. My heart soaring with every dip and turn of the kite, as if I were flying along, instead of standing with my two feet on the ground, squinting against the sun to see the dance.

What if it fell?

What if the breeze took it away?

I counted the seconds until I could reel it back in.

I was that kite.

Fragile against the wind. Soaring one minute. Spiraling straight down the next. Just looking for something to hold me up.

Before I spun out of control and flew away.

Disappearing from sight.

Chapter One

~~~~~~~~~~~

*I'm on my way to Ireland! I've pretty much lost a
whole night's sleep on the plane, but who cares?
Great things are waiting for me. I know it.*

—Travel Journal of Will Sinclair, Abbeyglen, Ireland

~~~~~~~~~~~

Miss?"

I pulled out an earbud as the flight attendant leaned over me. "Yes?"

"We have a few seats available in first class. Would you like to have one of them?"

Seats like recliners, meals that didn't taste like burned Lean Cuisines, and no guy in front of me leaned back 'til he was in my lap? "Yes, please."

I grabbed my backpack and followed the woman through the narrow aisle, dodging two ladies on their way to the bathroom.

Five more hours of the flight to Shannon, Ireland. I couldn't get there fast enough. But a cushy seat would surely help pass the time.

"Here we go." She smiled widely, and her eyes brimmed with an excessive amount of enthusiasm for a good deed she surely did every day.

Thanking the flight attendant, I slipped into the seat, the leather crunching beneath me, and set my backpack at my feet.

"Have fun," she said.

Have fun?

I glanced at the guy beside me. He leaned against the wall, his head propped into his hand, a Colts hat covering his head and shielding his eyes from view. From the stillness of his body, he had to be asleep.

I settled in, pulled out my travel pillow, zipped up my hoodie, and burrowed. Reaching for the newspaper, I opened to the second page, where the article from the front left off.

. . . The latest bombing in Iraq has been claimed by terrorist Hassan Al Farran, ringleader of the al Qaeda cell thought to be responsible for the deadly blast in Afghanistan that killed a schoolhouse of children, as well as CNN correspondent and humanitarian Will Sinclair, son of hotel magnate Marcus Sinclair. On the Most Wanted list, Al Farran is number four in command in the Taliban and continues to elude capture.

As the familiar churning began in my stomach, I took a few deep breaths. One day the pain wouldn't be as fresh as if the loss of my brother had just happened. Instead of two years ago. My counselor said I should've been past the anger stage. But I wasn't.

But on October twentieth, perhaps I would be.

I continued to read the article, but it provided no new information, and soon the words swam and blurred until I finally had to close my eyes and rest for just a bit in the dimmed lights of the plane.

⤙⤚

"The captain has turned on the Fasten Seat Belt sign. Please remain in your seats and refrain from moving about the cabin."

Somewhere in the fog of my sleepy brain, the flight attendant's voice registered, but I couldn't seem to pull myself to the surface. So tired. And warm. And comfy.

"Sir, your friend needs to put her seat belt on."

"As much as I like a lovely girl leaning on my shoulder," a lilting voice whispered near my ear, "I think you might want to listen to the flight attendant."

My head lifted with a jerk as the plane shuddered. "What?" *Where am I? What time is it?*

The boy beside me laughed, and after I blinked a few times, I saw him more clearly.

Snapping myself in, my cheeks warmed. "Was I just—"

"Sleeping on me?" He nodded his head, his blond hair peeping out from his cap. "Yeah."

"And did I—"

"Drool?" His voice carried a hint of Ireland. "Not much."

Gray eyes. Chiseled cheekbones. A grin that revealed a dimple. A voice low enough to send chills along my aching neck. A smile that would send most teen girls into a squealing fit of adoration and hyperventilation.

"Oh my gosh—"

"*Shhh.*" He pressed one finger to his lips. "Don't say a word. I've gotten this far without being bothered."

"Beckett Rush."

He flashed that million-dollar grin again. The one that earned this nineteen-year-old the lead role as the darkly romantic Steele Markov in a franchise of films such as *Vampire Boarding School* and *Friday Night Bites.*

"If you stay mum about this, I'll give you an autograph." He leaned close. "But you should know I've given up signing body parts."

I blinked twice, my mouth open in an O.

"I know, it's shocking," he said. "I guess the flight attendant thought she was doing you a favor sitting you next to me, but—"

"I don't want your autograph," I finally managed.

Beckett tilted his head and flashed those gunmetal grays. "Okay. One picture. But later. After we land, and I've had my breakfast."

"I don't want your picture either." I scooted away from his seat. "The last thing I want, Mr. Hollywood Party Boy, is to be photographed with you, where it will surely land in some trash magazine. As if I need any more of *that.*"

His frown was the first genuine facial expression I'd witnessed. No doubt, Beckett Rush was not used to anything but fawning and fainting from teenage girls. *And* their mothers.

"Have we met?" he asked.

"No." Digging into my backpack, I pulled out a magazine and flipped past the glossy cover. None of the girls looked like me. They were all rail thin, unlike my size nine. Scrawny legs, where my own were muscular from years of cheerleading. And their hair displayed artful compositions of chaos and grace, while my long, dark locks were stuffed into a messy bun on top of my head after an endless day of travel.

"Are you sure, so?"

"Quite." Returning the magazine to my bag, I retrieved the sheet music I'd been working on for weeks. My audition piece.

"Because now that I get a good look at you, you seem familiar."

I swiped my fingers through my brunette bangs until they offered a little coverage. "I have one of those faces."

"And you've certainly a strong dislike of me." I could feel his eyes study me as I reread the first eight measures. "As if I've done something to you."

"You have not."

"Then—"

"It's your type," I said, without looking up. "I know your type."

"Well now, that's interesting."

His cologne filtered my way and clung to my shirt where I'd fallen asleep against him. I probably had crease marks on my face from his shoulder. How embarrassing.

"Did you have a good nap, then?"

Boys like him were only after one thing. And I was done with him and his entire species. "Fine. Thank you."

"Since we've established who I am . . ." He lifted a blond brow when I didn't respond. "The next line is where you tell me your name. I think if you're going to drool on me, we should at least be on a first-name basis."

I sighed and looked toward the window where I saw nothing but dark sky.

"You look like a Myrtle to me," he said to himself. "Maybe a Mavis. But I could be wrong."

"Finley." I tried to rearrange my mussed hair with my fingers. "Finley Sinclair."

Silence. Then his eyes widened. "Of the hotel fame?"

Here we go. "My dad might own a hotel or two."

"One or two *thousand*." And then new understanding dawned. "You've had quite a year. I think I saw you on the cover of *People* some months back. 'Hotel heiress sneaks into club and parties the night away.'"

"That was last spring." And I had worked my tail off making amends, getting away from what my dad had called my crazy season. Thank goodness any small amount of notoriety I had did not extend to foreign countries. I would start over with a clean slate. "The article was grossly exaggerated, and I'm sorry I took a photo op away from you. But don't worry, your Wild Child title is safe. I don't want it." Not anymore, though you couldn't tell it from my list of escapades last year. And I was done associating with people like Beckett, or my ex-boyfriend, who just wanted to have a good time and didn't care about the costs.

I didn't miss the flash of Beckett's eyes before his amiable mask returned. "Since you're not a member of my fan club, let's talk about something else," he said. "A safer topic perhaps. What brings you to Ireland?"

Years of manners drilled into me made it impossible to totally ignore him. But I wished I were still asleep, blissfully unaware of the choppy skies or whom I was sitting next to. "I'm going to Abbeyglen. Foreign exchange program." And I was two weeks overdue. Instead of leaving last month like I was supposed to, I had opted for an orchestra camp instead. Now I would arrive mere days before school began.

My body jolted as we hit another air pocket.

"So your parents wanted you out of the country."

"It was my choice, actually. My brother Will came here for his senior year and I wanted to do the same. I hope to see every place he went." I thought of his travel journal in my backpack, sandwiched between a romance novel and *Seventeen*. And Will's violin, stowed in the front of the plane, the one I would use to get into the New York Conservatory. I'd stay in Abbeyglen through March, then go back to Charleston and graduate with my class. Just enough time to soak up the culture, buy my parents some souvenirs, and totally change my life.

Beckett put his elbow on my armrest and leaned my way. "I'm sorry about your brother."

"How did you know about Will?"

"What happened to him got the whole world's attention. I've already read two scripts based on your brother's life."

Anger had a stranglehold on my throat, and I considered pulling down one of those masks until the black spots went away. "Will's life was more than some Hollywood opportunity." How dare they commercialize the event that ripped my family in two? I'd seen enough of the real video footage to last me the rest of my days.

"I know that must've been hard."

"Thank you," I finally said. "Life can be hard. In the real world." What did Mr. Vampire know of difficulties? He lived in a magical palace where girls threw him rose petals and their never-ending loyalty. His movies' opening-night revenues could build a hundred of the schools in Afghanistan my brother had worked so hard for.

His smile was a slow lift of the lips. "Just a piece of advice. You might want to brush up on your people skills if you're going to make it in Abbeyglen. The Irish are some of the nicest folks on earth, to be sure. They won't take kindly to your surly attitude and sullen looks." Beckett's eyes took a lazy stroll over my face. "Pretty though those looks might be."

The boy was unreal. "Does that seriously work on girls?"

"Yes." He scratched his chin as he contemplated this. "Yes, it does."

I delicately cleared my throat and studied my nails. "Did absolutely nothing for me."

"Interesting. I guess there's a first time for everything." He shrugged. "So you don't care to sit by me. And you don't want my autograph. What is it you do want, Finley Sinclair?"

Some peace. Some healing. To hear God's voice again.

I wanted to find my brother's Ireland. To put it into song.

And I wanted my heart back.

"I'll know it when I find it." I looked past Beckett and into the night sky. "Or when it finds me."

Chapter Two

Call when you arrive. You know how your
mother worries. And be careful of strangers.
Can't trust anyone these days.
—Dad

Sent to my BlackBerry

I f I never got on a plane again, it would be too soon. All I
wanted to do was crash into a bed and stretch out my tired
body until I passed out into sleepy bliss.

After some unsuccessful small talk, Beckett and I spent the
remaining hours alternating between sleeping and ignoring one
another. Just when I had started to feel badly and thought to
attempt some kindness and genuine conversation, I opened a new
OK! magazine, only to be greeted by an article about the movie star
beside me and his wild night in Los Angeles weeks ago. A yelling
match with his producer. Dinner at Spago with three blond starlets.
A hotel room carelessly trashed.

So I watched one of the in-flight movies instead.

"Enjoy your stay in Abbeyglen." Beckett Rush grabbed his bag from the overhead bin as the passengers in front of us shuffled to the exit.

"Thank you." I hitched my backpack tighter and finally met his laughing eyes. "Nice to meet you." My voice was flat as my wilted hair.

Those full lips quirked. "Right. And you as well, Felicity."

"It's *Finley.*"

"I had a grand time sitting beside you." His accent made his words sound almost sincere.

"Uh-huh." I stepped into the aisle, grateful to be minutes from escape.

"Who knows?" he said. "We might run into each other again. Our paths might cross. Our circles might intersect."

I turned away from my inspection of the slow-moving woman in front of me and stared at this arrogant boy. "Pretty sure I don't hang out in the same circles as you."

"That's not what the tabloids say."

"My party days are over." My look dismissed him from the top of his Colts cap to his designer shoes. "A temporary lapse of judgment for me. Not something I want to make a career of."

"A little fun never hurt anyone. In fact, it pays my bills."

"There are more important things to care about." Like my audition. I wouldn't blow it again.

Beckett stared for one second before he threw his head back and laughed. "You take care of yourself, *Frances.* I hope you find just what you need in Ireland. And maybe even . . . a little fun."

"My name is—" I snapped my lips together. Never mind. The boy was an actor. Not a rocket scientist. Clearly he wasn't blessed with an ample amount of brain cells. Just stunningly good looks. And a voice that could charm a weaker girl into handing over her purity ring with one syllable.

The line in front of me finally moved. Two teenage girls ahead turned and gawked at Beckett.

"Is that—"

"Could it be him?"

"It's not," I said loud enough for them to hear. "Just his body double. Not nearly as cute." I lowered my voice to a stage whisper. "And a little s-l-o-w, if you take my meaning."

Leaving Beckett Rush behind forever, I grabbed my beloved violin, then followed the line that emptied into the Shannon airport. Stepping out of the traffic of busy travelers, I called home. My mom's sleepy voice answered on the fourth ring.

"I made it."

"Good to hear your voice." I heard a rustle of blankets and my dad mumbling in the background. It was ten p.m. there, and my parents were early birds. "Your father said he loves you and to call him later."

"Did he just roll over and go back to sleep?"

"The man sleeps through hurricanes." My mom yawned. "Now, Finley, don't forget what your counselor said."

"I know." Would I ever outrun my past? "I'll call her if I get stressed or overwhelmed."

"Or if those feelings start to come over you again."

"I've been okay for six months, Mom." No anxiety meds, no more depression talk. "You promised you wouldn't push."

"We love you. We just want you to take care of yourself. It's been a long haul for you, and I don't want anything to mess it up."

"I have to go. The O'Callaghans are probably waiting."

"I miss you already."

"Talk to you soon."

"Stay away from the black pudding."

"Mother—"

"And don't ride your bicycle on the wrong side of the road."

Ten minutes later I made it to baggage claim, where the machine gave a mighty groan and bags began to file out like weary soldiers. It was a long, tiring wait before I saw mine appear.

"Excuse me." I tried to step past a large gentleman standing in the way. "Sir, if I could just—" No! There went my suitcases. Using a little more elbow than manners, I nudged by the man and reached for the handle of my bag. I wrenched one off the belt and made a grab for the other. "Sir, would you mind grabbing that?" Fatigue pounded into me like a high tide. I swiped for the bag again, my fingers making contact. But couldn't keep hold.

I moved back and took a seat on the floor, knowing I'd have to wait 'til it came around again. So tired. And hungry. And smelly. And in need of caffeine.

Lord, I do not want to sit down and bawl right here in the middle of the airport.

"I believe this is yours?"

I looked up and saw Beckett Rush standing over me, my rogue suitcase beside him.

The guy could've put somebody into a trance with those eyes. "How did you know that was mine?"

"I just got a hunch." His arrogant smile quirked on his lips. "Like when I saw you nearly swan dive onto the conveyer belt."

"Your vampire instincts are uncanny." My fingers brushed his as I pulled my suitcase to me, my face burning at the sight of his smirk. "Thank you."

"Welcome to Ireland, Fiona Sinclair." And with that, Beckett Rush dismissed me and walked away.

I probably should've gotten his autograph.

And sold it on eBay.

Wearily tugging my stuff, I might as well have been dragging a mountain. I finally made it to the reception area and searched the small crowd for a redheaded girl with large brown eyes that matched the picture on my phone.

"Finley?"

Exhausted and hopeful, I turned at the voice.

A teenage girl stood behind me, eyes bright and smile wide. "You are Finley!" She crushed me to her, and my arms wrapped around her thin frame. She couldn't be any more than a size two, standing a head shorter than my five-eight. "I'd recognize you anywhere. You look just like your picture!"

I hugged the girl and laughed. "I guess you're Erin." At least I hoped she was my host sister. Otherwise, this was way too much PDA.

"Did you have yourself a good trip?" she asked.

Across the way I saw Beckett surrounded by what must've been his entourage. "A little turbulence."

"Come meet my family." I followed her to a smiling trio. "This is my mam, Nora. My dad, Sean."

"Very fine to meet you," Nora said. She gave me a light hug, and I shook Sean's hand. Erin's parents reminded me of the Jack Spratt nursery rhyme. Her mom was just as short and plump as her father was tall and thin. They all looked very perky for three in the morning.

"And this is Liam," Erin said with less enthusiasm.

"I'm twelve." His chestnut hair matched his father's, one shade darker than my own brown wavy locks. "But I'm mature for my age. In case you felt like dating a younger man."

"Mature?" Erin snorted. "You still play with Legos."

"Just practicing for my future in engineering." His voice cracked in an unintended squeak. "Mam says one day girls are gonna fall for my intelligence." Liam wiggled those brows toward me. "Better get me while I'm still available."

"Don't scare her away, dear." Nora pulled her son to her side. "He imagines himself a little Romeo, this one does."

Erin eyed her brother. "And you know what happened to Romeo."

As Sean drove, the family took turns pelting me with questions and throwing out random tidbits about each one of them. I wanted to tell them my brain had turned to mush hours ago, but I just smiled and nodded instead.

"We inherited a bed-and-breakfast," Erin said as one topic crashed into another. "It's a lot of work, but quite fun to live in. My father just retired from the army, and now he's unclogging toilets and burning scones. Show Finley your hand, Dad." She laughed as we cruised down the road. "Mam has to bandage a new wound every day."

"At one time in my life, didn't I dodge mortar fire for a living?" Sean O'Callaghan navigated the car on the roundabout. "Now I take hits wearing an apron and making jam."

"And a right fine job you're doing too." Nora patted her husband's arm and sent a wink to us in the backseat.

The busy intersecting highways finally lost their American big-city appearance and gave way to fields, too dark to see. My chest filled with an empty ache as I tried to imagine the beauty hidden by the night. In the daytime, I knew the meadows would be as green as though Photoshopped by God, like in my brother's pictures. We sailed by a farm with what looked like the remains of a castle tower just sitting out by the fence, and I leaned past Erin's brother to get a closer view.

"They're all over the place," Erin said. "Just some ruins. We have one on our property."

"It looks like a princess used to live there," I said, more to myself than to anyone else. "Maybe she was besieged by an angry dragon. And one day her prince finally came to save her."

Sitting beside me, Liam patted my hand. "I'll save you anytime, Finley."

I'd had too many moments when I had needed saving. But I wanted those to be over. This stay in Ireland marked that new beginning. No more trouble. No more desperate mistakes.

And definitely, no more drama.

❧

"Here we are!"

Following Erin, I slid out of the car with my heavy limbs and took in my temporary home, aided by the lights of the small parking lot.

The house perched on a hill as if it were spying on the town below. Cobalt-blue shutters popped against the cream-colored wooden siding. A flower box sat beneath each window with blooms and greenery spilling out over the edges. It all beckoned me to come inside and be happy.

"Give us your violin, so." Liam reached for the case I was holding.

"It's no trouble." I didn't trust it in anyone else's hands. Will had gotten the instrument in junior high. He hadn't stuck with it, but he'd given it to me when I was in fourth grade, and I would've run into a burning house for my violin.

Walking across the front step, I had to sidestep a faithful chocolate Lab that sat on guard duty, wagging its tail.

"Cute dog." I petted the soft, smooth head.

"That's Bob." Erin opened the door. "He's just a visitor, that one is."

Sean and Liam took my things upstairs as Erin and her mom showed me around.

"This is the living quarters," Nora said. "On the other side of the kitchen is the guests' part of the house."

"The good part," Erin said. "The part that doesn't have a leaky roof."

The home was cozy, yet large, filled with three bedrooms, a living room, a gigantic kitchen, and a breakfast nook where a scarred oak table was snugly tucked in the corner. It looked like it'd been through many meals, but I couldn't find a speck of dust, and I knew my dad would approve of that. A family lived here. One who didn't have to share the space with sadness and regret.

"Take her upstairs and show her where she's staying." Nora O'Callaghan gave my back a motherly pat. "I'll have a nice, big breakfast ready when you wake up."

Erin and I climbed the oak steps, my shoes landing on wood worn until the shine had dulled. Walking behind Erin, I noticed the cut of her jeans. The familiar style of her gray sweater. I didn't know what I expected, but every Irish person I'd seen so far had been dressed like the average American. Erin's outfit could've come from the mall back home.

On the second floor, Erin showed me her brother's room, where robotic sounds drifted through the closed door. "I'd advise you to stay as far away from Liam's room as possible." Her heart-shaped face scrunched. "It smells like feet."

We peeked into Erin's room, which was two doors down. The yellow walls were a natural match to her personality.

"My mam thought you'd prefer the room we fixed up in the attic. She said you'd want your own space where you could practice undisturbed. Can't hear a thing from up there. So to the top floor we go."

The stairs steepened and narrowed, and my tired body struggled with every move. When I hit the top, moonlight streamed through a window as big as the O'Callaghans' car.

"It's said the daughter of the original owner of Birch Hill House would climb up here and keep lookout for her fiancé, a seaman." Erin stood before the window, a smile playing about her lips. "One time he was scheduled to return, and she took her post. And she waited and waited." Her voice dropped to a sad whisper. "After two weeks of doing nothing but staring out toward the ocean, she finally had to accept the cold truth."

I looked toward the horizon where I knew the ocean lay. "His boat had dashed against the rocks, plunging him to a watery grave, never to return?"

"No." Erin blinked. "That he had horrible navigation sense and would have to be a cobbler like his father if he expected to ever be her mister." She eyed me warily. "You're a wee bit dark, aren't you?"

Before I could answer, Erin did a happy spin before the window, her red ponytail swishing the air. "I think Abbeyglen will be exactly what you need. You're going to love it here."

"I hope so." I smiled at her enthusiasm. "I'm certainly going to try."

"Good night, then. I know you're exhausted, so I'll quit talking and let you get some rest." She hugged me again and tiptoed out, leaving me to stand there contemplating the same window, the same vast darkness beyond it.

God, my brother felt your presence so strongly here in Ireland. Will you be here for me?

But, as usual, there was no answer. There hadn't been in some time.

After brushing my teeth, I found Mrs. O'Callaghan had turned down my bed, and on a small table beside my pillow burned a lamp, the only light in the room. I unpacked, placing my pants, all perfectly folded, in drawers. I hung my shirts and skirts by color on a clothes rack, then went about lining up my shoes, adjusting their angles until each was symmetrical to its mate and peace settled in my mind.

For the moment.

I flopped onto the bed, not even bothering to change into my PJs, and grabbed my backpack, pulling out my brother's travel journal.

As Handel softly streamed from my laptop, I gave into the pull to rub my hand over the soft leather cover of the book, then opened to the first page and saw Will's familiar handwriting. The loop of his upper case, the dips of his lower.

Travel Journal of Will Sinclair
Foreign Exchange Program
Abbeyglen, Ireland

Mom had given me the journal after my brother's memorial. Two days later the call came confirming my acceptance into the program to study abroad. Same country. Same town. Will had loved it here, even returned a few times.

After I got the placement, I knew—my audition song would

be for Will. For his Ireland. So far my composition was inspired by every picture in his journal. Except I lacked an ending.

Though I had the first page of his journal memorized, I read the words again.

Arrived in Abbeyglen. I'm excited to look at it all. Do it all.
This place is awesome.

It was the last page that plagued me. The travelogue was filled with journal entries and a few photos, each one meticulously explained. But toward the back, pressed into the center of the paper, was a picture of a single cross gravestone. No explanation. No commentary. I wanted to see every single spot my brother did. Feel what he felt. Feel . . . something. I would set foot on each landmark Will had and see it with my eyes and my brother's words. And when I found that Celtic cross, I knew I'd have what I needed to write the finale to my audition piece.

And perhaps I'd find Will at each of the stops. As each day passed, my grief over him seemed to widen, but my memories of him only lessened. And that couldn't happen. I wasn't going to let it.

My weary eyes drifted to the final sentence in his first entry.

God, I see you in everything.

I shut the book. Turned out the light.
I, too, wanted this place to be awesome.
But God?
I couldn't see him anywhere.

Chapter Three

- Two eggs, 200 calories
- One glass of orange juice, 110 calories
- One slice of something similar to bacon, approximately 2 grams of fat

My ability to rattle off nutritional information was one of my few talents, learned when I'd need to lose some quick weight each year for cheerleading tryouts. I couldn't remember a single math formula, but the nutritional breakdown of a chalupa? Embedded forever.

On Monday morning, I sat in the breakfast nook with Liam and Erin. The sun streamed in through the bay window as I took a drink of juice and watched Sean and Nora buzz about the kitchen, cooking for their guests as if they were in a race. Still jet-lagged, it made me tired just watching them.

"Sean, hand us that toast." Nora zipped past her husband, doing three tasks at once. "Finley, I'm sorry we didn't get out and about this weekend. It's a busy season here at the B and B, but as soon as things calm down, we'll take you to some good places."

"Like the stalactite cave," Liam said. "It's dark and creepy. And kinda drippy."

"Your brain's drippy," Erin said. "Mam meant the really important places."

"There are some I'd like to see soon." I thought of the pictures in my brother's journal. "Like the Cliffs of Moher."

"Beautiful spot near Doolin," Sean said from the stove. "Not too far, so."

The O'Callaghans were kind enough to give me the grand tour of Abbeyglen this weekend, but the demands of their inn didn't allow for too much time away. I hated being without a car. If I had my own transportation, I'd have just driven myself. But even Erin didn't have a car. She said hardly any of the teens did. Such strange torture.

"Are you nervous about school?" Erin asked.

"A little." Who wouldn't be? I'd been at the same private school all my life. And now I was going to an all-girls Catholic school. What if the girls at Sacred Heart didn't like me? What if they made fun of my Southern twang? What if I didn't catch on to their Catholic school ways? What if this uniform skirt cut off my air supply?

"Here's the plate for table six," Sean said. "French toast, eggs, and fruit."

"Young man." Nora peeked beneath the table at her son's feet. "Where is your other sock?"

Liam shrugged. "I could only find one."

"We have to leave in fifteen minutes. Go find it."

"I looked." Liam's pubescent whine came out like the honk of a flat horn.

"Och, the first day of school always affects him like this." Nora grabbed her son by the arm. "Let's go. I have a feeling you didn't look too hard."

Sean nudged an egg in the skillet. "Can someone take this plate out?"

"I will," Erin said.

"No!" Nora stopped, her foot poised on the first step. "Not after last time you won't." Her kind eyes turned to me. "Would you mind?" She jerked her highlighted pixie head toward Erin. "This one can't be trusted. Last time she served a guest breakfast, we found her thirty minutes later, sitting at the table rattling on about her earthworm collection."

Erin bit into a piece of sausage. "I like to share my passion for science."

"Our guests do not want to hear about worm droppings at the breakfast table." She gave Liam a small push. "Go on with you."

"Table in the corner by the fireplace." Sean handed the plate to me, then adjusted the strap of his ruffled apron. "Did I mention I used to ride in a tank for a living?"

Pushing the door open with my shoulder, I walked into the dining room where six tables draped in white cloths filled the space. At eight o'clock, only four of the guests dined, and their low chatter bounced off the hardwood floors.

The guest in the corner sat toward the fireplace with his back to me, a book in one hand, a cup of tea in the other.

"Here you go." I placed the warm food on the table.

And got a look at his face.

"You."

Beckett Rush lifted his head and smiled. "Good morning t'you, as well." He put down his book and glanced at his plate. "You didn't spit on me toast, did you now?"

"You're staying here?"

"I am."

"Here? At Birch Hill House? In one of these rooms? At this B and B?"

Beckett grinned at my babbling. "Don't you go getting any ideas about stealing the spare key and sneaking into my room." He covered his mouth in a whisper. "The innkeepers' daughter already tried it."

Of all the host families to stay with, I was residing with the one housing Beckett Rush. Unreal.

"Since I'm here for a while working on a movie, I guess we'll be seeing each other around." He picked up his syrup and poured a whorl of it over his plate. "Only in Ireland for a few days, and you've already found your pot of gold."

This was the O'Callaghan's customer. I couldn't snark off to him. I couldn't.

Oh, but I wanted to. What was it about this guy that had me itching to bare my claws?

I somehow managed to unclench my teeth. "Have a nice day."

He pierced a bite with his fork. "Dream about me while you're at school."

"Would that be with or without your false teeth?"

He gave me a slow wink. "They're fangs."

"Kind of sad you have to use props to get the girls."

"It's absolutely tragic, isn't it?" His smile reached his eyes. "Be sure to put me on your prayer list."

⸺ ❧ ⸺

My socks cut off my circulation, my uniform sweater itched, and my underwear seemed to be staging some sort of revolt to make me as uncomfortable as possible.

And these were the good points of the day.

I sat in fifth period and listened to the English teacher, Mrs. Campbell, give a preview of the year. No matter the country, it was the same spiel. If you didn't do your homework, you were going to flunk. And if you flunked, you'd never get your dream job. And if you didn't get your dream job, then you'd need to start practicing the phrase "Did you want biggie fries with that?"

As she lectured, I glanced down at my desk and realized that sometime during the hour, I'd rearranged my supplies. Three pens rested in a perfectly aligned group at a ninety-degree angle to my notebook, which rested in the exact center of the desk.

I did so like order. After Will died, when I wasn't sneaking out of the house, I was organizing the family closets.

"Students, you are sixth years." Mrs. Campbell paced the front of the classroom, her eagle eyes somehow falling on every one of us. We all looked like carbon copies in our dark shoes, plaid skirts, and navy cardigans. "After you sit your leaving cert this spring, you will be released into the real world. Do you know what you want to do? Where you're going? Do you know who you want to be?"

My stomach tightened with her every question.

How was it I was eighteen? A senior? On this ledge of two lives, preparing to jump off and go to college and leave my childhood behind?

My brothers both shot from the birth canal with their destinies stamped to their butts like signatures on a Cabbage Patch Kid. Alex picked up his first football at two and never looked back, becoming one of the nation's most beloved quarterbacks. And Will had gone on a mission trip in the eighth grade and forever championed for the plight of the less fortunate, whether through his work on CNN or his foundation to build schools in Afghanistan.

So far I was the family screwup.

But that was going to change.

"Every year we ask our sixth years to complete a final project." Mrs. Campbell stopped near my desk, which was unfortunately at the front. "This year's theme is serving," she said. "We don't want to just send out intelligent young women into the world, but kind, compassionate ones. Please take one of these sealed envelopes and pass it back."

I picked an envelope from the top and handed the stack to the girl behind me and tried to smile.

"I'm Beatrice Plummer," she whispered. "You may have heard of me."

"I don't think so."

She ran a manicured nail under her envelope. "My dad is the principal. Mr. Plummer."

"Must be hard to have your dad as principal."

"Actually I find it quite useful. Do you know Taylor Risdale?"

"The actress?"

"My third cousin, she is." Her braggish tone scrubbed over my nerves. "She's filming a movie here."

"I believe I did hear something about that."

"I'm in it." Her pleased grin let me know that it was an honor she was even talking to me. "So you're the new girl. The American?"

I nodded.

"Would you like to sit with me and my friends for lunch?" It came out with enough confidence to be more of a statement than a question.

We girls can sometimes be like wild animals, able to sniff out the strongest among us. Within seconds, I took in the total picture of Beatrice—her black sequined headband, the way her dark hair fell with perfect symmetry over her shoulder, diamond studs twinkling in her ears. Even her regulation socks somehow looked cooler than the rest of ours.

I'd just met Sacred Heart's queen bee.

"Thank you. But I'm eating with Erin." I gestured to where my host sister sat on the opposite side of the room. "Want to join us?"

Beatrice's glossy lips curved into a facsimile of a smile. "A word of advice?"

"Um, okay."

"You could aim a little higher." She delivered her sales pitch with all the finesse of a used car salesman. "With some guidance you could be one of the cool girls here, so."

"Like you."

She flipped her hair. "Of course."

"Thanks for the offer. I'll give it some thought." I might've been born privileged, but my momma hadn't raised no snob. Well, just when it came to egomaniacal actors.

I turned back around as Mrs. Campbell cleared her throat for attention.

"Students, please open your envelopes."

I peeled open the flap and reached inside.

Cathleen Sweeney.

"On your paper is the identity of a person you will be spending a lot of time with." Mrs. Campbell clasped her hands together, her eyes alight with excitement. "Each one of you will be adopting a grandparent from one of our nearby nursing homes."

Okay, I could do this. A chance to cheer up an elderly person? How hard could that be?

"You will be expected to see your grandparent at least twenty hours by the term's end. You will read to them, talk to them, get to know them, become a part of their lives. And before our Christmas holiday, you will turn in a portfolio to me." Mrs. Campbell passed out a pack of papers, and the classroom filled with the sound of thirty girls flipping through the stapled pages.

Mrs. Campbell explained each assignment and how we'd be graded. "My plan is that this experience teaches you more than any textbook ever could." She paused and her eyes panned the room. "My hope is that when you walk away from this . . . you are not the same."

An assignment that could change my life?

Sign me up.

Chapter Four

The people here are so nice. They do hospitality
better than any Southerner back home, and that's
saying something. Haven't met an unkind soul yet.

—Travel Journal of Will Sinclair, Abbeyglen, Ireland

*N*o cafeteria.

What kind of school was Ireland running here?

Erin bit into her sandwich. "Why is that weird?"

"You're missing the joys of healthy cafeteria fare like fries, cold pizza, and mystery meat." Not that I ate that trash. The last few months I had really cleaned up my diet, but school food was a teenage right of passage. Of course, so was driving, and they didn't get that one either.

"We either bring our own lunch or go off school grounds," Erin said.

Off-campus lunch. Maybe it wasn't such a bad idea after all.

"Ugh, there goes Beatrice and the Poshes." Erin's friend Orla pointed to the group of girls crossing the street.

"Where are they going?"

Orla took out a compact and covered the shine on her forehead where her blond bangs swung. "That's the boys' school. St. Raphael's."

"What did you call them? The Poshes?" I ate my peanut-butter-and-jelly sandwich, scraping off some of the strawberry jam, ripping away the crusts.

"Posh," Orla said. "Like fancy. Think they're better than the rest of us, sure they do."

"We used to be friends," Erin said. "That was before they got so uppity and . . . daring. We don't mind a bit of fun, but we're not party girls."

"Yeah." Orla opened her brown paper bag and peeked inside. "We know fun. Like two weekends ago we stayed up all night watching a documentary marathon on the brain." She rolled her eyes toward Erin. "We're positively wild."

"You forgot to tell me Beckett Rush was staying at your house." I was quite proud of how casual my voice sounded. As if it were every day I was sleeping under the same roof as a teenage phenomenon.

Erin craned her neck and looked all around before speaking in a hush. "Mam has made me promise not to so much as open my mouth one peep about him. Something about a contract she had to sign when he checked in. The whole town knows, but our family still can't say a word. It's been the hardest thing I've ever had to do. You can't talk about him either. We don't know who could be press in disguise. One word to them, and we lose the B and B, our possessions, and our life savings."

"Wow."

"I know. Isn't it awesome?" Erin gave an airy sigh. "Beckett's lovely, don't you think?"

"I guess." I took a drink of water. "If you're into his type."

She smiled. "The tall, blond, and ruggedly good-looking type?"

"I'd be careful with him, Erin."

"Oh, I know. My mam's already warned me. But he's been at our house for three weeks and been nothing but a gentleman. Hasn't made one single overture toward me." She sighed. "It's been a total disappointment."

"Bea's one of the locals the *Fangs in the Night* crew hired, don't you know," Orla said.

Erin nodded. "She has a small speaking part."

Orla took out a package of cookies. "But you'd think she was Scarlett Johansson."

"It is something to be proud of," Erin said.

Orla snorted. "And proud that one is. Her cousin got her the gig. Bea has all sorts of connections, and believe me, she uses them. She'll run over anyone to get what she wants. Best keep your eye on her. I've seen the way she looks at you, Finley. Like you're new competition."

I lined my bread crusts up neatly in a row on the table. "That's ridiculous. I don't want anything she has."

Erin looked toward St. Raphael's. "Just make sure you keep it that way."

→←

That night I woke up. Sweat glued my shirt to my skin, my heart pounded loud enough to wake the whole village, and tears coursed down my cheeks. Another dream where I saw Will. Yet I couldn't get to him. And he couldn't get to me.

One thirty a.m.

I rolled over and sighed, realizing that I was starving. Dinner had been some sausage concoction, and I couldn't swallow more than a few bites. Sometimes meat just grossed me out. Maybe this was God telling me to be a vegetarian.

Deciding to take my mind off of my growling stomach, I flicked on the bedside lamp and opened my brother's travel journal. I'd read this thing from cover to cover. Yet I still felt so drawn to it, as if it had something more it wanted to say.

I had to find a way to get out into the countryside and really see Ireland. The O'Callaghans were so busy, there was no telling when there would be a chance to get away. Patience had never been my strongest suit.

Or rolling my *r*'s.

God, I know we haven't talked in a long time, and you seem to be playing the quiet game, but if you could open some doors for me to get a car. I want to see the land my brother fell in love with. Talk to the people he never forgot. View the world as he saw it. He believed this was the most beautiful place ever. And I could definitely stand some beauty.

My tummy rumbled again, and I knew I had to do something about it. Last year I would occasionally forget to eat. My counselor called me depressed.

I called me devastated.

I slipped on a sweatshirt to go with my Mickey Mouse pajama bottoms and fuzzy bunny slippers and made my way down the two flights of stairs, straight for the kitchen.

The room came to life as I flipped the switch and investigated the refrigerator.

I spied the milk and remembered the impressive cereal

collection in the closet-sized pantry. Just as I reached in to grab the container, a low whine came from behind me.

I turned and listened.

Nothing.

Going back to the fridge, I pulled out the milk.

And heard the whine again. A pitiful sound, desperate and mournful, as if an animal writhed in pain just outside the back door.

I went to the door and my heart clenched at the lonesome wails. Turning the knob, I stepped outside and onto the back deck.

The kitchen light shone like a spotlight on the chocolate Lab I'd spotted on the front step the day I arrived.

"Hi, boy." I moved slowly, just in case the thing was crying over a new rabies diagnosis. "What's wrong, huh?"

The Lab remained at attention, but wagged its happy tail.

"Are you lonely? Do you need someone to talk to?" I reached out a tentative hand and scratched his head. "Because I totally relate."

"Do you now?"

I jumped at the voice behind me.

There in the corner, holding a small book light and a script, sat Beckett Rush.

"You scared me." My heart thumped wildly in my chest.

"I can see that." He closed his script. "Were you going to brain me with that?"

His gaze traveled over my head, and I realized I was holding the milk like a weapon. "I apologize for my catlike reflexes," I said, lowering the jug. "Clearly you were milliseconds from devastating pain."

He smiled. "Death by dairy products."

"The dog was crying. I . . ." I was standing there in my pajamas.

In front of Beckett Rush. The Hollywood movie star. "I wanted to check it out. See if he was hurting."

"The only thing Bob's hurting for is food." Beckett held up a plate. "I made myself a sandwich. Bob's a big promoter of sharing."

"He should've been around at dinnertime. I would've gladly shared."

"That bad? I have half a sandwich here."

I eyed him warily, as if the space between us were littered with land mines.

"I'm just going to throw it away." Beckett tapped the seat beside him. "Sit. Eat. I promise you're safe. I'm too tired to tick you off."

"You say that like you do it on purpose." With another scratch to Bob's panting head, I slipped into the vacant seat.

"It passes the time."

In the stingy light, I peeked beneath the bread and found ham, cheese, lettuce, and mayo. I scraped off the mayo, lost half the meat, and set aside one piece of bread.

"Picky eater."

"I have discriminating taste." I took a bite and smiled.

Bob gave another whine, then with a resigned sigh, dropped himself at Beckett's feet.

"See?" He scratched the dog's ear. "Some people like me."

"He's just lonely."

Beckett's eyes locked on mine. "I believe you said you were too."

"That was a private conversation. Between me"—I swallowed my bite of sandwich—"and Bob."

"So what are you really doing up?" His voice was sleepy deep.

"Just woke up. You?"

"Running lines." He held up his script. "I've been inside all day and needed to get out. Get some air." He ran his hand through blond hair that looked like it should've come with a surfboard and sunscreen. "Seems the scenes didn't go so well today." He took off his coat, stood up to his height that must've been at least six feet, and hovered over me. I held my breath as Beckett moved in close, and I smelled the detergent on his shirt as he settled the coat over my shoulders. "You look cold."

"Thank you." I let myself breathe again and snuggled into his jacket as Beckett sat back down, angling his body toward mine.

"I'm about to ask you a favor."

"And I'm about to tell you no."

"It's not a make-out scene. Though I'd be willing to rehearse that."

"Still, no."

"Dig deep into that cold, callous heart of yours, Frankie."

"It's Finley."

"Dig deep and find some kindness." He held out his script. "I've a need for someone to read the part of Selena."

"Selena the mutating vampire duchess? The woman who eats frogs, whose lower body is covered in scales because her mom had a fling with a merman?"

"I knew you were a fan."

Dumbest movies ever.

"I'll give you a tour of the set."

I rolled my eyes.

"I'll get my friend Jake Gyllenhaal to call you."

"Already have him on speed dial."

"I won't tell your friends about your sleeping attire." His gaze dropped to my feet. "Nice bunnies."

"Fine." I grabbed the script and put aside my half-eaten sandwich. "But tomorrow we go back to ignoring one another."

"Page fifty-one." The dimple in his cheek deepened. "And as for girls who try to stay away from me—my charm always wears them down."

"I'm up-to-date on my shots, so I'm pretty much immune to everything."

Beckett just tipped his chair back and laughed. "Famous last words, Flossie. Famous last words."

Chapter Five

From: jaynelson@newyorkconservatory.com
Subject: Audition Preparations

This message is to confirm your audition time at 1:00 p.m. on October 20 at the New York Conservatory. Please bring instrument, music, and any accompaniment needed, as it will not be provided. We look forward to meeting you and welcoming you to our esteemed campus.

On Tuesday, I skipped lunch for my first music lesson.

Since Sacred Heart didn't specifically have an orchestra, my parents arranged for a teacher to give me private instruction in violin and piano to help with my audition.

While my violin was my first love, if I was going to be taken seriously as a composer, I had to get better at the piano. I'd been taking lessons for three years, and I was still no Beethoven.

I slipped into the music room and, with my backpack still in my lap like a shield, I took a seat at a piano old enough to have been carried over on the ark. The room was small, quiet.

A sanctuary.

It was always this way for me. The stored instruments in the closets called out like old friends. The bent and scratched black music stands welcomed me into their home. The oily smell, a perfume. It was like . . . church.

I ran my fingers over the keys in a concert B-flat scale and let my thoughts wander. Last night had been weird. I helped Beckett with his lines until 3:00 a.m., when neither of us could talk for yawning. As he got into his scenes, the arrogance and antagonism disappeared. In its place was a guy who was a perfectionist about his craft. Who relentlessly attacked the same few pages repeatedly until I had the entire thing memorized too. He was serious, subdued. Much like me and my violin.

And for a few hours, I almost liked him.

I returned my attention to the front of the room and stopped playing when I spotted a picture of Christ hanging on the wall. The silence filled my ears, and I found myself . . . waiting.

Not really sure for what. A connection. A sign. A voice from the rafters to tell me how to get my life back?

"I've been telling Principal Plummer we need to redecorate in here."

I startled at the voice behind me. "Oh, hello."

An older woman walked into the room, smiling with two rows of oversized teeth. "Sister Maria. Resident musician, I am." She looked around the room, and I followed the path of her stare. Wooden floors. Wooden paneling. Pendant lights that hung from chains that were probably once brass, but now were more a shade of dusty.

"Except for two hours a day, it's a nice place for peace and quiet,"

Sister Maria said. "But it's a bit drab and dark for my taste. I keep hoping Mr. Plummer will bring it into this current decade, but so far we seem pretty partial to the 1970s." She shook her head and muttered, "Sacrilegious harvest gold."

"So you teach here?"

"Part-time. Principles of faith." She looked toward the cross. "It's an elective."

"Sounds like a good class," I said for the sake of small talk.

"Maybe you can get into it next semester."

With the way my faith was going, I'd probably flunk it. "And you give lessons?"

"Right. We're supposed to make your audition piece perfect for some fancy school and get you up to speed on the piano. Do I have it right, so?" She laughed for no reason, a full-bodied sound. The sort of chuckle that turned heads and made people smile.

"Yes." Perfection was exactly what I wanted in Will's song. "I have most of the composition done, except for the ending."

"Where do you come from again?"

"America. South Carolina."

"Ah, lovely place."

"It can be."

"But it wasn't when you left?" She dropped herself onto the piano bench beside me.

"It's complicated."

"You're a teenager. It's all complicated."

"It's just . . ." I hugged my backpack to me. "This isn't what I expected."

"What—life? Abbeyglen?" Smiling, she angled her head and regarded me with blue eyes that reminded me of my mother's. I'd spent the last two years turning away from all sorts of varieties of pity and understanding. But I didn't look away from Sister Maria.

"I really don't know." I shook my head. "It's nothing. I shouldn't be rambling on like this."

"I'm giving you some homework."

I mentally poked holes in all those warm, fuzzy grandma feelings.

"Get out and see the town. Get to know the land, the people." Her eyes sparkled with joy. "It's a beautiful place. Full of life. Everywhere I look, I see God."

"Sounds like my brother. He came here his senior year and fell in love with the place."

"Then you need to discover the Ireland he saw."

"I'm trying. The people I'm staying with run a B and B. They barely have time to sleep."

"God will open that door for you." Sister Maria put her wrinkled hand on mine. "There's nothing you're searching for that can't be found in Ireland—God, good music, beautiful landscapes, wonderful food, maybe even parts of yourself. You just have to be brave enough to look."

"You make it sound so easy."

She laughed again. "You know what comes after homework, right?"

"Normally a quiz. But I have you pegged for someone who's nicer than that."

"Wrong. Next time we meet there will be a quiz."

"Can't wait."

"So don't be thinking you'll get out of here without playing your piece." She clapped her hands. "Get to it now."

Without needing to take the sheet music out of my bag, I set my fingers on the keys and dove into Will's song. My execution was flawless, my timing a dream. For a full two minutes, every note just right.

And then I stopped.

"That's all I have."

I expected her to brag, to compliment my advanced skills, my creative vision.

"Your ending needs work."

"I don't have one."

"A requirement for every song, I'm told."

"I'm working on it." I told her about the journal, finally extracting it from my bag. "Have you seen this cross?"

"Sure."

"You have?"

Sister Maria squinted as she pressed her nose closer. "A few thousand of them. They're all over Ireland."

"But I have to find *this* one."

I waited for her to laugh, to tell me I was being foolish. But she just studied me for a moment before pursing her lips. "So that's where your ending is?" She tapped the picture.

"Yes."

"Then you must find it. But in the meantime, you continue to practice." She gave my hand a squeeze, her skin warm against my own. "No one bothered to tell me your name."

"Finley Sinclair."

"A beautiful name." She smiled. "Do you know what it means?"

I glanced at my watch. "Girl who's going to be late to class?"

"Warrior." Sister Maria stood, her form short and slightly stooped. Her uniform just like the other teachers'. "It means fair warrior." Her palm rested on my head, like she was bestowing a blessing. "And Finley Sinclair, I have a feeling that's just what you are."

❧

The sun shined. The birds sang. The trees swayed. It was a fine afternoon to adopt a sweet, elderly grandma.

I walked the half mile from school to the Rosemore nursing home. After presenting my paperwork to the head nurse, I followed her directions to hall C. The building smelled of cleaning solution and other things I didn't really care to think about. I passed by a yellow-haired woman with a walker who smiled at me and waved.

"Hello!" she said. "Hello!"

I waved back and kept walking. Old people were so nice.

I knocked on door 12 and went on in.

There in a wheelchair sat Cathleen Sweeney. White hair porcupined on her head. Pink pajama pants longer than her spindly legs. Fluffy blue slippers. Sleepy gaze.

Oh, she looked like the sweetest thing.

"Hello, Mrs. Sweeney. I'm—"

"Get outta my room!"

I took a step back as the woman roused like a waking dragon. "But I'm Finley Sinclair and—"

"I don't care if you're the Blessed Virgin herself, get out."

My heart tripled in time. "I'm from the school. You were assigned to me and—"

She peered over her bifocals, and I swore her eyes were mean enough to shoot lightning. "You have five seconds to remove yourself. I don't want any schoolgirl reading me stories or interrupting my day. Go do your work somewhere else, why don't you now?"

Out of fear, shock, or complete brain freeze, I stayed rooted to the spot, my feet locked to the floor.

"Nurse!" Mrs. Sweeney yelled. "Nurse!"

Oh, shoot. Oh no.

"Nurse!"

"Okay! I'm leaving!" I held up my hands as if Mrs. Sweeney had a pistol pointed at me instead of her bony finger.

"*What* is going on here?" The director of nursing stepped into the doorway, her scrub-clad body filling up the space. "Cathleen, stop that yelling."

"Then get her out."

"This young woman is from Sacred Heart. Haven't we been talking about this for weeks? Remember our conversation?"

"The one about me eating more prunes?"

The nurse took a deep breath and slowly released it. "The one about being nice and not scaring children."

"It's okay," I said, pulse galloping. "She didn't scare me." Much.

"Well, I meant to." Cathleen rested her hands on her wheels and glared. "I told you, Belinda, I don't want any company. I didn't last year, or the year before, and I don't today."

"Too bad." The nurse walked over to Cathleen, leaned down until they were eye to eye. "She stays. You'll not be chasing this one off."

This was not how I'd pictured this experience. I was *so* not going to bring her any of Mr. O'Callaghan's cookies. Not even the burned ones. How did someone get to be this mean?

"I think I should go." I tugged up the strap of my backpack. "I'll . . ." Mrs. Sweeney watched me as I backed out the door. "I'll just see if I can be reassigned. Shouldn't be a problem." I bid them both good-bye and all but ran out the door.

"Wait!"

I was halfway down the hall when the nurse caught up.

"I'm sorry for Cathleen." She panted with every word, winded after her little jog. "She can be . . . difficult."

Two-year-olds were difficult. That woman was a terrorist. "Really, it's not a problem. I'll just get a new assignment."

The nurse's brown skin wrinkled as she frowned. "I wish you'd give it another try. I know Cathleen is a bit harsh, but she needs someone right now." She dropped her voice and locked her eyes with mine. "Cathleen has cancer. She has a couple months left—at the most."

"She's dying?" They'd set me up with a *dying* grandma?

No way.

There was no stinkin' way.

"Um . . . I better get back home. Lots of homework to do."

"Please consider it. Cathleen needs you."

"No, ma'am. Pretty sure she doesn't." I shook my head, unwilling to explain, desperate to leave. "Good-bye." I mumbled another apology and raced out.

In the lobby, the yellow-haired woman with the walker smiled and waved again.

"Come back soon!"

Chapter Six

Hey, sis, got your text last night. Lucy says to
tell you she's so proud of you. She also says
not to be kissing any Blarney Stone. Love you
and missed you at family dinner Sunday. I had
to console myself by eating my pie . . . as well
as the piece that would've been yours.

Love you,

Alex

Sent to my iPhone

---

ut you have to give me another assignment."

I splayed my hands on Mrs. Campbell's desk Wednesday after school, letting her see the desperation, hoping she got a whiff of my fear.

"Finley, if I reassigned you, I'd have to reassign half the class, and I'll not be doing that."

"She's mean!"

"What she is, is a lonely woman who just needs some compassion, 'tis all."

"I can't go back there. Surely there's something else. Like volunteering for a church or a local orphanage?"

Mrs. Campbell shook her head. "If you don't complete this project you don't pass. It's as simple as that." She stuffed a stack of papers in a file. "Chin up. You can do it."

"But—" I choked on the words. And tried again. "She's dying."

Mrs. Campbell reached out and gave my shoulder a squeeze. "All the more reason Cathleen needs you. Do you realize what a special assignment you have here?"

I just stared at her. Special assignment would be like interviewing Lady Gaga. This was just cruel and unusual torture.

"It's not negotiable." Mrs. Campbell flopped open another folder and rifled through it. "Make it happen."

"She demanded I leave."

My teacher sat down in her chair and took out her grading pen, her focus on her work. "Then I guess you'll have to try harder, so."

"I can't just—"

"Yes, you can. And you will. Try not to make this about you. Make it about Cathleen."

"But *Cathleen* isn't the one flunking."

Mrs. Campbell gave a small smile. "Just pray about it."

Yeah. Because that's solved a lot lately.

With a weary sigh, I walked out, following the tile down the hall and out the door where Nora waited in the car.

"No luck getting it switched?" Erin asked from the front seat.

"No." And I had no idea what I was going to do. I'd had enough of death to last me until it was my time to go.

"We just got a reservation for the weekend with a scrapbooking club," Nora said. "They're paying extra to have lunch and dinner."

Erin looked at her brother like he was pond sludge. "So I have to keep an eye on Liam."

"That's fine," he said beside me. "That will give me time to hang out with Finley." His thin eyebrows waggled. "Show her what a real man can do with Legos."

Nora hung a left out of the school parking lot. "Finley, love, we'll have to put off sightseeing again. But I promise we'll get to it." Her eyes watching me in the rearview were tired, and I couldn't help but feel sorry for her. "We're still adapting to this B and B thing. We'll get our balance soon. The good news is Sean picked up a new bicycle just for you, so you'll be able to get about town."

The car climbed up the hill to the house, and I watched the ocean in the distance, feeling a twinge of homesickness for the Charleston coastline.

Nora put the car in park and we piled out, just as an old, green truck shuddered and rumbled as it stopped in the driveway.

"Behave yourself, Erin," Nora warned. "Liam, do not play twenty questions."

Before I could question Nora's odd tone, I got a closer look at the man behind the windshield. And it all became obnoxiously clear.

"Hello, Mrs. O'Callaghan," Beckett Rush said as he climbed out of the truck. With wagging tail and floppy tongue, Bob jumped from the back of the truck bed.

"Hello, dear. Did you have a good day?" Nora asked this as if he'd just returned from his desk job as an accountant.

"Wonderful as always." His gray eyes lit on me as he pulled Nora in for a side hug. "Probably due in part to your brilliant French toast this morning."

"You should really branch out. Try something else on the menu." Nora's pale cheeks turned pink. "Oh, and you might want to lie low this weekend. Scrapbook group coming."

"A bunch of girls with scissors," Liam said. "That's never ended well for me."

"And poor Finley," Nora said. "We were going to take her around a bit this weekend. But now we can't." She patted me on the back. "Girl's probably going to turn us in for neglect. She hasn't even seen the Cliffs of Moher yet, has she, Erin?"

Erin just stood there, her glazed eyes on Beckett. Her mouth tilted at an odd angle, as if she'd been struck dumb by lightning. Or the sight of an international teen heartthrob.

"I could take you."

We all stared at Beckett Rush for an uncomfortable moment until he repeated himself.

"I'd be glad to take you to the cliffs." He stood so close to me, I could smell his shampoo. I'd expected him to wear the scent of his own cologne sold by the finer department stores. Not something that reminded me of Pantene.

"That's okay." *What is the boy up to?* "I'll just wait 'til next weekend."

Nora's frown deepened. "Next weekend we're helping with the Donnelley family reunion. They love Sean's gooseberry crumble. Oh, Finley, I feel terrible."

"I really don't mind," Beckett said. "I've got the rest of the afternoon off. It's just a few miles away." He leveled his gaze on me. "You'll be safe enough."

"If it's just a few miles, I can walk. Some exercise would do me good and—"

"Nonsense." Nora regarded me as if I were touched in the head. "You two go on. Have a lovely time."

Oh no. "But I—"

"Would you care to join us, Erin?" Beckett asked.

Erin blinked twice. "No. No, thank you. Homework. I have homework."

"All right, then. Good-bye!" Nora wrapped an arm around each kid and escorted them inside. Erin walked backward, her mouth wide-open, still wearing that blank stare.

"Bob, let's go." As Beckett opened the passenger door of his truck, the Lab hopped in the back behind the cab. "You getting in, Finley? Or did you want to ride with my dog?"

"I'd rather not go at all."

"Clearly this is weighing on Mrs. O'Callaghan. You don't want to let her down, do you?"

Why wouldn't I have expected Mr. Casanova to have just the right words? "Fine." I struggled with the step until he took my hand and helped me up. "But no funny business."

His face was all innocence. "That hurts."

The tires of Beckett's rickety truck spun beneath us as we drove the short distance to the Cliffs of Moher. I stared out the window, rolling it down and inviting the wind to swoop inside, even though we were both in our jackets. Beckett didn't say a word, giving me the chance to watch every bit of Abbeyglen we passed, storing it all in my head.

"It's a beautiful town, isn't it?" He turned off the staticky radio. "I never get tired of it."

"Are you from here?"

"Lived in Galway the first ten years of my life before moving to America. But I'd come back with me da' to see me grandparents. They'd take me all over."

"And your mom?"

"She died, God rest her soul, when I was just a baby. Me da' quit his own acting career for me. Me parents were young, only nineteen when I was born. Da' did some work on a soap opera, and things were just taking off. Then I came along, and he had to take on a day job. The calls just stopped coming."

Beckett parked the truck, and Bob pressed his nose to the window to check our progress. "The door sticks. I'll be around to get it." He walked to my side and let me out. I tried not to stare at his blond hair dancing in the breeze. Because that would've been dumb. And something every other girl would do.

"Why'd you offer to bring me out here?"

He hesitated as we walked across the street to the entrance. "I was grateful for your help last night. I, um, I've had a bit of trouble with my scenes lately. Just hasn't been going well. It's caught the director's attention. But today"—he put a hat on his head and gave a curious smile—"after I ran lines with you, it was just solid. My director said Steele Markov came alive."

"So I have the power to raise the undead."

"Something like that." His eyes on mine darkened. "It made a difference."

"Well." Unexpected delight shimmied through me. "Glad I could help."

He stopped as we reached the first steps. "I have a proposition for you."

"Not on your life."

"Hear me out—"

"I'm not interested."

"It's nothing dodgy." His accent had grown stronger, and I wondered if I'd hurt his feelings. But that would've been impossible. "I want you to be my assistant."

51

I laughed as I zipped my jacket. "Is that what you call it?"

"I'm serious." He shoved his hat farther down on his head to block his face. "You'd just have to work a few hours a day after school. Help me with lines. That's all. I promise."

My eyes narrowed. "And what would I get in return, bragging rights? My name linked with yours in the magazines? No thanks."

"I'm asking you because . . . you're different. You're not into me. I'm not into you. There's no risk here."

Well, that had all the charm of a razor cut to the ankle.

Of course he wasn't into me. Why should he have been? He was around beautiful actresses all day.

"What I mean is, you're not impressed by my name or what I can get for you." He shook his head as if he were trying to dislodge the idea. "I know it's crazy."

"And what would I get in return?"

"I'll take you around Ireland. Show you the sights." He lifted his hands in the air. "No strings attached. And no *funny business*."

"I don't know."

"Do you want to recreate your brother's steps or don't you?"

"Yes." Desperately. For Will. For me.

"I could really use your help, Finley."

The raw appeal on his face had me wondering if I'd be crazy to get involved in anything Beckett Rush was a part of. "Let's just see how much of a tour guide you are first."

The wind picked up even more as we got closer to the cliffs.

"It's the ocean breeze," he said. "Wait 'til you see the water."

We walked up a series of steps until I finally stopped him so I could take a good look.

"The better view is up there." He pointed beyond us.

I dug out my camera and started clicking. "You can't rush me."

"You didn't tell me there were stipulations on my sightseeing duties."

I took a shot of the water below. "I'd like to actually *see* the cliffs. Not just drive by them." In the distance there they stood, jagged and majestic, green grass topping them like icing, the azure-blue waves below. I wished I had my violin to provide the harmony.

"What are you looking for?"

At this, I lowered my camera. "I don't know," I said honestly. "I just know I'm supposed to look."

"Come on. I'll take you to the best spot."

I tagged along behind him, practically running to keep up with his long strides. We walked a way, passing other tourists. A man in ugly but comfortable shoes. A woman sporting a fanny pack. People taking pictures. A family posing as a stranger captured the moment forever. Beckett kept his head down and his sunglasses covering those famous eyes.

The trail narrowed, and as we followed the sidewalk around a corner, I spied cows in a field as green as emeralds, munching on clover and ignoring those of us in search of the best view. We walked past the fenced-in cattle and I took another picture.

"They're cows, Finley."

"We don't have a lot of these in Charleston."

We reached the lookout at the top, and I had to tell myself to breathe again. The cliffs stretched out and wrapped around on either side of us. Beneath us the waves crashed and tumbled. Birds swooped in and dove toward the sea, only to land and perch on the rocks.

The wind sent my hair into orbit around my face, and I lifted an unsteady hand to hold it back.

I knew this place. These rocks. That water. That sky.

I breathed it all in. Tried to memorize its smell, the taste of it on my tongue. It was completely new, yet familiar all at the same time. My eyes failed me, as I couldn't take it in fast enough. Couldn't see it all without swiveling my head and looking in turns.

Beckett stood beside me. "Some people say they're just cliffs."

"But they're not." I shook my head, turned to look up at him. "And you don't believe that either. It's . . ." I struggled with the words. There didn't seem to be any to capture what I saw, what I felt.

His chest rose as he inhaled, his eyes still on mine. "Follow me."

I managed to get a few pictures, taking some as I walked. We left the main path until we came to a sign.

"Please don't go beyond this point," it said.

"I'm kind of trying to follow these sorts of warnings these days." I stared at the sign. "Maybe we should turn back."

"It's just so herds of tourists don't come any farther. Mind your step."

I stayed right where I was.

"If I'm going to be your bloomin' tour guide, I'm going to do it right." He held out his hand. "Do you think I'd take you somewhere dangerous?"

"You bite people for a living."

"Don't be a chicken."

"If you push me over the edge, my parents will be seriously ticked."

He grabbed my hand and pulled me along. "They'll probably send me a thank-you note."

Beckett Rush was holding my hand.

For the purpose of rudely speeding me along.

But still. For five whole seconds, his hand covered mine.

We came to the peak. And the panoramic view had tears stinging my eyes.

The sun skimmed along the water, making a luminous path. A castle tower loomed from the opposite side, just begging me to come and explore. It looked to be whole, unlike the others I'd seen around. Small yellow flowers danced at our ankles as I stared at the view that went for miles.

"I got it right," I said. "The piece of the song I wrote from Will's picture. It fits this perfectly."

I remembered the scripture beneath the picture of the cliffs in Will's journal. "Lord, Your faithful love reaches to heaven, Your faithfulness to the skies." Realizing I'd just spoken the words out loud, my cheeks burned. "When my brother came here a long time ago, it made him think of that verse."

Does your love reach this far, God? And if it extends to heaven and beyond . . . why can't it seem to find me?

"It's beautiful," I said, my voice clouded with embarrassment.

"It's more than that." He watched the ocean below. "It's like God painted it himself, then spun it into motion." Beckett angled his head toward me, took his aviators off, and let his eyes burn into mine. "*This* is Ireland, Finley. It's rough. It's wild. And it is holy."

I couldn't look away from him. The breeze tossed my hair, bit against my jacket, and all I could do was watch this mercurial boy.

His piercing gaze still holding mine, his fingers eased toward my face. I closed my eyes as his skin brushed mine, his thumb tracing a path across my cheek.

Behind me a seagull called, its cry piercing the air.

And the spell was broken.

Beckett cleared his throat, dropped his hand. "It was . . ."

Insanity. Ridiculous. A moment of crazy.

It was seconds of heart-twisting awe.

"It was a bug." He pulled his jacket tighter. Sniffed against the chill.

"Right." Of course.

"Finley?" he whispered.

"Yes?"

"Do we have a deal?"

Praying I wasn't about to return to a life of trouble, I gave him my answer.

"Yes."

Chapter Seven

Everyone hangs out in pubs. It's a family place, not like a bar back home. It's where you talk with your neighbor, hear some music, eat a hot meal, and listen to the stories firing all over the room.

—Travel Journal of Will Sinclair, Abbeyglen, Ireland

T he whole town is daft over St. Flanagan's Day," Erin said to Orla and me as we passed through the doorway of Molly Delaney's pub. The lunch crowd filled the long oak bar as well as the wall-to-wall tables.

"Well, if it isn't Sean O'Callaghan's daughter."

Erin smiled. "Good afternoon, Molly."

A short, white-haired woman toddled over to us and gestured with her chin. "I've just the table for you girls. Right by the window so you can see if any fine fellas walk by." She gave us a saucy wink as we giggled. "Didn't I raise five girls of me own? Sure. I know how you ladies come in for more than just the finest stew in Abbeyglen. Have you got your dates for the dance, so?"

I pulled my finger down the sticky menu in search of a salad. It was hard to concentrate on food with the man in the back corner playing his guitar. All I wanted to do was watch and listen. "What's this St. Flanagan's?"

"Och, have you not warned her then? That she has a full day of dancin' and eatin' ahead of her?" Molly shook her head. "You need to find this girl a date."

"It's just a holiday," Orla said. "With some silly tradition of girls asking boys to the dance."

"Silly tradition?" The old man at the table next to us put down his glass mug and shoved aside his plate of fish. "Why, it's almost the most important day of the year."

Molly *harrumph*ed and leaned toward me. "That's Ennis O'Toole, the mayor. Doesn't give a fig about the history. Just smells the money when the tourists come round."

"I heard that, Molly." Mr. O'Toole rose from his chair and joined us. "It was 1477 and none other than Christopher Columbus himself sailed into our harbor with a vessel unlike any ever seen before in Abbeyglen." The mayor's eyes shone beneath drapey lids. "So Columbus gets sick, he does."

Molly clucked her tongue. "Thought he was a goner."

"'Tis true. But Father Patrick Flanagan had the gift of healing in his hands, he did. So as Columbus's crew prepared for the worst, and while Columbus tossed and pitched with the fever, Father Flanagan prayed for Chris twenty-four hours straight. He took no food or drink. Just prayed for the man. Columbus's men thought the good priest was surely administering last rites." The mayor's voice pulled us all into the story, and I saw it unfold in my mind.

"By sunrise the next day, Columbus woke up a new man, asking for his ship."

"And a pint of ale," Molly said.

"A great party was had to celebrate his miraculous recovery," Mr. O'Toole said. "It lasted as long as the prayer vigil. And as the famous explorer left, he called out a blessing on Abbeyglen, wishing prosperity for one and all. And ever since then, our fishing nets have been full and our cows have been fat."

"And there's a stupid dance," Orla drolled.

The mayor shuffled back to his table. "It's where I met me wife."

"And why do the girls ask the boys?" I asked.

"Because Father Flanagan was too shy." Mr. O'Toole popped a fry into his mouth. "He'd have never asked a lady to dance."

"He was a priest," Orla said.

The man shrugged. "Technicality."

"It's just an old tradition is why," Molly said. "Been around for generations."

"Molly, going to be a quarter ring around the moon tonight. Rain. And you know what that means?"

"That you watched the weatherman?"

"Time to plant the onions."

"No," chimed in another man walking by. "That's if you find three crickets belly up on your front stoop."

"Very helpful, you are." Molly rolled her eyes. "Let these ladies get to their lunch. They have big things to plan." She took our drink orders and bustled back to the kitchen.

"The dance is a huge deal round here." Erin propped her chin in her hands. "We have an all-day festival, then at night bands play and the whole town comes for the dance. It's all outside. Very romantic . . . or completely depressing."

"Erin didn't find a date last year."

"I don't know why we make such a fuss," Erin said. "I've been stressing about it, and I'm starting to break out in zits."

"All right, girls, what'll you have?" Molly returned and set a trio of waters on the table.

"Hamburger." Erin handed back the menu.

"Me too," said Orla.

My good intentions for a salad wilted away. I'd just make up for it later. "Make that three." Though with all this home-cooked food, it was obviously time for me to get back to running. Before my skirt got any tighter.

"So," Orla said as Molly walked away, "any ideas on who you'll ask to the dance, Finley? Anyone here you fancy?"

At that moment, we watched a crowd move up the sidewalk to the door. In walked Beckett, followed by five more cast members. Including a girl I recognized as his beautiful costar.

Beckett waved to a man behind the bar. His eyes scanned the room as he greeted the good citizens of Abbeyglen.

Then he saw our table.

His gaze locked onto mine.

He smiled. A small, slow curve of his lips.

"No." I looked away, bringing my attention back to the girls. "Definitely no one here I fancy."

>€

After school I hopped on my bicycle and rode to the location of *Fangs in the Night*, sliding past the makeshift barricades lined up to keep obsessive fans away. I probably should've gone to visit Mrs.

Sweeney, but for some reason I just wasn't in the mood for her verbal harassment or stares of death.

That blissful fun would have to wait another day.

In the middle of filming an outdoor scene, the crew hovered all around the grounds like bees in search of honey, and, looking to the background, I could see what drew them to this particular town. A giant stone castle sat boldly in the meadow. But this wasn't just a ruin, a piece of a tower. Though worn and battered, it was, from the outside, standing nearly whole, as if waiting for someone to lower the drawbridge and commence with court. With windows missing and turrets crumbling, whether by time, weather, or man, I knew it was nothing that couldn't be fixed in a good editing studio. I envisioned women with big, sweeping dresses inside and men riding up on steeds after a day of hunting and warring.

Members of the crew walked past me as if I were invisible. Two women with ghostly white-powdered faces. A man carrying a light. A lady balancing three coffees. All these people, and yet, bless my sweet luck, Beatrice was the first person who took notice of my presence.

"What do you think you're doing?"

Beatrice stood there in a skintight bodice and ballooning skirt that dragged the ground, holding a brownie and Coke. My brain went into calculator mode, and I totaled up her fat, calories, carbs, divided by the square root of her obnoxious scorn.

"I asked you a question," she said.

I took a step back as another girl approached. Taylor Risdale, the queen of twentysomething movies. She was even more beautiful in person with her spun-honey hair and waifish figure. Her skin was airbrushed perfection; I couldn't find a single blemish. I could hate her for that reason alone.

"What's going on?" Taylor asked. "Another intruder?"

"I, um, came to see Beckett." Why had I agreed to this? Because I needed Beckett's truck.

"You came to see Beckett. Isn't that sweet?" Beatrice bit into her brownie, and my stomach pulled at the sight of her red lips chewing.

"This is a closed set," Taylor said with a little less hostility than her cousin.

"I know." I looked past her for signs of Beckett. "I'm not here to stalk. I—"

"That's what they all say." Taylor laughed.

"Seriously, if you'll let me explain."

"Don't embarrass yourself further." Beatrice shook her head like a hassled mother. "Have a little dignity."

I was losing my patience. And my courage. "Beckett asked me to be here."

"Sure he did." Beatrice took a delicate sip of her Coke. "And I'm the Queen of England."

"Is there a problem?"

At the sight of Beckett, I wanted to weep with gratitude. Bob trotted along beside him, a soggy tennis ball in his teeth, and I knew I was rescued.

"I'm taking care of it." Taylor slithered up next to him and wrapped her arm around his bicep. "Just another silly fan girl." According to the tabloids, these two had been dating for months in an on-again, off-again relationship that was as volatile as it was mysterious.

Beckett gave the girls a bland smile as Bob wagged his tail against his master's knee. "I invited Finley."

Taylor's face froze as if she had just sat on a pair of fangs. "Beckett, can I talk to you?"

"Later." He extracted himself from her grip and stood beside me. "Finley's my new assistant. Mary left, and I need some help." I looked ridiculous standing next to Taylor. She was a model. A goddess. Beatrice might've been pretty, but she wasn't perfect. She had some curves. And a bump on her nose.

"I could help you," Beatrice said.

"No." Beckett's voice was smooth as an alto sax. "You have too much to do already. We need you fresh for your part. I couldn't stand the thought that I had taken you from your true calling."

"But—"

"Thanks anyway."

Beckett took hold of my arm and steered me in the other direction. "Very smooth," I whispered.

He looked down and grinned. "Beatrice? She's not too bad."

"Yeah, because when she's around you she gushes with charm and oozes with kindness. Before you got there she'd sprouted demon horns and was hissing smoke."

"Don't worry. I've got her number."

"Oh, I'll just bet you do." On speed dial.

Beckett laughed, then pointed to a trailer. "That's mine. Go on in."

"If your next line is 'make yourself more comfortable,' I'm pretty sure my daddy would expect me to punch you in the nose."

"Ciara's waiting for me in there to touch up my makeup, and we can . . . what? That's funny to you?" He opened the trailer door and Bob hopped inside.

"You come with your own makeup crew. I'm just going to need a minute to process this, Mary Kay."

A muscle in his jaw ticked as he held the door for me to step inside. "Finley, this is Ciara, one of the makeup artists." He handed me a script as he took a seat in front of the woman and her magical box of cosmetics. "Finley's going to be helping me out, so make sure she feels at home."

"Welcome, Finley." Ciara looked about the same age as Erin's mom, and her own face was makeup free and framed by a cherry Kool-Aid stripe of hair on either side. Her smile revealed a gap between her teeth that added to her rebel cuteness. "Oh." She reached for a powder brush from a tool belt around her waist. "You-know-who showed up today."

I flipped through the script and tried to fade out of the circle of their conversation. But looking through my lashes, I saw Beckett's lips thin and his fingers tighten on the arm of the chair. "Thanks for the heads-up." He turned to me, the smile back in place. "Page fifty-two. Let's start from the top."

As we read the scene, I watched Ciara touch up his vampire look. The makeup should've feminized Beckett, but somehow it didn't. Ciara's deft hand had only sharpened his edges, making him even more rough . . . dangerous . . . earthy. His clothing came straight from the 1800s, and the cut of the charcoal pants and jacket gave me a new appreciation for historical detail.

"There you go, boss." She gathered up her brushes and put them away. "See you in ten."

"Thanks, Ciara. Now take a break. You've been on your feet all day."

"I'm gonna go read that book you gave me," she said. "This boy"—she gave his shoulders a sisterly squeeze—"always reading books and passing them on. He's yet to suggest a bad one."

Ciara shuffled out of the trailer and the wind slammed the door shut, jarring Bob from his growl time with his ball.

"So . . . ," I began.

"Don't believe a word she said."

"You read. And often, it seems."

"She just said that to make me sound smart."

"It almost worked."

He tapped the script. "Start again."

I flipped the page back to the beginning of the scene just as the door opened again. Bob's ears twitched and his tail stopped wagging.

"Hello, son."

A man who could've been Tom Cruise's twin stepped inside. He pulled off his Ray-Bans and surveyed the room. "And you are?"

My eyes widened at his curt tone. I opened my mouth to respond, but Beckett beat me to it. "This is Finley. She's my temporary assistant. Finley, meet me father, Montgomery Rush."

"Pleasure to meet you." Mr. Rush held out his hand, and a large diamond sparkled on one of his fingers. "Beckett," he said, dismissing me, "did you get that script I overnighted you?"

"Yeah. *Bite Night* the sequel."

"And you read it?"

Beckett reached into a small refrigerator and pulled out two water bottles, handing one to me before twisting the cap on his own and bringing it to his lips. "Haven't read it yet."

"Get on it. We need to negotiate. Those terms they sent us are quite unacceptable. Read the script."

"What's the point?" He set his water down and eyed his father. "It will be a slightly altered version of this movie. And the one before it. And the one before that."

"And that's why they pay us the big bucks. And this time"—his eyes lit up like Christmas—"they're going to pay you double. I've got it all planned out."

Beckett snapped his fingers for Bob, then opened the door, staring into the cloudy sky. "I'm just sure you do."

Chapter Eight

- Breakfast: grapefruit, tea, no sugar/cream
- Lunch: soup, apple
- Calories: 425
- Exercise: 2 miles on bicycle
- Days 'til audition: 40

Dysfunction was apparently a family epidemic. I had it. I didn't know anyone who didn't.

Bundled up against the wind, I sat at lunch outside the school with the girls and pondered the previous day's weird exchange between Beckett and his dad. I'd read that his dad was his manager and very hands-on in his career. But apparently it'd been a successful formula. Otherwise Walmart wouldn't carry Steele Markov dolls on their shelves and teenagers wouldn't come in spastic herds to see the midnight openings of his movies.

"Don't you like your soup?" Erin lifted her spoon to her mouth and peered at the barely touched thermos her mom had packed for me. "It's still warm. You know, vegetables provide powerful antioxidants, which can delay the aging process. I was just reading this fascinating article yesterday—"

"Biscuits." Orla popped a cookie in her mouth. "Become the doctor who figures out how to get antioxidants into biscuits."

"It's good," I said. "I guess I'm just not hungry today." It was the stress. My counselor told me when those feelings started to creep up I was supposed to pull out my favorite verse and say it out loud. Or in my head. Sometimes I got so sick of those verses. Other times I wished God would come by and skywrite them in the clouds. "Have you guys ever seen this?" I plundered through my backpack until I drew out my brother's journal. It opened right to the last page. "This cross?"

Orla took a look first. "They're all over the country."

"You have to find that exact one?" Erin asked.

I quickly explained. "I can't finish my song without it. And if I don't finish my song, I'll mess up my audition with the New York Conservatory. Again."

"Cross yourselves." Orla glared over my shoulder. "Here comes Beatrice."

The queen bee and two of her ladies-in-waiting sauntered up to our table. "Hello, girls. What's new in your little world?"

"We were just talking about music," Orla said. "Music and soup."

Beatrice tapped her long nails together as she speared me with her dark brown eyes. "What exactly do you think you were doing at the set yesterday?"

In no rush to respond, I stirred my spoon in my thermos and watched some carrots and potatoes do backstrokes in the broth. "Working?"

She planted a hand on her hip. "I know what you're up to, and frankly, it's pathetic."

"Back off, Beatrice," Orla said. "You're just mad Beckett chose Finley and not you."

Beatrice ignored this and continued to stare me down. "If you think he likes you, you're delusional. He would never date a commoner. He only goes for actresses."

"It's a job. Not a dating opportunity. I don't want to be part of your little movie clique. I agreed to be his assistant and in return, he's helping me . . . with a project." That's all she was getting. I wasn't telling her one more detail.

Anxiety spun like a cyclone within me, and the food suddenly became a solid mass in my stomach. I shoved it away to get it out of sight. The pasta started to look like worms, the meat greasy wads of some poor, sacrificed animal.

In all these things, I am more than victorious through Him who loves me. In all these things, I am more than victorious through Him who loves me. In all these things, I am—

"Oh, I'll just bet he's helping you." Beatrice's top lip curled. "Just watch yourself. The movie business is a world few understand and few can handle."

Orla bit into an apple. "You've done a walk-on part for one movie and a commercial for socks."

Beatrice lifted her pointed chin. "I'd hate for you to . . . get hurt or get in any trouble and have to cut your stay short in Abbeyglen. That would be terrible." Her smile made my insides curl. "I'm just looking out for you. Like a friend. As the principal's daughter, I feel it's just naturally my job." She flounced away with her two bodyguards, who cast dark looks over their bony shoulders.

"Was that a threat?" Orla asked. "I don't like that."

"Beatrice just has her nose out of joint," Erin said. "She's under the misconception that she has a chance to get in Beckett's inner circle, and Finley's become an unexpected threat. And the fact that you're associating with us, instead of her—even worse."

"It really is just a job." I twisted the lid on my thermos. Ireland was supposed to be where I finally found peace.

God, why is turmoil following me like I'm in a bad soap opera?

"You've nothing to worry about." Orla pointed to my soup. "You going to eat that?"

"No."

"Can I have it?"

"Yes." I slid it her way. "I think I've lost my appetite."

☙❧

After school I hopped on my bicycle and pedaled away from Sacred Heart and toward Rosemore nursing home. Maybe I had caught Mrs. Sweeney on a bad day. Maybe she hadn't felt good, and it had made her uncharacteristically cranky.

God, help me get through this. Because I've got nothing to offer someone who's in the last stages of her life. Nor do I want to be around her. Please . . . help me.

Walking through the doors, I waved at Belinda the head nurse, smiled at the old woman in the wheelchair in the middle of the lobby, and followed the linoleum floor to hall C.

It's about Mrs. Sweeney. It's about Mrs. Sweeney.

Standing in front of room 12, I tapped my knuckles on the door, then peered inside. "Hello?"

She glared at me from her bed. "Go on with you."

I stepped inside. "I think we got off to a really bad start, ma'am."

"Don't make me get out of this bed, child."

I swallowed and kept on walking, getting closer to the dragon's nest. "My name is Finley Sinclair. And I want to be your friend."

She stared at me like I'd just offered her a time-share in the desert. "I don't have the energy to deal with you today, so I'm telling you, leave my room!"

"I can't do that, Mrs. Sweeney." I inched in more. "You and I are going to hang out a bit. I brought a book." I pulled out *Pride and Prejudice* from my bag.

"I don't like reading."

I unclenched my teeth. "Well, that's no problem. I'm going to read *for* you."

"D'you think you're better than a television?" She threw her head back and gave a frail laugh. "At least I can press the mute button on the telly."

Lord, you probably think this is funny, don't you? I guess somehow I deserve this.

"Have you ever read *Pride and Prejudice*?"

"No," she snapped. "I've no use for such romantic tales."

I took a seat in the chair beside her. Then scooted it back three inches, just in case I needed to make a hasty exit. Or in case she ate children. "It's a great book." Actually I hadn't read it. I figured everyone in the world had but me. Apparently, it was like the single girls' Magna Carta.

"I don't want to hear it." Mrs. Sweeney turned her head and faced the wall. "I don't know you, and I certainly don't want to hear your voice prattle on."

"I introduced myself. Do you remember that I'm from the school and—"

"Young lady, I do not have much time left." Mrs. Sweeney shot every word like a bullet. "And I do not want to spend what little remains with the likes of yourself!"

That was *it*.

"You know what? I'm here to spread some dang goodness and light, and I can't do that with you yelling at me!" Bloodshot eyes stared back at me as I stood. I might've been scaring her into a heart attack, but I couldn't stop. "I have had it up to *here* with death, and guess who I get assigned for this dumb project? You! Not some sweet old grandma. Not some storytelling grandpa. You!"

Mrs. Sweeney crossed her bony arms over her flannel-covered chest and huffed.

"Now, you need me." I stomped back toward her bed. "And I need to get my hours in. So we're going to be friends. Whether you like it or not."

"I'm calling the nurse." She reached for her button. "I pay too much money for this place. I don't even feel safe." Her breath wheezed, and I felt a stab of guilt. "If this is what young people are like today, then the whole world is doomed. Doomed, I say!"

"I'm not leaving."

"'Tis downright sinful to treat your elders in such a manner."

I eased back into the chair, shoved it back another few inches, then opened the book. "'It is a truth universally acknowledged, that a single man in possession of a good fortune must be in want of a wife.'"

"Gibberish!" Mrs. Sweeney held her bony fingers over her ears. "You're talking nonsense. Where is that nurse?"

The door flung open and Nurse Belinda rushed inside. "This better be good."

Mrs. Sweeney took two deep breaths, and again I reconsidered my stance. "This young girl here will not leave. She has taken over me room and invaded me privacy. I want her removed at once."

"Did you do that—invade her privacy without her permission?"

I clutched the book to my chest. "Yes."

"And did you refuse to leave after Mrs. Sweeney asked you to do so?"

My pulse skittered in my wrist. "Yes."

Belinda shook her head. Then smiled. "Good on you." She clapped me on the back and chuckled. "Now that's what I like to see. Cathleen, you can shout all you like, but Finley is welcome to stay. In fact, I'm prescribing it."

"You can't prescribe anything," Mrs. Sweeney said. "You're not a doctor, sure yer not."

"Then I'll get him to write an order. You ladies have a fine day." Whistling to herself, Nurse Belinda sauntered out, closing the door behind her.

With her lips pressed tight enough to vacuum seal, Mrs. Sweeney stared at me from her bed.

On the wall the third hand of a clock ticked off the seconds, reminding both of us time was slipping away. Time in that day. And in our two lives.

"If it's any consolation," I said after a moment, "this went much better in my head."

Those eagle eyes didn't even blink.

"I, um, I'm sorry. I don't deal well with stress."

She *harrumph*ed and deflated into her pillows. "Get us a drink of water."

At least she was acknowledging me. "Yes, ma'am." I walked to her side table and poured from a pink pitcher with her last name written on it in rushed, uneven letters.

She took the cup from my hand, shaking as she lifted it to her cracked, gray lips.

I returned to my seat and opened the book. "'It is a truth universally acknowledged, that a single man in possession of a good fortune must be in want of a wife.'" And as the seconds stretched out like warm taffy, I read for the longest thirty minutes of my life.

By the time I stuck a bookmark between the pages and shut the tome, Mrs. Sweeney's head tilted at an angle as she snored louder than a four hundred–pound man.

I slid the book into my bag and eased from the chair. Walking on tiptoes, I crossed the room and peeled open the door.

"Get a better book."

I froze with my hand on the knob.

Mrs. Sweeney opened one puffy, heavy-lidded eye. "I said, get a better book. That one is absolute rubbish. Featherbrained girl running after some silly boy? I won't have it."

I turned my head until I could cover my smile. "Yes, Mrs. Sweeney." I couldn't have agreed more. "Is there another classic you'd like to hear instead?"

"I should say so," she said as I pulled open the door. "Bring me something by that fella Stephen King."

Chapter Nine

STEELE MARKOV

I'm trapped. In this vampire body. In a world that
doesn't understand me. I don't want immortality . . .
I want my freedom.

Fangs in the Night, scene 5, page 24
Fierce Brothers Studios

When I get to heaven one day, I'm going to ask God how it's possible that time moves so much quicker on the weekends than on school days. Saturday and Sunday flew by as I helped the family with the scrapbooking guests, did my homework, Skyped with my parents, talked with my brother Alex and his wife, Lucy, then treated myself to some more of Will's journal.

Sitting in the music room Monday before school, I pulled the journal out and let my eyes memorize every detail of the picture on the eighth page. The photo was kind of blurry, but he'd captured a town. Houses painted in Crayola colors and drenched in early morning sunshine, surrounded by more of that grass that was so green, fairies must've repainted it every night when the people slept. Beneath the photo, Will's boyish cursive proclaimed a verse from Psalms.

Lord, You light my lamp; my God illuminates my darkness.

I knew dark. Dark was the dreary sky outside the windows of this room. It was the shade of the cloud that followed me every minute of the day. It was that voice that whispered I was never going to get this song right. Never going to close up the canyon in my soul where a brother used to be.

I rested the book in my lap and looked around. Since I had the place to myself, I let my ears open to the sound of the space. The hum of the lights above. The muffler of the car outside. The bird chirping in the drizzly distance.

God, where are you?

No answer.

I squeezed my eyes shut and tried harder.

Helllew, God.

It's me.

What did it take to get some attention here?

I have things to tell you, but I don't think there's any point. It's like you took a can opener and peeled the lid off my heart and leaped out the day Will died. Why are you so silent? Of all times to leave me alone.

"Sleeping or praying?"

I turned my head and found Sister Maria walking toward me. Her lined face had a rosy glow that, on any other woman, could only come from a Sephora counter. But I couldn't say I'd ever seen a sister buying up the MAC. Her khaki pants were perfectly ironed and her Sacred Heart polo tucked neatly inside her stretchy waistband. As she slid into a chair beside me, I caught that same twinkle in her eyes, as if she were only seconds away from delivering a clever punch line.

"I, um, I thought I'd have a little time with God before we started." That made me sound so mature. So holy. Never mind that only one of us had showed up to the divine meeting.

Sister Maria looked straight ahead, a smile pressing into her round cheeks. "It's a good place to sit and think. I come here quite a bit myself. And it has great acoustics. I've found it's the best place to practice my Beatles tunes. I sing the part of Paul, of course. My pitch is just about perfect on 'Let It Be.' The trick is to stay away from dairy. Clogs the throat." She directed her focus on me. "Now, we were talking about you."

"We were?"

"I believe I gave you some homework. How did it go?"

"My keyboard was delivered yesterday. I practiced for three hours last night."

"Not that homework."

"Oh." I hugged my backpack to me, resting my chin on top. "I went to the Cliffs of Moher."

"Good girl. And?"

"And that's it."

"What did you see?"

"The cliffs." My mind took me back, and I could almost feel the nip of the air on my face. "The birds. The ocean below us."

"Those are the basics. What did you *really* see?" Sister Maria waited for me to continue, with a look on her face that made me want to get the answer right.

"I guess . . ." That deep stuff—it was like wading through

pudding. "I saw what my brother did when he was here a long time ago. I could've stood in the very same spot. I watched the same waves and climbed on the same rocks. My brother said it reminded him of the verse about God's faithfulness reaching to the skies, like the view."

"Hmm." Her lips pursed as she considered this. "And did *you* sense God there? Did you hear him then?"

I gave a faint laugh. "God isn't exactly hanging out with me these days."

"Nunsense." She snorted and elbowed me again. "That was a joke. It gets Sister Mary Theresa every time. Of course she's also touched in the head, not that you heard that from me." Her face straightened into a mask of seriousness. "Finley, you simply must keep praying."

Like I hadn't been? Well, sorta. "But he's not listening."

"Oh, he's listening all right."

"No. Trust me." I jerked my chin upward, where a ceiling hung overhead, blocking me from the sky. Me from God. "Haven't heard a peep from him in over a year."

"So the line's clogged up. Sometimes when we get bad mobile reception, we don't know if it's our line or the other person's." She set some scales on the stand. "Hard to tell. So much interference with the signal these days." She set some scales on the stand. "I believe God spoke to you at the cliffs." Her hand came to rest on the top of my head. "But perhaps you weren't truly listening."

❧

From my place below the set, I watched Beckett stand in a tree, thirty feet above us, attached to a series of cables. Taylor Risdale, wearing a cranberry silk dress with a waist I couldn't fit one leg into, fluttered her Chinese fan.

The director grabbed his megaphone. "And . . . action!"

Beckett flew through the air, his hair blowing in the breeze, and his white shirt, unbuttoned to midchest, undulating as he swished through the forest like a noble prince. With really sharp teeth.

"They'll use CGI to make those cables disappear." Mr. Rush stood beside me, one eye on his son, one on his BlackBerry.

"Looks scary," I said.

"They're very careful. Effects have come a long way since my day."

"I guess lots of things have changed since then."

"Some. It's still a game of survival." He lowered his phone. "I hope you don't get any ideas about me son. Do you understand what I'm saying?"

Why did everyone say that to me? Did I look desperate? "I'm just here to help."

"You seem like a nice girl, and I don't want you to get your hopes up. I see it all the time. Girls throwing themselves at him." He laughed. "I remember those days meself."

"So you manage his career and his love life?" Had I really just said that?

"Make no mistake." He gave me his full attention. "His love life *is* his career."

Ten minutes later Beckett joined us, wiping sweat off his temple even though it was only sixty degrees.

"Da'." Beckett nodded his head at his father, then bestowed a smile on me. "Hello, Frances."

Cheeky boy. "Here's your water." Our fingers touched as I handed him the bottle, and electricity shot up my arm. *No. This*

*can't be happening. I am not attracted to him. Gotta think of some-
thing to distract myself from his blazing hot looks. That shirt. Please.
Might've been stylish in the 1800s, but now the only men who wear
flouncy shirts also have a collection of heels and handbags to match.
And his hair. He totally needs a haircut. And the pants?*

Oh. Who was I kidding? Beckett was as masculine as pickup
trucks and Stetsons.

"This coffee is cold." Mr. Rush stopped an assistant walking by.
"I would be forever in your debt if you'd get me another one, please.
One cream, two sugars." He gave her a grin, and I saw Beckett's
charm was stamped right in his DNA. "Thanks, dear."

"These people don't work for you, Da'." Beckett massaged the
muscles in his neck.

"If they work for you, they work for me. Now, about that
contract."

"Later. Finley and I are going to rehearse."

Mr. Rush studied me once again, and from the look on his face,
I could tell I didn't pass his test. "I'll come along. I'd like to talk to
you about—"

"I'm working."

A familiar giggle had me groaning. "Dad? Did you say dad?"
Beatrice shimmied our way, a predatory smile on her lips. "Are you
the famous Mr. Rush?"

Montgomery Rush gave Beatrice his camera-ready smile. "Me
son is the famous one."

"As are you, sir." Her voice became Marilyn Monroe light.
"You're renowned. How you've built Beckett's career, supported him
since he was just a little boy with a dream? Positively inspirational."

"There was never any choice." Mr. Rush regarded his son, his
eyes assessing, as if weighing the loss and gain. "When me boy got

the acting bug so young, I just had to move him to Los Angeles and nurture his dream."

Beckett's jaw tightened. "I don't remember telling you I wanted to be an actor."

"Of course you did. 'Da', I want to be in the movies.' That's exactly what you said."

"I was six. I also wanted to be an astronaut and a Shetland pony."

"My goodness, he was something at those auditions. Doing the name proud, he was." Mr. Rush rested his hand on his son's back. "Still is. And will for years to come."

"You're a wonderful father, Mr. Rush," Beatrice cooed. "And your son has been so . . . helpful to me on the set." Her viper eyes zeroed in on me. "He's just gone above and beyond to . . . make me feel so at home."

My temper simmered at a low boil, but it wasn't out of jealousy. It wasn't. I simply wanted Beatrice out of my sight. Removed. Like to another planet.

"Beckett, let me know when you're ready to run lines," I said. "I'm going to go grab something to eat from the craft services table."

"I'll join you." His fingers circled my upper arm, and for a second, I got a flash image of Taylor's winsome limb. Bony. Almost as slender as her wrist. What did he feel when he held mine? Was my arm fat? Flabby?

Suddenly a snack was no longer calling my name.

"I'm going to talk to your director," Mr. Rush said. "Nice to meet you . . ."

"Beatrice." She glared at me before putting her pretty face back on. "I'm sure I'll see you around."

I dislodged Beckett's grip and walked to the area that housed the food. Two tables sat beneath a tent, covered in food easily eaten on the go. Sandwiches, fruit, chips, pastries, granola bars, candy. All for the taking.

I picked up a sugar cookie and watched the sprinkles leave a crystal trail. My teeth sank into that first bite, and my taste buds sang an aria.

"Lots of snacks to pick from," I said as Beckett came in and picked up a protein bar.

"It's a trap." He tore into the wrapper. "It lures you in, then next thing you know, you can't button your pants."

I swallowed my bite of cookie. It made a slow crawl down my throat, and I wished I could bring it back up. Wished the fat wouldn't multiply in my cells. Tossing the rest of the cookie, I reached for a Diet Coke instead.

Beckett grabbed another water from a cooler, then stood beside me, with only inches between us. "I'm not messing around with Beatrice."

Placing the cookie in a napkin, I let it crumble in my grip. "I didn't ask."

"I know." His sigh was weary. "I just . . . I don't need those kind of rumors started—that I'm chasing girls from Sacred Heart."

Like me.

"I'm here to be your assistant and get a ride around Ireland. That's it. Besides"—I patted his white shirtsleeve—"we all know your reputation."

"Finley, I—" He clamped his mouth shut.

"Yes?"

"Nothing." He tore open his protein bar and threw the wrapper on the table. "Forget it."

"Beckett." Montgomery Rush held up his BlackBerry as he

walked toward us. "Did you check out yesterday's E! News main headline?"

"I'll look later. Let's go, Finley."

His dad read from his phone. "'Beckett Rush spotted in London Saturday. Tinseltown's It Boy reportedly had three dates with three different girls at La Trattoria . . . all over the course of six hours. Two of the ladies discovered the duplicity, and a catfight broke out. Taylor Risdale broke up the fight before storming out. Beckett's camp could not be reached for comment.'" Mr. Rush laughed. "You know what this means, right?"

"That once again my name is trashed."

"That your DVD sales will spike at least 5 percent." Mr. Rush grinned and looked to me to join in the odd celebration. "Isn't that great?"

"Yeah. Great." I looked at Beckett, remembered how it felt to stand beside him on top of the cliffs. The guy was nothing but a player.

And I wasn't going to forget it.

Chapter Ten

*The air seems cleaner, the colors sharper, my head . . .
quieter. It's like I can actually hear myself think. And hear
God talk. And that's usually a good thing . . .*

—Travel Journal of Will Sinclair, Abbeyglen, Ireland

I'm debuting me homemade banana-cranberry scones for a taste test." Erin's dad passed around a basket at the dinner table and waited for each one of us to take one. He watched our faces in nervous anticipation, wearing an apron that said "I Gave Up Big Guns For Sticky Buns."

"Well?"

"It's great, Dad," Erin said.

Liam crammed the whole thing in his mouth. "It's my favorite."

"That's what you said about the chocolate chip last week," Sean said.

Erin reached for the butter. "And the strawberry before that."

"Is it my fault Dad keeps topping himself? He's a genius."

"Don't ignore your dinner." Erin's mom passed the platter of fish around the table. "Finley, how are you getting on at school?"

"I like it. So far most of the girls have been really nice." I cut the battered cod into tiny pieces as the day's stresses twisted and twirled in a tattered ballet in my mind. My song, my audition, English project, Beatrice, Beckett. I'd thought this foreign exchange program would be one big vacation.

Erin bit into a fry, or as she called it, a chip. "Beatrice has been beastly to Finley."

"Really?" Nora asked, her face full of concern. "I'm glad you finally got away from her, Erin. Ignore her, girls."

Liam pushed up his sleeves. "I'll take care of it if you want me to. Sometimes these things just need a man to step in."

"That's not really necessary." I circled my fry through some ketchup, holding back a smile. "Besides, I know her type. She'll forget about me eventually and move on to a new target." I hoped it would happen soon. I was running out of energy to deal with her.

"Is it not any good?" Nora gestured to my plate. "Do you want something else, then?"

"No, it's great." I swallowed a bite of fish and felt the grease seep over my tongue. Taking a drink of water, I forced it down my throat. Along with my growing unease.

I felt overwhelmed.

Strange.

Just . . . off.

I couldn't explain it. But everything was out of place. Spinning.

Heads turned as a knock came from the door leading to the guests' dining room, and Beckett Rush walked in.

"Welcome!" Nora jumped up and went to the cabinet. "I'll get you a plate. I'm so glad you could join us after all."

"Are you sure you don't mind?"

"No!" the entire O'Callaghan family said.

Erin just stared in her starstruck trance. "Hey."

Sean pulled another chair to the table, and we squeezed together 'til you couldn't fit a dishrag between us. My knee touched Beckett's as he sat beside me, and I saw him look at me out of the corner of his eyes and smile.

Nora sat a plate in front of him. "Your father didn't want to join us?"

"No. He had meetings tonight."

"It's a shame we didn't have another room for him here," Nora said.

"He's fine with the rest of the crew." Beckett helped himself to some fish and chips. "They've got a great hotel about thirty minutes down the road with the many amenities me da' requires."

"And why didn't you stay there?" I couldn't help but ask.

"And miss this?" He took a bite of fish and his eyes rolled back in bliss. "Heaven."

Erin's mom laughed. "Stop that."

"It's true."

"Tell us how the movie's going," Sean asked. "I know Erin's dying to hear all about it. Right?"

"Um . . ." Her mouth opened and closed like a guppy. "Yes. Yes, I would."

That response had actually been understandable. I called that progress. Next she'd be able to articulate a few more syllables and make normal human eye contact.

Beckett talked about *Fangs in the Night* for a few minutes, but then turned the questions back on the family. He asked Sean about running a bed-and-breakfast and listened intently as Sean told him about two overflowing toilets on the second floor. After quizzing Nora about her day, he discussed video games with Liam.

When Beckett's plate was cleared, Nora brought out the coffee and apple crisp for dessert. Soon, amid the clank of cups on saucers and forks on plates, the room was full of stories and laughter. I sat back and watched as the family smiled at one another. Finished each other's sentences. Laughed before the punch line arrived.

And it made me miss my family.

The way we were. Before we changed. Before we were one less.

God, it's so unfair. Why would you pick my family to tear apart? Why take my brother? Why not some loser on death row? Some child abuser who deserves it. My brother was good. He was kind. He lived every day for you. And for what?

I pressed my napkin to my lips, then rested it on the table. "I think I'll just go for a little walk while there's still some light out. See that ruin on the property Erin mentioned." I smiled at Erin's parents. "Work off some of that amazing dessert."

"Would you like someone to go with you?" Nora asked.

"No, thank you. I won't be long."

I grabbed my coat off the peg near the door and headed outside. The gray sky threatened to rain, and by the smell of earth and moisture, I knew it wouldn't be too long in coming. I put my earbuds on and pulled up my own creation on my iPod.

I barely got out of the yard before I saw a familiar Labrador running along beside me. "Go home, Bob."

His soulful green eyes stared into me, as if he was sending me comfort and love. The world was so simple to a dog. I scratched his head and stopped. "You have to turn back. Beckett will think I kidnapped you."

"That's right, he will." Beckett walked toward us in his brown jacket, his hands stuffed in his pockets and a baseball cap on his head. "Bob, don't trust this girl. She looks innocent, but we know her type."

I turned off the music. "I'm sure you do. And every other type."

He clutchd his heart. "Another sweet insult from your lips. Are you like this with all guys or—"

"Or just infamous troublemaking actors?"

His smile faded as he walked beside me down the hilly driveway. "Why'd you leave?"

"I wanted to walk."

"You were sitting in there like you'd lost your best friend."

"Delayed jet lag."

"Really?" He slowed his steps and watched me. "Interesting."

"Go back inside, Beckett."

"I hired you to be my assistant. So if anyone is going to be bossing someone around, it's me."

"I'm off the clock." I kicked a rock with my shoe. "Go find one of your groupies."

"And end this riveting conversation?" He tossed a stick for Bob, and we both watched the dog race after it like a life was at stake.

I turned my attention back to Bob's owner. "Why do you stay at the B and B?"

"Because they cook good."

It was true, but I didn't buy his reason.

"So where's our next tourist stop?" he asked.

"They're not just tourist stops." It was more than that. It was like using the same map my brother did all those years ago, my longitude and latitude matching his. "I don't know where we're going next. I've been too busy with homework and practicing lately to think about it."

The night wind blew past us, and I huddled deeper into my jacket. South Carolina girls were not used to forty-degree temps in September.

"What's it like—going to school?"

I stopped at the sight of some wildflowers along the side of the road and reached to pick one. "School?" I shrugged. "Hectic. Busy. Loud. You go to a bunch of classes and learn a ton of stuff you care nothing about and will probably never use, and you pray the morning flies by so you can get to lunch and see your friends. You sweat through the indignities of PE and wish you had a double block of English and study hall because the rest of it is just grueling."

His lips spread into a smile. "It sounds grand."

"Right."

"No, I mean it. You're lucky."

"I passed out in pig dissection last year, hit my head, and had to wear a giant Band-Aid on my forehead all week."

He took the flower from my hand, and my skin tingled where his fingers brushed mine. "But you have those memories."

"And you don't." His voice had been neutral, as if he'd just been making casual conversation, but the tinge of sadness in his eyes had given him away. "Did you go to school on the set?"

He nodded. "Usually me, a few other child actors, and a tutor. I graduated last year."

"So no prom, no homecoming dance, no smelly gym class."

"No."

"Do you regret that?"

My breath stopped as Beckett reached out and tucked the flower above my ear, a wistful smile about his lips. "I regret a lot of things." His face was inches from mine as he studied me.

"I'm sorry you didn't get that experience," I whispered.

"Nobody said life was fair."

"It should be."

The air stilled, suspended with unspoken words, heavy thoughts, and two people who couldn't look away from one another.

Finally Beckett smiled, and that dimple popped.

The moment broke like a bubble in the breeze.

"So you're a big senior, or sixth year." Beckett cleared his throat and looked toward the darkening sky above us. "I'm sure the daughter of hotel magnate Marcus Sinclair and sister of two celebrity brothers has her whole future planned out."

"In October I audition for the conservatory. If I get in, I'll study there. Double major in violin and composition. That's if I pass the audition."

"Of course you will."

"It's my second time to try." I hadn't meant to say that. Something about the music of nature and the dimming light loosened my tongue. "Music is my life. The only thing that's made sense the last few years."

"I can't imagine you failing at anything." He raised his eyebrow, turning his statement into a question.

"That first audition . . . I didn't even make it into the building." The old shame barrelled through me as the memory unfurled. "My parents let me out at the entrance. I went to the auditorium while they parked, walked up the steps, went to the big double doors." I could still feel the metal under my skin. "Then I turned around and walked away." The doors had been so heavy, my arms couldn't seem to open them. My head wouldn't hold the tempo of the audition selection. My fingers wouldn't stop shaking enough to even grip the violin. "I just couldn't do it. My parents found me sitting on a bench in front of a dorm." Hands belted around my knees, humming my piece, and crying hot tears. "That was six months ago." When I got a new counselor. A lady who told me I wasn't crazy. Just broken.

"And how's that new song coming along?"

"It has to be perfect this time. And it's not." Last time I had prepared a generic audition piece. But this composition would be personal. It would be Will's.

"Anyone ever tell you you're too hard on yourself?"

"All my life. And you?" It was time to turn this conversation around. "Is acting the career you want?"

"Who wouldn't want my life?"

"That doesn't answer my question."

"So it doesn't."

"Do you ever miss your mother?"

"I never knew her, so no. But I miss what could've been." He tilted his head. "It's nothing like what you went through, is it now? It was a horrible story, about your brother. How do you get over something like that?"

"You don't."

The stitches on the old wound unraveled within me as I thought about the answer. "I held on to hope that he was alive for almost a year." I wiped my nose and told myself to stop. I'd never even told my counselors that. "I prayed by the hour during those months. I had faith then. And where did that get me? Where was God when my brother died? When my world imploded?" My voice broke and I covered my face. "I have to go." I dashed past Beckett and walked as fast as I could.

With Bob running ahead, Beckett caught up with me in three strides. He reached for my arm and pulled me to a stop. "Wait."

"I should be over this. I know I should. But I'm not." Through my tears, I saw concern staring back at me. And it just added another knot to the dark tangle inside. "I want to be me again—to have faith, to feel hope, to feel . . . something. Something besides this . . . this . . ." Ugliness. I closed my mouth and just shook my head.

"Hey. It's okay to be mad." Beckett slid his arms around me and enfolded me in a hug. "But you can't give up on your faith."

"What do you know about it?" I asked against his jacket.

"I watch a lot of TV."

He rubbed circles on my back while I held on, despite my better judgment. I blinked away the last of the tears. "I just spilled my guts to a vampire."

"It's one of our many tricks." He took a step back, and the wind filled the space between us. "Before I'm done with you, you'll be craving type O and hanging out with bats."

Reaching into my pocket, I pulled out my phone and touched the screen. "Do you recognize this?"

His hand on mine, Beckett drew the phone toward him. "It's a Celtic cross."

"I have to find it."

He looked at me and gave a low laugh. "They're all over the country. There are thousands just like that."

No, there couldn't be any just like that one. "This one apparently captured my brother's attention. And I have to find it. It's the last thing he put in his journal. If I don't locate it, my trip is incomplete—my audition piece, incomplete. I will find this."

"It's going to be next to impossible."

"It was important to my brother. And now"—I shook my head, knowing I sounded like I'd lost it—"now it's become this obsession." I seemed to have quite a collection of those.

Clouds darkened overhead, forming a canopy of gray. "But what if you've let your grief become your guilt?" His voice was as soft as the night breeze. "It's okay to let it go."

I shook my head and moved out of his grip. "I can't," I said. "Not now. Not yet."

And sometimes I feared . . . not ever.

Chapter Eleven

- Lunch: one apple, two plain rice cakes, Diet Coke
- Calories: 150
- Taste: zero
- Days to audition: 32

As I pedaled my bike, a man I recognized as the local butcher strolled with his wife, an umbrella over their heads. "Good day to you, Finley from America."

"Good day to you, Mr. and Mrs. Walsh." I loved the sound of their accents.

"Sure, we saw you running this morning," Mr. Walsh said as I stopped, putting my toes to the ground. "We called out to you, but me wife said you had in those ear thingamabobs and couldn't hear. Running so fast, you scared the coats right off me sheep."

I laughed, my legs still jelly from pushing myself four miles. Pretty good for not putting on running shoes in a month.

"Next time you come round, you stop in for tea," Mrs. Walsh said.

"I'll do that." As I pedaled away, I thought how back home, we threw out invitations and knew it was just polite talk. In Ireland? It meant I'd better see you at my house soon.

A light misting rain peppered down on this chilly Wednesday afternoon, and I held my own umbrella while steering my bicycle with one hand, a skill I was proud to have acquired. And one that was necessary. I was sure I hadn't had a frizz-free day since arriving. I guess it was the price you paid to be in one of the most beautiful places on earth.

Hopping off my bike, I wheeled it under the awning of the Rosemore and went inside. Every time I opened the door, a wave of disappointment washed over me. The nursing home looked the same. Smelled the same. Felt the same. I didn't know why I kept hoping for it to magically transform into Disney World or some other place of happiness and smiles. But it was never going to do that. This was a building where old people came to spend their last days. Where they came to die. Like Mrs. Sweeney.

I said hello to the nurse on duty at the front desk and found my way to Mrs. Sweeney's door. "Hello?"

I waited for Mrs. Sweeney's usual command to leave, but heard nothing.

The room was dark, save for the dim light coming through the window. I flipped on the lights.

"Mrs. Sweeney!" She lay on the floor in a heap, eyes wide, shaking. I rushed to her and dropped to my knees. "Are you all right?"

She closed her eyes. "Does it . . . does it look like I'm all right?"

"Let me call the nurse."

"No." Her whisper sounded loud in the still room. "Just help me up. I'm . . . I'm too weak."

"You might've broken something. I don't think I should try to move you." What would Erin have done? She'd have known all that medical stuff.

She lifted her head and glared. "Am I not eighty-three years old? I believe I would know if something was broken. I just can't get meself up. Quit your prattling and give us some assistance."

Reluctantly, I eased my arms under hers, and together we slowly raised her from the floor. The woman weighed no more than Erin's stick of a brother, and as I settled her into her silver wheelchair, she heaved a long breath.

"Thank you." She rested her elbow on the chair and leaned her head into her hand.

"Are you sure you're feeling okay?"

"Fine."

"Because you just thanked me."

"'Twas an accident." She continued to take deep, quivery breaths with her eyes closed, as if she was trying not to relive those last few moments on the floor.

"What happened?"

Mrs. Sweeney remained quiet for a long stretch before finally answering. "I had to go to the loo. Normally I can take meself." She lifted her head and took some steadying breaths. "It was dark. I was groggy. Tripped over my slippers." Holding up her hands she grimaced. "No harm done."

"This time," I said. "And how long had you been on the floor?"

"It doesn't matter," she snapped as the color returned to her cheeks. "Make yourself useful and get us a glass of water."

Biting my tongue, I did as I was told, letting my heart return to its regular pace.

"Aren't you supposed to be at school?"

"It's lunchtime." I forced my voice to speak in notes of calm.

"You crazy Irish folk let your teenagers run all over town for lunch."

"Where you do nothing but find trouble."

"The more scandalous the better. Like visiting nursing homes." I handed her the cup. "I still think I should call the nurse. Have her check you out."

"Don't you dare. I've been poked and prodded all day."

"And nothing hurts?"

"Just me ears."

"From my prattling. Yes, got it." I smiled just to annoy her. "I brought us a book to read."

She *harrumph*ed as I sat down and pulled it from my bag. "Stephen King." I showed her the cover. "*Carrie.*"

"I read that years ago." Mrs. Sweeney rubbed her elbow. "I guess I could give it another listen. Until you find me another."

"Since it's about a girl who ends up terrorizing people, I thought maybe you could pick up some new tricks."

She slid me a look. "The only evil in this room is you. Impertinent girl."

She was half right. Sunday as I sat with the O'Callaghan family in the seventh row of their church, I found myself tuning out. After I doodled my name fifty-seven times on a bulletin, I started strategizing my approach with Mrs. Sweeney. The assignment wasn't going away. I needed to deal with her in a way that would keep her at arm's length—because I would not be getting attached—yet I needed to be friendly enough to get her to cooperate.

My church-inspired conclusion was that she was obviously a proud woman, so if she was anything like me, sympathy over her situation would not win her over. After my brother's disappearance, there was nothing I detested more than people oozing with softly spoken words and hugs that went on way too long. And Mrs. Sweeney didn't need that either.

At least that was the theory. And since I came up with it in a church, surely it was inspired by God. Or boredom. Either way, I thought it was sound. I'd just have to log in those twenty hours as quickly as possible, then I could say good-bye to the crabby woman.

"Are you ready for me to read?" I took her outstretched cup and placed it on the bedside table.

"I was ready ten minutes ago. If you wait any longer I'll have time to write a novel meself."

"Yes, ma'am." I opened the book and read, filling the sentences with an animated voice and pausing for suspense at all the right places, composing a soundtrack in my head, heavy on the strings.

By the time I got to chapter three, Mrs. Sweeney's eyes had closed and her breathing came slow and even. I'd have been insulted, but I decided I liked her this way.

"Knock, knock!" Nurse Belinda stuck her head inside and smiled. "Cathleen, I brought the mail. Oh." She lowered her booming voice. "She's asleep."

I double-checked to make sure Mrs. Sweeney was truly out. "She fell this afternoon," I whispered.

"Did she now?" Belinda shook her head, and the salt-and-pepper bun on her head tottered. "She's had a rough week. Hardly gets out of bed now. It breaks my heart." She held out an envelope just as an alarm went off somewhere down the hall. "Do me a favor and stick this in her top drawer. I've got to go check on a resident. Cathleen always tells me to throw her mail away, but I know she just digs these letters out of the trash and saves them." The alarm continued to squawk like an angry bird, and Belinda sailed out of the room.

I tiptoed around Mrs. Sweeney's bed and to her dresser. I reached for the top drawer, and the thing wouldn't budge. Gripping the pull, I gave it a yank. On the third try, it flung open and letters spilled onto the floor.

Peering inside, I saw stacks and stacks of letters. Same white envelopes. Same address. To Fiona Doyle, Galway. From Cathleen Sweeney.

Each one marked return to sender.

Just like the one in my hand.

"Now, we're just looking today, Erin." Nora O'Callaghan held up a soft ivory dress that shimmered under the lights of Hargood's House of Formal Wear, a store that mostly carried a small selection of custom bridal wear and custom pieces.

"So the girls wear white dresses and the boys wear . . . ?"

"White shirts," Erin said. "Nice pants, many wear suits, usually in light colors."

"I was hoping the guys had to dress like Columbus." I flipped through two racks of white flowy dresses, the kind you'd wear on a summer night on the beach or frolicking through an Irish field of wildflowers looking for fey folk and leprechauns.

"Do you see anything you like?" A woman popped her head between two racks, a measuring tape dangling from her neck and a pincushion wrapped around her wrist.

"Deirdre here makes them special every year," Nora said.

"Sure. Me and me daughter. We order some too. Those folks in China make a good St. Flanagan's Day dress as well."

"Nothing compares to yours, and you know it."

Deirdre held up a humble hand. "You get the dress in one of the four sizes," she said to me, "and we alter it to fit."

"Och, Erin, what about this one, then?" Nora held up a white thing with a ruched top and tea-length skirt.

"That one's made just for your tiny frame," Deirdre said.

"What do you think, Finley?" Erin asked.

"You'd look beautiful in it."

Nora grabbed an armful of choices and pushed us toward the dressing rooms. "In you go. I'll pass the garments over. I've left your dad and Liam at home fixing a broken washing machine, so quickly, if you please. I'm afraid, given too much time, Liam will have the thing torn apart and refashioned as a robot."

"Who are you asking to the dance?" I asked Erin from my dressing room as I lifted my sweater over my head. The full-length mirror in front of me framed my body, and I stepped closer and stared. My eyes traced the line of my hips, my convex stomach, the legs beneath my jeans.

What did the world see when they looked at me?

"I've a mind to ask Samuel Connolly," Erin said from the other side of the wall. "He's a fifth year, but mature for his age. Very smart. Not much time left to ask though. Why don't guys get as stressed out about this as we do? I think he likes me, but I'm not sure."

"He'd be an idiot if he didn't like you." I pulled a dress on, letting it slide down my arms and cascade over me. The material lay soft against my skin and I tried to imagine myself dancing in a cute guy's arms. Beckett Rush's smiling face came to mind, and I blinked it away. Silly thoughts.

Reaching for the door, I stepped outside. "What signs have you seen that Samuel's interested?"

"Oh, lots of them," Erin called. "He said hello to me on Tuesday.

Waved at me from his bicycle last Sunday. And I'm fairly certain he smiled when we passed him in our car on Friday. But I could be wrong. He also might've been sneezing. It was from a distance. Hard to tell." The dressing room door creaked as Erin stuck out her head. "So basically either he's madly in love with me . . . or he doesn't even know I exist." With hesitation on her face, Erin joined us.

Nora dug in her purse and pulled out her phone. "Oh, if your father could see you now, he'd burst into tears."

"Mam, no pictures!"

"It could be your last festival dance. Next year you'll be gone. I have to document the memories." The camera flashed twice. "And, Finley, you're a vision, you are." She snapped two more. "Your mam will flip." Nora walked a circle around me. "Just a nip and tuck here and there. Deirdre will make this fit as if it were made for you."

Erin smiled. "I think it is."

We changed back into our clothes, both Erin and I having our eye on our favorites.

"There's himself calling again," Nora said as she followed us out of the dressing room. "This is the third time your father's called. I better take it." She held the phone to her ear and walked toward the front of the store.

Just as Beatrice and the Poshes walked in.

"Oh great." I turned and faced the other direction, studying a rack of dresses with great interest. Mother-of-the-bride dresses.

"Hello, Bea," Erin said. "Shopping for a dress?"

"I'm helping my *friends* select theirs." Bea and her minions simultaneously smirked.

Erin's smile didn't falter. "Found your own already?"

Beatrice tossed her hair. "I had it special ordered, of course." Her chin lifted as she looked around. "My father had me order a few different gowns for the Hollywood premiere of the movie, so I went ahead and got a dress for the dance. If I'm not working on the next movie, I suppose I'll be at the festival. I do hope you can find yourself a date this time." She looked at Erin with feigned pity. "It was so sad last year, to watch you go alone."

Erin's mouth dropped. "Well, I—"

"And two years in a row?" Beatrice and her girls shared a snotty smile. "Total social death, I would suppose." Her lips curled in a smile. "Good luck with that."

"But . . ." Erin's cheeks glowed pink. "I . . . I have a date."

Like a bad paranormal movie, time seemed to stop as I looked at Erin. And she looked at me.

"Is that so?" Beatrice's voice dripped with disbelief as thick as cake batter. "Who?"

Erin cleared her throat and glanced at me again. "You'll just have to wait and see."

If was official. My host sister had crossed over to the dark side.

Desperation had just made this good girl go bad.

Chapter Twelve

- Days until audition: 34
- Breakfast: 2 eggs, 1 Diet Coke
- Calories: 108
- Exercise: 1 hour running, 30 min. talking to Mom and Dad

With the world heavy on my mind Thursday afternoon, I left school as soon as the lunch bell rang, hopped on my bike, and headed toward the nursing home. I had to get my hours in and wrap up the Mrs. Sweeney experience. She was deteriorating, and I didn't want to be there to see it. And I shouldn't have to be. What kind of school would put that on a kid?

The sun warmed my face as I pedaled, and my mind drifted to that morning. After my run I had nothing else to do, so I picked up my worn Bible and cracked it open to Isaiah 43, where the ribbon marker took me.

Do not fear, for I have redeemed you; I have called you by your name; you are Mine. I will be with you when you pass through the waters, and when you pass through the rivers, they will not overwhelm you.

If that was all true, where was God when my brother died? Where was God when I was at rock bottom last year making stupid choices, seeing two counselors, with parents who watched me for fear that I'd never come out of my bedroom again?

And where was God now?

Arriving at the home, I threw the kickstand down and reached into the basket, lifting out a small cooler. It was Nora O'Callaghan's idea.

"Bring Mrs. Sweeney a picnic," she'd said. "Get her outside. She needs some sun."

If she melted on my watch, I was *so* flunking English.

"Good afternoon, Mrs. Sweeney." I knocked twice, then walked on inside. As usual, the room's dimmer switch was locked on depression mode, and I decided I'd had enough. All this darkness couldn't be good for the woman. Assuming her pain was low today, she was about to get some Vitamin D therapy. "How are you feeling?"

From her bed, Mrs. Sweeney swiveled her head in my direction as I walked to her window. "Who are you?"

"The same girl who was in here Wednesday. And every glorious visit before that."

"I've never seen you before in my life." She pointed her finger toward the door. "Leave my room at once."

"Nice try. Despite my protests, Belinda assures me there's nothing wrong with your mind." Pulling with both hands, I jerked the curtains apart, and sunlight flooded the room.

Mrs. Sweeney gave a yell from the back of her throat and threw up her arms to cover her face. "I can't stand that sun!"

I turned around and smiled. "I see the vampires have gotten to you too."

She blinked against the light. "Rude, impertinent child."

I walked to her bed and fluffed her pillows, appreciating the organization of her bedside table. "I see you had a shower today. But that hair needs brushing. Tell me where a brush is or I go through all your drawers. You don't want me to discover your secret stash of *Enquirer* magazines, do you?"

"What?" She flopped her hand toward her pine chest-of-drawers. "Top drawer. But my hair is fine."

"If you want birds to nest."

"I mean second one!" Mrs. Sweeney sat up, spitting crackers. "Stay out of the top drawer!"

But it was too late. I opened the drawer and saw the piles of returned letters again. The envelopes seemed to jump out and beg for me to touch them, to deliver them from the cold recesses of the drawer.

"I said to shut that," Mrs. Sweeney snapped.

Biting my tongue on the million questions, I got the brush and went to work, slowly getting out the day's snarls. "I shopped for a dress yesterday." That was my new tactic. I was just going to talk like Mrs. Sweeney gave a rat's tail. Like my life was the most fascinating thing ever. "Erin and I both found dresses. But then we ran into Beatrice."

Mrs. Sweeney closed her eyes as if she were sleeping.

"Beatrice is the villain in this story, in case you're keeping up. I guess she has a history of harassing Erin and her friends. Erin told Bea she had a date for the dance, and now Erin is going to ask Samuel, but if he says no, it's gonna be bad. But who would say no to Erin? She's gorgeous. And I know I should pray for Beatrice, but, well, my prayer list is very long now that I've met you, and I simply don't have time. Should I continue praying for your bunions?"

Her gray lips tightened.

"I'll take that as a yes." I set the brush down. "Where was I? Oh, I was taking you on a picnic."

Her eyes popped open. "A what?"

"Picnic," I said with more enthusiasm than I felt. "You'll love it."

A knock sounded from the door, then Belinda and an assistant walked into the room.

"Just in time," I said. "She's all ready."

"No, I'm not!" Mrs. Sweeney sputtered as the two nurses gently eased her into her wheelchair. "Put me down. You can't manhandle me. I'm a sick woman."

"You told the doctor you feel good today," Belinda said. "Finley's offered to take you outside to get a little air, get some food." Reaching into Mrs. Sweeney's closet, the nurse took out a coat and eased the woman into it.

I grabbed a blanket from the end of her bed and draped it over her legs. "Ready?"

"No." Mrs. Sweeney's eyes were wide, whether with anger or fear, I wasn't sure. "No, I don't want to go. I want to eat my lunch here."

"It's beef and cabbage day," Nurse Belinda said. "You hate cabbage."

"Come on, Mrs. Sweeney." I released the brake on her wheelchair and gripped the handles. "I promise I won't keep you out past your curfew." I gave Nurse Belinda a questioning look, but she gave me two thumbs up and waved us out the door.

"Work on that tan!" Belinda called as I wheeled Mrs. Sweeney down the hall, carrying our picnic in the crook of my arm and praying this didn't end in disaster.

"Don't talk Finley's ear off, Cathleen," Belinda said as I pushed Mrs. Sweeney outside.

The sun shone down on us, and Mrs. Sweeney shielded her eyes with a shaking hand. "It's too bright."

"I can take care of that." I pulled the pink sunglasses off the top of my head and slipped them on Mrs. Sweeney. "You look fabulous."

"I want to go back inside."

"As soon as we eat."

"I'm not hungry."

"I know the feeling. My counselor said being in a funk will do that to you."

I pushed the wheelchair down the sidewalk. "You just let me know if you want me to pop any wheelies. We could totally catch air on this thing."

Mrs. Sweeney ignored me as she sat with her arms crossed over her chest, her hands tucked inside her coat sleeves. But when we passed by the bakery, her eyes fluttered closed and she inhaled the yeasty aroma.

"When's the last time you were outside?" We walked in front of a gift shop, and a woman waved from the window where she stacked St. Flanagan figurines.

"Awhile," Mrs. Sweeney finally said.

"Like last month?"

"No."

"Last year?"

She shook her head as she took in all of downtown, watching it as if it were a Spielberg film.

"When?"

"I don't know." Her voice was as soft as a thornbush. "Five years or so."

"You haven't been outside your nursing home room?" No wonder she was so miserable. "Why?"

"None of your business." She lifted a hand in greeting to a woman pushing a baby stroller.

"Mrs. Sweeney . . ." I followed the sidewalk to the left and took us to the small park. "Who is Fiona Doyle?"

Mrs. Sweeney coughed into her fist and shook her fuzzy head. "She's nobody."

I steered the wheelchair onto the grass, putting my weight into it to make the chair move. "How's this spot?" Taking off my jacket, I laid it on the ground, then went about setting up our lunch. "Nora packed this for us. Here's some chicken. Some sort of salad." I lifted out the final container. "And if we're good girls, she packed a few of Sean's chocolate chip scones. He's just perfected them." I fixed Mrs. Sweeney's plate, cutting up her meat in small pieces, then handed it to her. "So you were telling me about the letters. That's a lot of letters you've written to nobody."

"If I must be out here, let me eat in peace."

"I just thought perhaps I could find the right address for you."

Mrs. Sweeney glared as I helped her with her fork. "I have the right address. I'm not addled."

"Then why—"

"I will not discuss this." With a sigh she chewed her chicken, a signal the conversation was over.

Keeping one eye on our beautiful surroundings and one on my elderly charge, I noticed she ate like a bird. A very slow, tired bird, and it was hard to watch. As I continued to help her with her lunch, I kept up my one-sided conversation and was halfway through another Beatrice story when a man walked our way. He wore baggy pants, an old T-shirt, and his long, dark dreadlocks hung down like snaky ropes.

It was Beckett's worst disguise yet.

"Good afternoon, ladies."

I pulled out another piece of chicken for our guest. "Hi."

"Beautiful day out," he said in a Jamaican accent. "Not a cloud in the sky."

"Yeah. It's nice," I said. "Interesting Irish-Caribbean brogue you've got there."

Mrs. Sweeney eyed him with blatant suspicion. "I'm ready to go back anytime."

"Surely you don't want to leave yet." He smiled at me, revealing even, white teeth. "I hear there are actors in town. You might miss one."

I picked at my salad. "They're nothing special."

"I hear one in particular is good-lookin'. That Rush mon."

"I've seen better."

His grin deepened. "Have you now?"

"Besides Beckett Rush is kind of . . ."

"Charming and manly?"

"I was going to say feminine. And pasty."

He laughed and took the uneaten chicken leg from my hand and brought it to his lips. "Since you insist on ripping my heart out, the least you can do is feed me."

"Who is this man?" Mrs. Sweeney asked. "What's going on here?"

"This," I said, "is Beckett Rush. He's an actor." Mrs. Sweeney's unimpressed stare made me laugh. "He stars in vampire movies."

Her eyes widened with interest now. "Is this true?"

"It is, ma'am." He took one of her veiny hands in his and gave it a small squeeze. "Just one of my little disguises so I can go about without notice. We're making a movie a few blocks away. Finley's been kind enough to help me with my lines."

"Oh, she's real helpful," Mrs. Sweeney said. "Finley, get the boy a plate."

"He's too busy to eat with us. An important actor like Beckett probably has to eat with the cast or go to some meeting or sign autographs for screaming girls."

"I told you I would sign your shirtless Beckett Rush poster." He took a seat on the grass beside me, his knee brushing against my leg. "Now, Mrs. Sweeney, I would hate to impose on your tea party, but that chicken smells quite good. I bet you used to be a fierce cook, am I right?"

I blinked twice. Surely my eyes failed me. What was that on Mrs. Sweeney's face? Was it . . . a smile?

She flopped her hand and gave a small chuckle. "Sure, I cooked. But baking was my specialty."

"Ah." Beckett reached over me and grabbed another piece of chicken. His arm brushed against my shoulder, and I forced myself not to draw back. "So you were all about the sugar and spice." He shook his greasy finger at Mrs. Sweeney. "You're my kind of woman."

She laughed again, a rusty sound I barely recognized, as if her pipes hadn't played that tune in years.

I looked at Beckett and shook my head in shame. "You just can't turn it off, can you?"

He winked a gray eye. "Just part of me charm, Frannie."

"I can't ever remember her name either." Mrs. Sweeney's lips quirked as she slanted me a look. "Tell me about this movie."

And so Beckett did. As if he had all the time in the world, he explained the entire plot and every character, bringing the saga to life, with the storytelling skills of a born Irishman. Mrs. Sweeney leaned forward in her chair, hanging on his every animated word.

"Now that's a tale." She sat back when Beckett finished. "Not like that drivel she tried to read me."

"I said I was sorry. I won't insult you with Jane Austen again. How was I to know you had a taste for blood?" I put the lid on my water and placed it back in the cooler. "Though now that I think about it, it makes perfect sense."

"Disrespectful child," Mrs. Sweeney muttered.

But there was some color on her cheeks, and her frown didn't seem to be so severe. If I wasn't mistaken, she was enjoying herself.

An unexpected flutter of happiness shimmied through me. I'd just wanted a change of scenery and to get in some hours. But somehow . . . I thought I might've brightened Mrs. Sweeney's day.

With Beckett's help.

His phone buzzed in his pocket. He pulled it out and checked the display.

"Girlfriend number twelve missing you?" I asked, watching his forehead furrow.

Distractedly, he fired off a quick text. "Something like that. I've got to get back." His smile returned as he stood up, flipped his crazy dreads, and took Mrs. Sweeney's hand again. "It was an honor to meet you. Please don't let Finley here talk bad about me when I leave."

"I tune out every word she says anyway."

Beckett helped her with her sagging blanket, then leveled that deep gaze on me. "Thank you for lunch. That was . . . unexpectedly good."

I didn't know whether he meant the food or the company. Either way, coming from his lips, the words sounded as decadent as chocolate cake. *God, help me with my immunity force field with this boy. Falling for him would bring nothing but trouble. And I've had plenty already.*

"By the way, Bob said to tell you he's ready for another adventure."

I brushed the grass off my uniform skirt. "I'd hate to upset a Labrador. What do you have going on this weekend?"

"Filming. I've some downtime though."

"I'll pick a place."

"See that you do." And with another grin to Mrs. Sweeney, Beckett walked away.

"'Tis a fine young gentleman there," Mrs. Sweeney said.

"Yeah." I watched him until he disappeared around the corner. "He's okay."

"Okay?" She flicked crumbs off her lap. "He's first-rate."

I slipped my jacket back on, picked up the cooler, then reached for her wheelchair. "He's also a total player and wild as the Irish wind."

"Psshh." She grumbled as I pushed her back onto the sidewalk. "Don't tell me I don't know what I'm talking about. I said he's a good boy." Resting her chin into her hands, she slumped in her chair as if the day had suddenly caught up with her. "I can spot a bad one a mile away. I know their kind too well."

"I'm a really good listener, if you'd like to expand on that." I hummed a new scrap of melody that popped into my head. "Maybe tell me about those letters. Confession *is* good for the soul."

I expected her to tear into me yet again, but instead she stayed silent for several seconds, running her fingers over the trim of her blanket. "I do believe my soul is past the point of helping."

"That's not true. It's never too late."

She looked at the town as we walked by, her eyes heavy with

fatigue. And an ache so deep, it didn't have a name. I'd seen that look in my own mirror.

"I gave up that right many years ago," she said. "My fate is like those envelopes—sealed and tossed aside."

Chapter Thirteen

- Hours of practice: 3
- Hours of sleep: 4
- Hours looking for cross: 2

The piano bench groaned as I sat down in the music room Friday during lunch. I opened my brother's journal to the page I'd read twice already that morning.

Went to Galway tonight. People everywhere, enjoying life, smiling, and just slowing down to let the world take care of itself for a few hours.

The feeling was contagious. Especially when I stepped into McPherson's Pub to grab a bite of the special and listen to some traditional Irish music. The fiddle made me want to dance myself, and many did. The drum beat like my very own heart. And some little flute that looked no wider than a pencil reminded me of the Aran Islands floating not too far from Abbeyglen.

God was here tonight. In the strings of the guitar and the call of the singer's voice. I realize how often I overlook him back home.

And I know I don't want to do that anymore.

The LORD will send His faithful love by day; His song will be with me in the night a prayer to the God of my life.

Psalm 42:8

"Happy Friday." Sister Maria walked into the classroom, a gentle smile on her face. This was the woman who could help me with my audition, who could make sure there would be no doubt I was ready.

"Hello." Funny how when I was in this room, I breathed easier. When I saw her, the muscles in my shoulders loosened. I could just . . . be myself.

I put up my journal and placed my fingers on the keys.

"Starting with the piano today, are we? Why don't you just warm up for me?"

I played some scales, enjoying the freedom of the familiarity, the echo and reverb of the notes.

"You play the piano by ear," she said as I stopped.

"I can read music."

"I know this as well." She nodded to the piano. "Just play."

"What?"

"Anything you like."

I thought about it a moment before launching into an old Black Eyed Peas song, jazz-style.

"No." She put her hands on mine. "You've something weighing on your mind. I want to hear that."

"How?"

She smiled. "Try."

I sat there as the minutes scraped by.

"Anytime."

This felt . . . wrong. It was invasive. It was too . . . personal. Like she was asking me to cut open my heart and let her see the ugly mess of it all.

"I can't."

"Finley," Sister Maria said. "There's no perfection here. Music is never perfect. It has flaws, it has character. It has to start rough. Especially when that's what you feel." She crossed her arms over her chest. "Now begin."

My fingers hovered over the worn, ivory keys. My breath came faster, as did the unexpected pressure of tears.

"Close your eyes."

The woman was bossy.

But I obeyed.

Please, God.

And then I played.

From the pit of my soul, the place where the bleakness crouched low. Where the week's anxieties gathered like the calories, the music began.

Three minutes later my hands moved over the black, my fingertips pressed into the white, until it all made sense. My foot held the pedal as I heard the ending in my head seconds before my hands repeated.

Tears dripped onto my chin, my hands, slapping me out of my trance.

"I can't do this."

I stopped.

Sister Maria just looked at me, no expression on her face. No judgment. "Feel better?"

"Not really."

She smiled and slowly nodded. "You've the gift, Finley Sinclair. Believe in it."

"I have to finish this audition piece."

"And you will. Don't rush it."

"But I can't get the ending until I—"

"When you're ready to hear the rest, you will. Just like today." She stood to her feet and wiggled her fingers toward my violin case. "Now before I hear you play your song again, why don't you tell me what's on your mind?"

I got up and unpacked my violin, running my hand over the maple scroll. "I can't stop thinking about Cathleen Sweeney, the woman I visit as part of my English project." And heaven knew I didn't want to think about her.

She nodded. "I've heard of her."

"Do you know anything about her?"

"Just that she hasn't any family. I hear she's a little bit of a pistol."

"She's lonely." Had I just taken up for Mrs. Sweeney? "I mean, she's sick and dying, and she thinks it's too late to make amends with God."

"So maybe you're the person to help her see the light."

"But God and I aren't speaking, remember?"

"Still?" Sister Maria looked to the ceiling and let out an exaggerated breath. "How long is this standoff going to last, then?"

I shook my head. "I feel sorry for Mrs. Sweeney."

"Understandable," she said. "But not entirely useful."

"What should I do?"

Sister Maria held up her hands in a shrug. "Nothing?"

"But . . ." Ideas spun and sputtered in my head. "I think I have to do something."

"Ask God."

I felt like we'd worn this topic out. "I told you we're—"

"Ask him anyway." Sister Maria chuckled. "You'd be surprised what he might come up with—if you're looking for it."

"Speaking in parables went out with the New Testament times."

"I'm trying to bring it back. That and the jitterbug." She glanced at my backpack on the floor, where my journal stuck out. "What does today's entry say?"

"My brother talks about going to Galway."

"A beautiful place. Can be quite lively."

"He seemed enchanted with the music."

"Ah, yes. Who wouldn't be?"

"I've heard some Irish music. Will it be so different there?"

"Depends. If there's a difference, I've every confidence you'll hear it."

I slid my bow against the strings two times, then let it fall. "Will heard God." I gave a small laugh, but it was an empty sound. "He saw God wherever he went and heard him in a pub of all places."

"I'm sure the Lord likes a bit of fiddle and bodhran too." She sat in an aluminum chair, lacing her wrinkled fingers in her lap. "So you said you've heard our music?"

"I have."

"But have you listened?" Sister Maria tilted her head and pierced me with those searching eyes. "Really listened? Maybe you should go check it out yourself."

"Are they playing hymns or something?"

She put some new sheet music in front of me. "Depends on who's doing the listening."

→ ⟵

"Hey, Finley." Beckett's makeup artist held up a wave as I walked onto the set. "Beckett's in his trailer. Go on in." Beatrice stood next to her and shot lethal darts in the form of an artful glare.

"Thanks, Ciara." I didn't get five steps away before Beatrice dogged my side.

"How much longer are you going to let this go on?" she asked.

"I have no idea what you're talking about."

"Being Beckett's *personal assistant*." She had the nerve to do air quotes. "Are you seriously so desperate for his attention that you've signed on to be his dog walker and coffee fetcher then?"

I wasn't about to explain my arrangement with Beckett to her. "I don't get his coffee." I got him water. "And Bob and I are friends." I waved at a passing camera guy. "I'm sorry if that's hard for you to accept, but I can no longer deny my strong feelings for the drooling beast."

"You're not Beckett's type."

Didn't I know it. "That's why we get along so well."

"And don't forget about Taylor. Do you think you've got something she doesn't?"

No. One look at Taylor, and I felt like I was fat, ugly, and clumsy all in one.

I picked up my pace, and Beatrice wobbled in her heels to keep up. "You're not what he wants."

"One of the many blessings I counted this morning."

"You think you're so—"

"Look." I pivoted hard on my heel until we were face-to-face. "Just back off. I'm not moving in on your fan-girl crush."

"Beckett and I are friends and—"

"I don't care." I blocked out the images in my mind. "What you two are is not my concern, and neither should I be any concern to you."

She lifted a perfectly waxed brow. "If you get between Beckett and Taylor, I promise it will mean trouble for you."

"Are they a couple?" I watched Beatrice closely. The only time I saw Beckett and Taylor together was in the tabloids. "Doesn't matter. I'm not here looking for autographs *or* a date, so I guess I don't have to worry."

She took a step closer, so close I could see the cracks in her lipstick. "I heard Mr. Rush warn Beckett against you with my own ears."

That shouldn't have hurt. But it did.

What had Beckett said to this?

I sighed like I was the actress. "It must be exhausting to maintain this much drama all the time." I glanced at my watch. "You heard Ciara. Beckett's waiting for me." And I walked away, with my hands clenched into fists and my cheeks burning on my face. The nerve of that girl. She totally needed a therapist. And I should know.

I knocked once on Beckett's door, then let myself in.

"I said I would look at the scripts."

Beckett held up a hand in greeting as he sat in one of the plush chairs next to his father.

"There's no time for you to read the script," Mr. Rush said. "Just sign the contracts. That will give you three movies for next year."

The tension in the room was thick as Mr. O'Callaghan's chocolate pudding. I slid past the guys and went to the tiny kitchen area, took out a Diet Coke and let the cold liquid burn down my throat.

"I want to read the material."

Feeling like an unwelcome guest, I reopened the fridge, hid behind the door, and began to arrange the contents by height.

"I'm your manager. It's my job to help you select the work. Would I lead you astray?"

"No, but maybe it's time to branch out."

"To what? We're building an empire here."

"To something that doesn't involve fangs and blood."

"That's what your fans want to see."

Beckett shoved his fingers through his hair. "I can't do this forever."

"Of course not. You only have a small window of time to play the teenage heartthrob, so take advantage of it before we move to the next stage in your career." Mr. Rush set the contracts on the small table. "Have these signed by the time I get back next week."

"Where are you going now?"

"Los Angeles. I want to have a talk with a guy about more Beckett Rush merchandise."

"The posters and unauthorized biographies weren't enough?"

His father didn't smile as he got to his feet. "You may not see it now, but one day you'll thank me for this." The door slammed behind him, leaving the trailer doused in awkward silence.

"So . . ." I stepped away from the fridge and fingered the hoodie I wore over my uniform. "When can I get my Beckett bobblehead doll?"

"Let's just run the lines, okay?" His tone was as sharp as a pointed stake.

"Fine." I sat down my drink and picked up his script. "Where do you want to start?"

"Page fifty-six."

"We've done that scene ten times."

"And it's still not right." He thrust the script at me. "I want it perfect." He pinched the bridge of his nose and closed his eyes as if warring with a headache. "Page fifty-six."

"Got it. Anytime you want to start." *Your royal crabbiness.*

Beckett sat there a moment longer, and just as I was getting ready to prompt him with a line, he looked up. "I'm sorry."

"No, that's not your line." I scanned the page. "You're supposed to say—"

He reached out, covered my hands on the script with his. "I'm sorry, Finley. I didn't mean to take my bad mood out on you."

His skin was warm against mine. "It's fine."

"Tell me about your day."

I blinked at the topic change. At the change in the boy. "Um . . . what?"

"Your day. Tell me about school."

"Don't you want to run lines?"

"It can wait."

"Okay." I licked my bare lips and regretted their lack of gloss. Taylor would never have naked lips. "I don't really know anything exciting."

"I don't want exciting." He leaned forward, as if he were about to divulge international secrets. "I want *normal.*"

"Well . . ." What I wouldn't have given to pull just one sexy thing from my boring day. "We're reading *Macbeth* in English, and

I made an 85 on a quiz in math." Was that seriously the best I could do? "I, um, failed to show my work and didn't get credit for a few problems."

"I hate when that happens."

I stifled a smile. "I had a music lesson at lunch. Hung out with Sister Maria."

"Is she hot?"

"For seventy, yes, I do believe she is."

He removed his hand from mine and leaned back in his chair. The harsh lines left his face and that L.A. smile returned. "What's your least favorite subject?"

I frowned. "Why?"

"Because I want to know."

"History. I get confused on all the dates and wars and names of men I'll never really need to know."

"I love history," he said. "The victories, the defeats, the stories of the underdog."

I reached for my Diet Coke and ran my finger around the rim. "Do you regret not going to school? Not having a normal childhood?"

He looked out a window framed by beige linen curtains with the blinds pulled up to let in the sun. "I've had an amazing life. Anyone would've traded places with me."

It was my turn to lean in. "That's not what I asked."

His chest rose as he took a deep breath "I can't complain about what I've had. I could quit work today and still be set for life. I have a garage full of cars in all five of my houses. Friends all over the world. A first-class seat on any plane going anywhere I want."

His face would rival an angel's. "But . . ." I tried to refocus. "Do you ever just want to be a regular guy?"

He shook his head. "I can't want that. It's not an option."

"But it could be if—"

"Now," he said, cutting me off. "Tell me about Mrs. Sweeney."

I studied his pensive face. "How come I'm always the one doing all the talking?"

"Because that's what I'm paying you for."

I let that go and filled him in on my adopted grandmother. "So I just need to get my hours in so I can be done with the woman." Before she got really bad. And died. "But Sister Maria thinks I need to help her."

"And what do you think?"

"I guess I could find this Fiona Doyle. Maybe it's an easy fix. Like maybe it's nothing more than Mrs. Sweeney owes her some money and has been trying to get it to her for years. Or she borrowed her favorite jeans a long time ago and wants to give them back."

His full lips quirked. "You know it's more than that."

"You're right. But I don't have time to figure it out because I have to find a pub in Galway."

"Any pub will do?"

"McPherson's, I think. One with music that will alter my life forever, give me eternal happiness, and make me see God. You know. One like that."

"So you need the magical sound of Ireland *and* some information about an Abbeyglen native. Francine"—Beckett's eyes danced in the streaming sunlight—"I'm about to solve your every problem." Beckett stood up and gave my hair a light tug. "Prepare to worship and adore me."

His smile was a strange poison, and I was drinking it in. "And when do we commence with this worshipping and adoration?"

"Saturday night." He walked to the trailer door and flung it open. "And Finley?" His eyes lingered on my school uniform, then back to my face.

"Yes?"

"Wear something pretty."

Chapter Fourteen

Galway is so different from Abbeyglen. Louder, busier, bigger. The Irish love their weekends, so everyone comes out on Friday and Saturday nights. The air crackles with excitement. Anything is possible . . .

—Travel Journal of Will Sinclair, Abbeyglen, Ireland

On Saturday evening, I looked in the bathroom mirror and took the straightener to the same piece of hair for the tenth time. Steam wafted from the flatiron, and I knew if I kept at it, I'd have a bald spot instead of an errant lock of hair.

After a quick blast of hair spray, I slid the shell pink gloss over my lips and surveyed my work. Smoky shadow highlighted my eyes with dramatic eyeliner and heavy lashes. My hair cascaded across my shoulders like I was a starlet in a black-and-white movie. I wore a sequined gray tank covered by a black fitted cardigan, a filmy charcoal skirt, and shimmery flats. The reflection in the mirror was one of a girl totally chic, totally put together.

And through my nerves, all I could see tonight was the extra flab hanging over the waist of my skirt.

My days of eating at the craft services table were over.

I jerked at the knock on the door and quit my inspection. I sucked in my stomach and opened the door.

"Beckett's downstairs," Erin said. "He looks . . . divine."

"That good, huh?" I spritzed some perfume on my neck and wrists.

"I can't believe you have a date with the hottest guy in the world."

I checked my teeth. "It's not a date."

"Whatever you call it, it's still totally cool."

"Do you want to come with us?"

She shook her red head and already I could see her morphing into awkward mode. "No. No, I can't. I couldn't. I'm going to Orla's tonight. We're going to do facials, then have a decent munch on as much pizza and fairy cakes as we can stand. At least with Orla I can make complete sentences. And after last night at dinner when I dropped the potatoes . . ."

"I don't think Beckett even noticed."

"They fell in his lap, Finley."

Beckett had stopped by at dinnertime again. Even though Erin got a little clumsy with the vegetables, he just laughed it off and spoke to her as if she were an old friend. And not someone who had just tried to scorch his crotch.

It was strange. It was almost as if he liked hanging out with the O'Callaghan family. Surely he had somewhere more thrilling to be on a Friday night. Yet there he'd been, sitting at the dinner table with us, eating roast and potatoes and laughing at all of Liam's jokes.

I walked down the stairs and into the living room where Beckett sat on the couch across from Nora.

"And then I started coughing and my fang shot out my mouth and . . ." Beckett lifted his head and turned those warm gray eyes on me. A slow smile spread across his face. "Hello, Flossie Sinclair."

My stomach did a quivery flip. "Hello, Beckett Rush."

"Here's your coat." Nora handed my jacket to Beckett. "Don't forget curfew."

"I won't, ma'am," he said, never taking his gaze off me. "I'll be the perfect gentleman."

Nora giggled. "I don't doubt that a minute." The phone rang from the kitchen. "I better get that. You two have fun." She scurried out of the room, leaving the two of us. Alone.

Beckett walked to me, and I smelled the hint of his cologne. "You look beautiful."

My skin heated at the intensity in his voice. "You do too. Not nearly as . . . pale." He looked positively heartbreaking in dark jeans, a button-down shirt, and a tweedy blazer that was mismatched so artfully, it could've been picked out by one of his stylists.

"I decided I'd leave all the makeup to you tonight." He held out my coat, and I turned around, pushing my arms through the sleeves. His fingers brushed across my neck as he lifted my hair out from the collar. "I like what you've done with your hair."

"I just brushed it." I shrugged one shoulder. "No effort at all."

An hour and a half later I strolled the streets of Galway with the boy most girls would've died a thousand deaths to be near. He wore a fedora slanted over one eye and a pair of glasses, giving him a studious, preppy look. It might not have made someone notice Beckett at first glance. But they would've by the second.

"How many more pictures can you take?" He stood across the

street in front of a restaurant with lime-green shutters and a door as red as a valentine. In Ireland, I'd seen color combinations that I'd never dreamed would work. And yet, somehow they did. So much more welcoming than the black iron gate that stood in front of my own house back home.

I looked in the shop window and saw hats like those worn to the Kentucky Derby or what royalty donned for fancy events. Magical pieces constructed of ribbon and plumes, lace and sparkle.

I continued my slow perusal, and the next building, painted turquoise and accented with flowers sprouting from every window and pot, stopped me. Peeking in, I found my own slice of heaven when I realized I was looking at a music store, filled with instruments that gleamed and shined, making me want to press my nose against the glass and tell Beckett to come back for me in an hour.

"We're going to miss it," Beckett called.

"Wait just a—" I was jerked into motion as he grabbed my hand and speed-walked down the cobblestone road.

He continued at this pace until we reached McPherson's Pub. Music surrounded us like air as we stepped inside and squeezed our way to a small table. It was another world.

Beckett pulled out my chair and gestured to the front where five men played. "Guy on the fiddle is Donal Murphy. A fine man. If there's information to be had about anyone in Abbeyglen, he's your man. He knew my grandfather. Rumor has it he's been alive since the beginning of time."

And he looked it. Wrinkles that stretched and pillowed across his weathered face. Hands made of more bone than skin. Pants that hung from his frame as if there was nothing to cling to. But it was his eyes that caught my attention next. They could belong to a twenty-year-old. So alive. Bright. Almost as if backlit by fire.

"This is his brother's pub." Beckett opened a menu. "Donal moved here when his wife died last year. But he still keeps up with what's what."

"He's playing without any music." Sister Maria would be proud.

Donal Murphy finished his song, held up his fiddle, and bowed to the crowd. They clapped madly, calling out his name, holding up their drinks. Old as dirt, and the man had groupies.

Beckett stood up and waved Mr. Murphy to our table.

"Beckett Rush. Is that you under that hat?" Mr. Murphy slapped him on the back. "Oh, but it's a fine evening now. What are you doing all the way out here?"

Beckett looked at me. "Research."

"And who is this lovely lady?"

"Meet Finley Sinclair from America. She needs some information."

"Bah. I'm an old man who knows nothing and needs to wet his whistle, so."

"Let me rephrase that. She needs some gossip."

Mr. Murphy plopped himself into the third chair. "Now that I might possess." His eyes glimmered with mischief as he planted his bony elbows on the table. "What do you want to know, Finley from America?"

"Sir, do you know Cathleen Sweeney?"

His face pinched in a wince. "Brooding woman. Did the books for a few stores in town. Quiet, sullen thing and always seemed to have a thorn in her saddle."

"She's dying," I said.

Mr. Murphy nodded. "I'd heard as much." He shook his wispy, white head. "Folks said it's the cancer, but I know it's her heart. The woman is eaten up with guilt. She's carried it around with her for more years than I can count. And it's finally rottin' that cantankerous heart."

I couldn't help but feel a little defensive of the woman. "She's not *that* bad."

Mr. Murphy hooted with laughter. "She'd scare the bark off a tree, that one. She's terrible. Everyone knows that. She left Mr. Sweeney only a few years into their marriage. Rumor has it he drank himself to death in his loneliness. You don't just go leaving your husband."

"But there had to be a reason," I said. "Mrs. Sweeney seems to have no family or friends, but she sends letters to someone named Fiona Doyle. There're years' worth of them—all returned to sender."

"Well o'course they'd be sent back unopened. Why would her sister want to talk to one such as Cathleen Sweeney?"

"Her sister? So something happened between them?" I asked.

"Oh, sure it did." He stood up, done with the conversation. "Now, I must go. Me fiddle calls."

"Wait!" I called. "Mr. Murphy!"

He stopped mid-stride and turned back.

"What happened?"

"Don't you know?"

I shook my head.

"Cathleen stole her own sister's fiancé."

And with that, he departed, weaving through the crowd, back to his beloved music.

"So there you have it," Beckett said. "Except—"

"Yes?"

"If Mrs. Sweeney is the man-stealer, why is she the one who's so bitter?"

"I don't know, unless it's because—" And then I recalled Mrs. Sweeney's cryptic words.

My fate is like those envelopes—sealed and tossed aside.

"Because she needs her sister's forgiveness."

With the crowd buzzing around us, we listened to the band, and I saw all the instruments my brother had described. But nobody played with as much life as Mr. Murphy. As the band picked up the pace, Mr. Murphy dropped his bow and began to dance a jig. The crowd clapped in time, and soon a couple got up and joined him. Then three more.

The music became a living thing in the room, as well as in my heart, where it sent powerful shock waves of . . . something.

"I wish you could see your face right now." I looked across the table to find Beckett's eyes on mine.

"I never can describe it. But it's here. Do you feel it?" I put a hand to my chest. "Do you feel it?"

His smile was a slow lift of his lips. "I feel it indeed."

"I've never heard anything like Mr. Murphy. He plays with everything he's got."

"Wish he danced half as good and—"

"*Shh.* Wait." I held up my hand, humming. "I gotta get this." Grabbing my phone, I pushed a few buttons, activating the voice recorder, and hummed right into it. "I need to change part of Will's song. I hear it so clear."

"From the band?"

"No, in my head. Sometimes it's like God just downloads it."

"The God who's not talking to you."

I smiled. The song would come together. "He sends me occasional love notes, I guess."

"You should play tonight."

I looked back at the band. Let the music fill every cut and scrape on my spirit. "I just want to listen."

Beckett watched me over the salt and pepper shakers. "Then let's dance."

"No, thank you."

He held out his hand. "If you want the full effect, you can't very well do it from your seat."

Before I could argue, he pulled me to my feet and out into the crowd. I thought there couldn't possibly be room for one more person, but Beckett wedged us in and turned his laughing eyes to mine.

"I don't know how to dance like this," I said, already feeling the embarrassment creep up my neck.

"You don't have to know the steps." He drew me closer, resting his hand at my hip. "Just feel the music." And with a look of challenge, he put us into motion. Spinning, skipping, clapping, he propelled us around the tiny space. My shoes stomped across the rough-hewn floor, and when I tripped over Beckett's feet, his firm hold steadied me at once. "I've got you." His face hovered inches from mine. "I won't let you fall."

The music swelled and crashed, the instruments playing their own tune, yet still coming together in perfectly mismatched unity.

"You're trying too hard." Beckett sang off-key in my ear. "Don't overthink it."

I assumed he was talking about the dancing, but it might as well have been the advice for every part of my life. The more I thought, the foggier things became.

So I just let go. My feet skipped to the frantic tempo, and I released my hold on Beckett, clapping my hands as I followed his lead. My hair whipped across my shoulder, in my face. I imagined I looked like a chicken having a fit, but I didn't even care.

The drum beat in a fierce staccato, and the pounding rumbled in my chest. Donal Murphy's violin sang the solo, calling out to every lonely, empty heart in the room—come and be happy. And mine longed to answer. The flute intertwined with the guitar, almost like angels orchestrated the notes.

The Lord will send His faithful love by day; His song will be with me in the night.

Are you here for me too, God? Or just there for those so strong in their faith like Will?

Laughing, Beckett took my right hand and spun me round.

And then I was laughing too.

It was the sound made by a girl who hadn't lost a brother. A girl who wasn't angry, who hadn't had her world upended.

The music exploded to a finale, and Beckett twirled me one more time. Completely winded, I clutched his shoulders to steady myself and catch my breath.

And stood straighter. As if a few ounces of the weight had lifted.

"Admit it," he said. "You had fun."

"I did." I tilted my head back and smiled. "You were right."

"What's that?" He cupped his ear. "I don't think I heard you correctly."

"You were right. And I was . . . wrong."

With his silver eyes on me, he reached out and pushed a strand of hair from my cheek. His finger stroked the delicate skin of my ear as he tucked the tendril in place. "You're not too bad, Finley Sinclair."

I couldn't have looked away from this boy if the room had caught on fire. "You're okay yourself. At times."

"But we can't get involved."

"No." I swallowed. "Definitely not."

His face lowered a fraction of an inch. "Because I'm infamously bad."

"And I'm staying away from trouble."

His voice was rough, husky. "It would never work."

I took a step closer. "Impossible."

He traced my cheek with the pad of his thumb. "We don't even like each other."

"I pretty much can't stand you."

And then his lips crushed to mine. In the middle of McPherson's Pub, as Mr. Murphy played his fiddle and total strangers danced around us. I curled my arms around Beckett's neck and pulled him nearer. My eyes closed as music and boy consumed me, his lips sliding over mine once more. It was both too much and not enough.

And it had to stop.

I moved away, bringing shaking fingers to my lips. "What just happened?"

Shutters fell over Beckett's eyes as he took a step back. "You just kissed me."

"I didn't kiss *you*. You kissed me!"

He cleared his throat, ran a hand over the light stubble on his face. "'Tis a matter of opinion."

"'*Tis* not. And what would Taylor think of this? I—"

Beckett placed one finger against my lips, locking his eyes with mine. "The blame lies with Donal Murphy and his magic tunes. We forget it." He dropped his hand. "We forget it. Agreed?"

Forget the kiss that went straight to my toes? That his hands held on to me like they'd never let me go? That my heart leaped out of my chest and fluttered like a bird?

I nodded my head. "Already forgotten."

Chapter Fifteen

- Number of cemeteries visited this week: 2

- Number of miles run today: 3

- Number of times I redid hair in last hour: 3

- Number of times I've thought of one certain vampire in last 30 minutes: 12.5

Beckett Rush. The hottest actor on the planet. Kissed me.

This was the thought that replayed in my head all day Sunday into Monday at school. Through all of church, I doodled hearts and swirly doodads, then realizing what I'd done, I scribbled big *X*s to cover them up. Erin peeked over at the finished product and gave a frown. I thought she now doubted my salvation. Or maybe just my art abilities.

And today in school had been the same thing. In trig, I got called on twice, and both times my intelligent answer was, "Huh?" And who could listen to Beatrice drone on as Macbeth when I heard Beckett's voice in my ear? Saw his sculpted face coming near mine?

All because Beckett Rush kissed me. Plain Jane me.

And I didn't know why. He didn't like me. I didn't like him. He had Taylor, and I was steering clear of the party life.

"We missed you at lunch again today," Orla said as we walked outside after school.

"I've got to get my hours in at the old folks' home." Mrs. Sweeney's clock was ticking, and I didn't want to be around when God pressed her eternal snooze button.

Erin ran to catch up. "There's a new documentary on tonight about organ harvesting. Who's in?"

"Hello, girls."

We all turned and saw Beatrice, flanked by her entourage of Poshes.

"How is the hunt for a date going?" Beatrice asked Erin. The two friends beside her shared a vicious grin.

"I've got my date," Erin said.

"Who was it you said you were taking again?" Beatrice asked.

"I . . . I, um, didn't."

Beatrice's laugh was like blunt nails on a dry chalkboard. "Let me guess . . . because he doesn't exist?"

"Are you calling Erin a liar?" Orla pushed her sweater sleeves up to her elbows.

"If the St. Flanagan's Day dress fits . . ." Condescension fizzed from Beatrice's lips. "But if she says she has a date, then who am I to doubt? Can't wait to meet him." Beatrice and her sisterhood of snobs gave us parting glares, then sauntered down the sidewalk in the other direction, completely dismissing a world where normals like Erin and the rest of us existed.

"I have *got* to find a date," Erin mumbled.

Orla popped her gum twice, still glaring at the back of Beatrice's head. "My cousin's still available."

"Your cousin wears eyeliner."

"It's just a phase."

"Finley, you should ask Beckett to go with you," Erin said.

I stumbled over a rock the size of a quarter. "There's no way. He doesn't like me like that." Did he?

"You've been humming ever since your evening in Galway." Orla's tone dared me to cough up some details.

"Just working on my song."

"You keep telling yourself that," Orla said. "But if I'd gone out with Beckett Rush . . . I'd be humming too."

I made four loops around town on my bicycle before finally stopping at the set. And that was just because I had to tinkle. Besides burning some calories from an overindulgent weekend of Mr. O'Callaghan's cooking, I needed to burn off some of my nervousness.

It didn't work.

I popped the kickstand and walked to the open field where the swarming crew fluttered around the actors in the scene.

The director spoke to Taylor, and as she nodded vigorously, her impossibly voluminous hair flowed around her like spun silk. Or really good extensions.

A dry tickle scratched my throat, and I coughed into my hand.

Beckett stepped away from his position beside Taylor. And looked right at me.

He wore another ridiculous outfit from the nineteenth century, but I doubted any man from the 1800s looked that dashing and ruggedly handsome. Or arrogant. Or charming.

Oh gosh. He was like a fever, a plague that none of us could resist.

"Action!"

The scene came to life as Beckett reached out and touched Taylor's flawless face. I averted my eyes and focused on the camera crew. It was just another reminder that Beckett had a girlfriend. And it wasn't me.

Nor did I want it to be.

"Cut! Take a half-hour break." The crew separated like ants in a sandstorm, and Beckett caught my eye, then jerked his head toward the direction of his trailer.

I might've worked for him, but I wasn't at his beck and call. How about a little *please* and *do you mind*?

As he headed to the trailer, I stopped and talked to Ciara and got some tips on shading with concealer. Then I paused at craft services and snagged a cookie, took a bite, then threw it away. No more table grazing for me. One bite of an Oreo was like five minutes of running. Not worth it.

After helping a cameraman with some equipment, I finally moseyed to trailer number six and knocked on the metal door.

My fingers barely make contact before the door swung open and there stood Beckett, leaning against the opening, his white linen shirt unbuttoned to midchest, his hair lying in waves of mussy perfection, and his eyes filled with lazy mischief.

"I called you Sunday," he said.

I pointed to his shirt. "Seriously? Is this 1975?"

He looked down. "It drives the chicks wild."

"Yeah, the ones who work at Hooters and have a thing for backseats."

"You didn't answer your phone Sunday."

I forced myself to meet his stare. "Are you going to let me in?"

"Are you going to answer my question?"

"I was busy."

"Doing what?"

"It's a holy day. I went to church and spent the rest of the time reflecting on the sermon and how I can apply its principles to my life."

"You don't even like that church."

"Fine," I said. "I didn't want to admit it, but I prayed for your dark soul. Now let me in."

"Careful," he said. "The step broke this morning." Beckett held out his large guy hand and pulled me until I was standing beside him in the doorway, blocked from moving inside. "It's touching to know you were praying for me." He looked down, pinning me in place with that gaze. "And to think I believed you were ignoring me."

Good heavens, Harry Potter didn't have any magic like the kind this boy was brewing. "Why would you think that?"

"I don't know." Beckett's voice was low and rough. "Thought Saturday night might've scared you off."

"Walking the streets of Galway?" I made my words as calm and unaffected as possible. "Dinner at the pub? A little dancing? Gossiping with your friend?" My eyes dropped to his lips, and I forced them back to his stare. "Why would that affect me at all?"

The laughter of girls came from behind us, breaking the spell and making me remember Beckett and I were not alone, but where everyone could see.

Beatrice and Taylor walked by. Taylor gave a weak wave, and I held up my hand in return. Beatrice stared at Beckett, then back at me, her eyes thinning like a snake about to strike.

"Get inside." He gave me a light push out of the way and pulled the door closed. Walking to the refrigerator, Beckett reached for a Diet Coke, popped the top, then handed it to me.

"Thanks." I took a sip, grateful for something to do. "Want to run lines?"

He stood too near, so close I could have reached out and traced the line of his jaw. As a furrow formed on his brow, his eyes searched mine, and my heart thudded twice before it remembered to beat again. The seconds ticked by.

Finally, I interrupted the silence. "Beckett?"

"I had a good time Saturday night," he said, as if he didn't quite understand it.

I didn't want to be pleased. Yet I was. "You did?"

His lips lifted in a lopsided grin. "Yeah."

"Oh." Seriously? He had fun? With me?

Beckett stepped away, and I took the opportunity to breathe. He moved to one of the chairs and sat down. Picked at a string on the upholstery. "One of those pictures in your brother's journal was Lahinch. I wondered if you'd want to take a drive there Sunday after we go to church."

As friends? As a boy and a girl who kissed after a whirling dervish of a dance in an Irish pub? Wait—

"We?"

"You go to yours," he said. "I go to mine."

"You go to church?"

"Church of Ireland, yes." I swore I saw his cheeks flush pink. "My neighbor used to take me when I was little. It's not a big deal."

For some reason I got a charge off this information. "It kind of is. Beckett Rush, America's party boy, attends Sunday services."

"Are you laughing at me?"

I sat down and crossed my legs. "Does your dad know you do this?"

"It's a yes or no question, Finley. Either you want to go or you don't. I just thought you might like to see some more of the local culture. That's all."

"You could just go with me and Erin on Sunday. No, wait, probably best we not attend together anyway. You'd probably try and kiss me during the invitation."

He quirked a brow. "You couldn't keep your hands off me Saturday."

"Me?" I pointed my finger in his face. "You were the one who insisted we dance."

"You loved every minute of it. Admit it." Leaning forward, Beckett braced his arms on his knees and stared right at me. "Finley?" He traced the plaid pattern on the arm of my chair, so close to my hand, I could almost feel it on my skin. "I had fun Saturday. I mean that."

Beside me a droplet shimmered down my can. "You already said that."

"I don't think you believed me either time. And that's just sad." He gave a small sigh. "When I'm with a girl, I like to make a good impression."

"I don't mess around with guys who have girlfriends."

"Don't believe everything you read in the tabloids."

"And what exactly does that mean?"

He gave a noncommittal shrug.

"Besides." I studied that face. "You said you wanted it forgotten."

He stood up, planted his hands on either side of my chair, and hovered over me, his lips a breath away from mine. "I don't know why I like hanging out with you, but I do."

"You actors aren't paid to think on a regular basis." And *I* couldn't think. Not with him so near.

"You." He shifted until his mouth was next to my ear. "Were the best part of my weekend."

I turned my head just slightly 'til our eyes met again and my cheek brushed against his. "I'm still waiting for you to address the Taylor issue."

I heard his sigh, a real one this time. "Can you just trust me that I'm not crossing any lines?"

"You have a girlfriend."

"And if I didn't?"

"Are you saying you don't?"

Behind us the door flung open, and Beckett pulled himself upright.

"Check out *People* magazine's website!" Taylor hoisted herself into the trailer, holding up her iPhone. "We made the day's headline." Beatrice stood behind her, a twisted smile on her face.

"We're running lines," Beckett said. "I'll look at it later."

But Taylor wouldn't be deterred. "I'll read it for you."

"No, Taylor—"

"*Fangs in the Night* cast has a wild Saturday evening in Doolin." Taylor laughed as she showed us the screen. Beckett stepped in front of me, blocking my view, but with an elbow to his side, I moved around him. And what I saw had my stomach folding.

It was a picture of Beckett surrounded by a group of castmates in some pub. His arm was slung around Taylor, and she gazed up at him like he held her world.

"'Hollywood's hot couple tears up the town,'" Taylor read. "Great picture, huh?"

I looked at Beckett, an invisible fist around my heart. "I guess that beats my Saturday night."

Chapter Sixteen

You sounded down on the phone yesterday. You
can talk to your old dad about anything, you know.
Except boys. And bras. And that Bieber fellow.
—Dad

Sent to my BlackBerry

The clock read a mean-looking four forty-five a.m. when I finally admitted defeat to a wasted night of zero sleep and got up. My eyes blurred and burned, and I didn't have to look in a mirror to know they were puffy and would require concealer applied like spackle.

Turning on the lamp, I reached into the drawer on the bedside table and retrieved my Bible. Not feeling particularly inspired, I flipped through the pages and randomly stopped. My finger landed on the second chapter of Ephesians, and I pulled the covers up to my chin and read the words. Finding nothing leaping out at me or whispering, "Finley, this is God talking to you," I closed my Bible after a few minutes and attempted to pray.

If there were crickets in the room, they would have provided the soundtrack to the silence that hung so loud.

God, I don't know if you're listening or keeping up, but I did not have a great weekend. It started out good. Galway was beautiful. The music was amazing. For a while, I felt so free and alive. And then things got complicated. Beckett kissed me, and it meant nothing. To him. I just fell into the lie that things were different. That he was different, and maybe because of me. Like he'd change his ways for someone like me. I'm just another girl he's wooed and kissed. Meaningless fun for him.

Total confusion for me.

I sat there for a few more minutes, just in case God wanted to speak from the rafters or send a trumpet-blasting angel to deliver some good news.

But nothing.

Why did I even bother?

Wide-awake and revved up on frustration, I jumped out of my Hello Kitty PJs and into my running gear. Grabbing my iPod, I tiptoed down the stairs and slipped out the back door into the dim light of dawn.

As old-school Crowder sang in my ear, I took off down the driveway, angling my body against the wind and downward slope of the road.

My feet hit the ground, and with every strike of my shoe, I breathed a little faster. And a little easier. This was familiar. This was comfort. The oxygen pumping through my veins, the movement of arms and limbs, the killing of the calories.

By the third Kings of Leon song, I realized someone was approaching. I looked behind me, my head jerking in a double take.

Beckett. Decked out in head-to-toe black, from his Nikes to his stocking cap, he picked up the pace. And so did I.

"Wait," I heard him say over a wailing guitar.

A cool girl would've kept an even clip. A sophisticated one would've pretended nothing was the matter.

Me?

I took off in a dead sprint.

Without even looking back, I knew he was gaining on me. I cut through Mr. Dell's rocky field and, using some of my old cheerleader agility, leaped over his stone fence. The grass snapped at my legs, but I pushed on, having no idea where I was going. And hoping Mr. Dell didn't own a bull.

"Finley!"

"Go away," I called back.

Five seconds later a hand grabbed the hem of my jacket. Then Beckett's fingers closed around my upper arm, forcing me to stop.

I ripped out my earbuds. "What?" My breath raged in and out of my lungs.

Beckett maintained his hold and stared at me as if I'd lost my mind. "I want to talk to you."

"I'm busy." I flailed my hand toward the meadow. "I have many fields to go before I'm done." I wrenched my arm free and began to walk deeper onto the property.

Beckett followed. "Are you mad?"

"That you're interrupting my morning run? Yeah."

"That's not what I'm talking about."

"I can't imagine what else you could be referring to."

"Cut the crap, Finley. Just talk to me."

"And say what?" I rounded on him. "That seeing you on the Internet partying with the cast after you dropped me off hurt me? Or maybe you want me to say that our kiss Saturday night meant something? Well, no—to all of the above."

"I'm not the jerk you think I am."

"You're right." I looked toward the rising sun in the distance. "I think you might be worse. But if you believe I'm going to be one of the legions of girls falling under your celebrity spell, you are mistaken."

"I don't think that."

"How could you not?" My voice rose. "Every single girl you so much as look at swoons at your feet. But you know what? I'm not impressed, Beckett." The lie hurt as it tripped off my lips. "I don't see what everyone else sees. Saturday night was fun, but kissing you was a mistake. We both agreed on that."

He ripped off his hat and tunneled his fingers through his hair. "What if I changed my mind?" His mercury eyes held mine. "What if I can't stop thinking about it?"

With a small laugh, I shook my head. "What is this—phase two of the Beckett Rush seduction plan?" I stabbed him in the chest with a pointed finger. "I'm onto you. I might not be as worldly as all those actresses you date, but I'm not an idiot."

"Finley—"

"I'm sure you and your friends had a good laugh at my expense."

In all these things, I am more than victorious . . .

"Did you tell them about your down-home evening with me and Mr. Murphy?" The tears were going to fall any second, but I'd be darned if he'd see me cry.

"No, it's not like that." Beckett reached for me, but I stepped away. "I meant what I said—Saturday night was . . . I loved every minute." His accent thickened as his forehead furrowed into a frown. "You can't believe everything you see or read in the press."

"So you and Taylor aren't a couple?"

He opened his mouth. Then shut it.

"What a good boyfriend you are." I forced my voice to be flat and even. "I'm positively eaten up with jealousy over what Taylor's got. I mean, what a moral, trustworthy guy. She's *so* lucky."

"I can't explain everything, but—"

"Because there is no explaining it." I stuck my earbuds back in, cranked up the volume, and ran back in the direction of the house.

Leaving Beckett Rush far behind me.

⊰⊱

I visited with Erin and the girls outside at lunch for a few minutes before throwing my apple core in the trash and hopping on my bicycle to see Mrs. Sweeney. Between her snoring through my reading selections, yelling for the police, and threatening to lob her pudding cup my way, it was an hour in which I was going to do nothing but store up some treasure in heaven. God owed me for this one. Meanwhile, Erin was matched up with some old lady who'd already knit her a hat and matching scarf.

"Good afternoon, Mrs. Sweeney." I knocked twice, then walked on inside. "How are you feeling today?"

A lonely tray sat on the cart next to Mrs. Sweeney's bed. "Go away."

"It's good to see you too." I pointed toward the covered plate on her tray. "What's this?"

"Bangers and mash."

"Uh-huh."

"Sausage. Mashed potatoes. What are they feeding you that you haven't heard of that?"

"Well, if it's so good, why aren't you eating it?"

"Because I don't want to." Mrs. Sweeney lay against her pillows, her wrinkles more pronounced in a room lit only by her reading light.

"Want me to cut it for you?"

"Am I a child that I can't cut me own meat?" We both knew she hadn't cut her own food in weeks. Lately I'd seen a nurse's aid helping feed her. "I'm just not hungry. And shut that lid." She turned her head, paling. "I can't stomach the smell."

"Do you feel sick?"

"Of course I do. I have cancer."

I covered the food and pushed the cart away. "You have to eat though."

She grumbled and rolled her eyes. "If they're not bringing me something greasy, it's brothy like I'm a wee baby."

I dug through my bag and pulled out some crackers from yesterday's lunch. "I have just the thing." I opened the packet and handed them to her. "Now eat."

"Anyone ever tell you you're bossy?"

"Anyone ever tell you your hair needs brushing?" I walked to her bedside and fluffed her pillows. Then grabbing her brush, which she'd begun to keep on her table, I gently smoothed out the day's snarls. "I see you had a shower today. Your hair smells nice and clean."

"*Hmph.*"

God, help me get through to this woman. And help her use sentences that consist of real words. Ones that contain vowels and everything.

"I know you're dying for an update on my life. I can see it in your seething eyes, so I won't keep you in suspense any longer." Mrs. Sweeney's lids closed as if she were sleeping, and I took that as an invitation. "I've been practicing night and day on my audition song. Nobody can identify the cross in my brother's journal, which means I still don't have an ending for it. It's not like I can just put any old notes in there. We still don't have a date for Erin. She's a basket case. And apparently when she gets stressed, she reads medical journals online. Beatrice is still harassing her. And she's not exactly nice to me either." I didn't even wait for Mrs. Sweeney to comment. Because I knew she wouldn't. "I guess every town has to have a bad seed." Lumberjack snores slipped from Mrs. Sweeney's cracked lips. I continued my easy strokes with the brush and kept talking.

"So I went to Galway with Beckett Rush Saturday night. You know, the actor you were drooling over at our little picnic. We ran into someone you might know." I teased the top portion of her hair to give it some lift. "Donal Murphy."

Mrs. Sweeney's closed eyes flinched.

"Said he's known you a long time. The man sure is full of information."

"A bloomin' busybody is what he is." Mrs. Sweeney's voice popped like a firecracker. "Can't believe a word he says."

I settled myself into the chair beside the bed. "I know about your sister."

"You had no right to go nosing around! You didn't just run into that man, did you?" Her hair flopped as she pulled herself up in the bed. "You're to stay out of my business!"

"How long has it been since you talked to her?"

"Just leave!" She flipped to her side and yanked the covers to her chin.

Fine. If I had to have this conversation with her back to me, I would. "I know you care about your sister." Silence. "Mr. Murphy said you, um, stole her fiancé. And while I've never done that, I have done some pretty terrible things. I've hurt people. Made my family cry. Lost some friends. I know what it's like to make bad choices—ones that seem right at the time. And I know what it's like to pay the consequences. And, Mrs. Sweeney, I don't know what you believe, but I think if you asked God to wipe your slate clean, he would. It's that easy. And that's something I can't do for you." Her breathing was slow and steady. I knew I'd probably worn her out until she truly did fall asleep. "But I think you want your sister's forgiveness too. And . . ." I hoped I didn't regret this. "I can help."

The clock on the wall ticked. The lamp bulb hummed.

But I got no response from Mrs. Sweeney.

"Okay. Here's the deal," I whispered. "Maybe you shouldn't trust me with this. Because God and I . . . we're not cool. And he's kind of mad at me right now. Or maybe he had to run interference for me so much last year, he's taking a Finley break. But I'm still going to pray about this. For you. Because"—I sniffed against unexpected tears—"it bothers me that you won't have closure. And believe me, you need it. We all do. You are the grumpiest woman I know . . . but it seems I care about you."

Oh, what was the point?

Walking around the bed, I crept to the door and pulled it open. "Finley?"

At that hoarse voice, I stilled.

"Yes, ma'am?" My eyes teared up again and I pressed my lips to hold back a smile.

"Bring your fiddle next time."

"Yes, ma'am."

"And Finley?"

"Yes?"

"Don't take any guff from that Beatrice."

"I won't, Mrs. Sweeney."

Behind me the lamp shut off.

And the room went dark.

Chapter Seventeen

STEELE MARKOV

No, I have no reflection in the mirror. I have no
reason to look upon it. I see who I am reflected in
your eyes. I know what you think about me. But
what if I told you, you were wrong?

Fangs in the Night, scene 8, page 48
Fierce Brothers Studios

"That's quite a book you're reading."

Beckett looked up from his biography on George
Washington and stared at me as I stood in the doorway of
his trailer, blocking the Wednesday afternoon sun. "It does have lots
of big words in it." He quirked a brow. "Maybe you could help me."

"Just sound them out." I shut the door behind me and stepped
inside. "I'm here to tell you I quit."

Beckett scratched his shoulder and yawned, an indulged prince
in his castle.

"I said I quit."

He went back to his book. "I heard you."

"Okay then." I stood there like a fool, counting the ways I'd love to tell him off. "I just wanted to say good-bye."

"Resignation not accepted." His long finger slowly turned a page.

My face flushed with angry heat. "Don't pretend like this bothers you—"

The sentence died as Beckett slammed his book on the table and pushed to his feet. He closed the gap between us in three steps and towered over me. "You want to think I'm a party guy, fine. You want to think I chase anything in tight jeans, I'll take that too. But at least I've been faithful to our agreement."

"And to Taylor? Have you been faithful to her?"

"You said you'd help me until the movie was done. *That* was our agreement, in case you need a reminder."

"But—"

"Haven't I driven you to wherever you asked?"

"Yes."

"Have I treated you badly on this set?"

I shook my head. "No, but—"

"Is this what you do? Just shut down when things get tough? Run away when it doesn't go your way?"

I flinched at his words. "You are such a jerk."

"Maybe so." His jaw tightened. "But not about our bargain. Looks to me like you're the one flaking out. I thought you were better than that."

Yeah, well, I wasn't. "Why can't you just let me go?"

His gaze slowly dipped to my lips, then slid back to my eyes. "Maybe I don't want to." He massaged the back of his neck. "I thought we were friends." Something swam in those eyes. Something searching, almost plaintive. "Finley, I know you're upset, and I'm sorry. But my life isn't my own. There are things about this business you don't understand."

"I understand more than you think." Like the fact that Beckett was a master manipulator and a total player.

"No," he said. "You don't. Besides, how are you going to get to all those destinations you have mapped out? Are you going to give up on that too?"

"I'll find a way."

"Or you let me take you. Like we originally discussed."

"Why? Why are you doing this?"

"Because I want you here."

His forceful words hung between us, balancing between his interpretation and mine. "What does that even mean?" That he liked me? That he wanted to spend time with me?

When he looked at me, the rogue was all gone. Instead I saw a guy who was tired, who was in high demand from everyone who knew him. "The director was threatening to replace me on the movie just a month ago." He spoke softly, as if his words might leak through the walls of the trailer. "Then you came along and helped me with my lines, and I had him shoving contracts in my face for the next deal."

"So I'm a good-luck charm?" Bitterness pierced my ego like a pin. Why did I even care?

Beckett reached out with both hands and slowly lifted my stocking cap off my head. He ran a hand over my hair and smiled. "Static."

I grabbed my hat from his grip. "Your improved acting skills have nothing to do with me."

He planted his hand over the space above my head again and sighed. "I can't explain it."

"Try."

"You're real, Finley."

You're flawed. You're not perfect like every other girl I see.

So what if I was real? I didn't live in Hollywood.

"I'm just . . . comfortable around you. Everyone else is so fake, so eager to kiss my butt, to tell me yes when the answer is no. That's not what I want. Nobody else but the director has the guts to tell me when I deliver a bad line or mess up a scene. But you. I need honest feedback right now."

"Ask your dad."

Beckett's eyebrows slammed together. "He'd yell anyone to the ground who suggested I wasn't delivering an Oscar performance with every word."

"Sounds very encouraging to me—"

"No." His jaw tensed. "I want someone who'll just be truthful. Do you have any idea how little honesty I see? I can't trust anyone. But you barely tolerate me." His lips quirked. "It's perfect."

"Sorry. Not interested. Our agreement was that I help out as your assistant. I owe you nothing more."

"Do you want to find that gravestone in your brother's pictures?"

"Of course I do. But I also distinctly remember you said it was impossible."

"I'll make it happen."

"You said yourself there were thousands—"

"Trust me."

My laugh was low and cynical. "I might not be at the top of my class, but I'm not a total idiot."

"I'm asking you to do this one thing for me." His voice was so sincere, but he was an actor. "Do this as my friend, and I'll find the site of the photo."

"Beckett?" I crooked my finger and he leaned close until my lips were near his ear.

"Yes?"

"Find yourself another friend."

Chapter Eighteen

In the Bible you said your constant love and truth will always guard me. I can't believe parts of the Dun Aengus fortress still stand. It made me think how as crazy as it is, even though this has been on Inishmore Island over thousands of years, you're always with me. You stay the same. Nothing wears you down.

—Travel Journal of Will Sinclair, Abbeyglen, Ireland

He kissed you?"

Erin stopped in her tracks right in front of the entrance to school, as if the shock had paralyzed her legs. "I can't believe you kept this from me. Finley, that's awesome."

"No, it's not. It's awful."

"I'd take that kind of awful *any* day," she said. "But be honest. Didn't any part of you just . . . hope?"

"It's not that I thought he liked me. I know that kiss was simply a diversion." Just something Beckett did on a regular basis with any chick with lips. "But still. There might've been the tiniest sliver of my heart in that. Some part of me who wanted Beckett to say, 'I've never felt anything like I did when I kissed you.'"

"It's like Shakespeare."

Then the fantasy continued with a few declarations of adoration, some proclamations of my intoxicating beauty. "Well, it's not going to happen. So pretend like you know nothing about a kiss."

Erin sighed. "Sadly, I don't."

I stepped through the doors of Sacred Heart and reality smacked me back to earth with the smell of disinfectant mixed with the perfume of a few hundred girls. My pulse scurried as I realized I'd forgotten two notebooks and a work sheet at home.

God, help me.

Erin and I walked into English class, and the temperature dropped a good thirty degrees.

I found the source of the cold as I took my seat in front of Beatrice.

My smile was friendly, as if I hadn't a care in the world. "Good morning."

"Is it?" She studied her notes for our quiz on *Macbeth*, not even bothering to look at me. "Taylor said you weren't too happy about her and Beckett in the tabloids."

"I really don't care. Beckett and I are friends. That's all." And no longer that.

She turned a page of notes. "You throw yourself at him at every opportunity. It's embarrassing really."

I threw myself at him? Me? "That's an . . . interesting perspective. But I think we both know it's not true."

"I know what I've seen." Her lip curled into a snarl. "You know it's best for both of their careers if they're a couple—as long as they're doing these movies."

"And Taylor's success means more roles for you?" Because this was more than Beatrice being protective of her cousin's "boyfriend." This was strictly about Beatrice.

"It's public knowledge he's with Taylor."

Was he? I just didn't know anymore. Nor did I understand why he wouldn't come right out and tell me. "I'm his assistant. That's it." Or I *was* his assistant.

"And wasn't that clever of you to get that job?" Bea sat back in her chair, her spine as straight as the wall behind her. "Watch yourself, Finley." She snapped her binder shut. "I'd hate for you to do something you'd regret."

"All right, class. Clear your desks." Mrs. Campbell passed out the quiz, and I turned back to the front.

I was reading question number six when I felt the first poke.

I glanced behind me, but Beatrice was writing furiously on her paper.

When I got to question number ten, she jabbed me again. "What?" I hissed.

I was going to rip that pencil out of her little manicured hand.

"Finley Sinclair," Mrs. Campbell said, her accent as sharp as the gaze over her bifocals. "Is there a problem?"

I darted a look at Beatrice, then shook my head. "No, ma'am."

After the quiz, Mrs. Campbell put us into groups to read the next act of *Macbeth*. Just as I was giving my best performance ever of Lady Macbeth, I saw Beatrice walk with Mrs. Campbell into the hall. I continued reading, though it was hard to totally throw myself into character when the role of my husband was played by a chick named Teresa Muldoon.

Mrs. Campbell stuck her head back into the room. "Finley, may I see you, please?"

Beatrice stepped back inside, and the hair on the back of my neck stood on end.

"Yes?" I said as I joined the teacher outside.

She held up my quiz. Then Beatrice's. "Would you like to explain this?"

I squinted to see the red grade. "We both need to study better?"

"Miss Sinclair, twice I caught you turning around looking at Beatrice's paper."

"I wasn't looking at her paper. She—"

"And then I see you two made the same exact grade. And not only that, but missed the same questions."

"But she was—"

"And *both* put some of the same ridiculous guesses. Now what do you say?"

I took another glance at the quizzes. "My guesses were completely original. And it ticks me off that she obviously copied them."

"Yes, your answer to the question of what makes Duncan a good king?" She read from my test. "He has a really cool crown." Her tone was dry as the pork chops Nora served for dinner last night. "Very impressive. You could've at least studied enough to know when you were copying a completely ridiculous answer."

"But I didn't copy. I came up with that ridiculous answer all by myself. *Beatrice* copied!" *In all these things, I am more than victorious through Him who loves me . . .*

"I saw you turned around myself."

"Because she was jabbing me with her pencil."

Mrs. Campbell regarded me as if I'd just told her the sky was purple. And even I heard how unbelievable it sounded. Because what eighteen-year-old girl purposely poked someone with a pencil as part of a diabolical scheme to get someone in trouble? Beatrice Plummer.

"I get how this looks. But I am telling you the truth." Heat crept up my neck. Frustration pressed at my temples. Because Beatrice had been at this school forever. Her father was the principal, and she was the one with credibility. I was just the heiress with a bad reputation that seemed to have followed me from America.

"I am very disappointed in you. I will have to report this, and it will go on your record." Mrs. Campbell lifted her chin and looked down her nose. "Let us assume it is your last disciplinary action."

"But I didn't do this. I promise I—"

"We're done here." Mrs. Campbell opened the door, and with my hands clenched, I walked inside the classroom.

Where all the girls watched me.

Including one who wore a telltale smirk.

❧❦

"You're going to love the Aran Islands." Nora parked by the dock and smiled at me and Erin as we unbuckled. "Beckett's such a busy thing, it's no wonder he hasn't been able to take you. I guess something got in the way."

Erin elbowed me as we walked toward the ferry. "Like his lips on yours."

"No matter." Nora handed our tickets to a burly man in a coat as the wind pushed right through my jacket. "With Sean and Liam taking care of the house, it finally gives me a chance to take you about. I've been remiss in my duties, I have. This will be just the thing to get your mind off that terrible Beatrice. That principal father of hers is no better." Nora continued to grumble as we climbed aboard the open ferry.

I had called her as soon as I'd gotten out of English, and she came and picked up me and Erin. After going nose to nose with Principal Plummer, which got us nowhere, Nora just checked us out and asked us what we wanted to do with the day.

I thought about my brother's journal and the next spot on the agenda. Who needed Beckett and his truck? And his laughing eyes. Or his chiseled form, voice of honey, and a face that proclaimed him as God's favored child.

Not me.

I pulled my hat farther down on my head as I stood at the railing between Nora and Erin. The wind on the water kicked up, as if it were mad that we were disturbing the ocean by traveling across. I knew exactly how it felt. I was ticked too. And if Beatrice had been on that boat, I'd have thrown her overboard.

God, help me to see what Will did. He had such unbelievable faith. Was he never shaken? Even in his last moments, did he not doubt, not wonder where you were?

Two hours later I stepped off the ferry onto the dock on rubbery legs, after being tossed about on the choppy Atlantic.

Nora rented us each a bicycle on the crowded quay at Inishmore, one of the three Aran Islands.

"Isn't it beautiful?" Erin asked as she pedaled beside me, her red hair whipping behind her as wild as the land around us.

The island was small but busy, a mix of bare nature and booming modern commerce. Shops and pubs beckoned us to come in and sit all day, but it was the stone and grass beneath the sunny sky that sang to me.

"I think this day calls for ice cream," Nora said.

"For lunch?" I asked.

"Sometimes a girl just needs to indulge." Nora steered us toward Joe Fitzpatrick's Cafe, where Celtic music blasted from the speakers overhead. Erin consumed a double scoop, filling us in on all the merits of calcium in dairy and antioxidants in chocolate. All I knew was the forty-five degree temperatures and the water-fed breezes made it much too cold to eat rocky road or vanilla bean. I took a few bites, then watched as it melted in the cup before I threw it away.

"On to Dun Aengus," Nora said.

My legs tired as we pedaled toward the visitor center, where we left our bikes and I bought another ticket. From here we walked for twenty minutes uphill, and I pulled out the gloves I'd taken to carrying in my jacket.

"Look at that," Erin said as we rounded the top.

My brother's fortress stood in its stark beauty against the edge of the water. People sat on rocks on the ground around it, taking pictures and letting children play. Nora walked off to snap some photos herself.

"Come on." Erin led as the two of us climbed on the ruins, the three remaining rings of stone slab walls.

Navigating loose rocks, she took me to the very edge where the land dropped off completely. "Another form of protection?" I asked.

"Hundreds of feet down." She pointed to some large pieces of overhanging slate. "Best view there is."

"We sit on it?" So close to the drop-off?

"No." She laughed, and her voice carried in the wind. "We lie on it. You won't fall." I watched as she walked to the slate and lay on her stomach. "Come see the ocean."

With gingered steps, I joined her. Though I was on solid ground and in no danger of falling, it was still a long way down. The ocean waves slammed into the rocks. "This island reminded my brother of God, his protection."

"And what does it make *you* think of, then?"

"Mrs. Sweeney," I said without thinking. "I get the feeling all she's known are hard times. I believe every time she got back on her feet, another wave knocked her back until it just wore her down." Kind of like me. But my audition was going to change everything. It had to. "Erin, do you know what happened to her husband?" It was past time to do some research.

"No. Have you asked Mrs. Sweeney?"

"She won't talk about her past."

Erin gave a small giggle. "I know just the ladies to ask. The MacNamara sisters. If there's something to be known, they'll have your information."

"Would they talk to me?"

"They'd talk to a tree stump. If you can stand their plastic-covered couches and fifteen cats, it would be worth the visit, sure it would."

"It's really none of my business, I suppose."

"Mrs. Sweeney is now your business, Finley. Don't doubt that."

We fell into a comfortable silence as we both watched the scene around us, painted by the strokes of God's majestic brush.

Minutes passed before the cold of the wind and the damp in the air finally got to me. "You know, we're surrounded by people, but it just feels so . . . lonely here."

Erin lifted her head, giving me a faint, thoughtful smile. "Only if you let it."

Chapter Nineteen

- Breakfast: one bite fish, 3 calories
- 2 Diet Cokes to chase down fish, 0 calories
- Exercise: running, 3 trips to bathroom to pee

The planet would have to explode for this day to get any worse. Mrs. O'Callaghan fixed us fish for breakfast, my socks were two different shades of blue, and I accidentally walked in on Liam in the shower, seeing enough to scar me for the rest of the year. I just wanted to get through this Friday and get to the weekend.

When we finally arrived at school, Erin stopped at her locker, but I continued walking down the hall until I got to number 328. The one that belonged to Beatrice.

I didn't even bother with a hello as she twisted her combination. "You totally framed me for cheating."

She took her time looking up, her bored expression only adding kindling to the fire of my temper. "I have no idea what you're talking about."

"Seriously?" I laughed. "Could you be any more immature? I mean, sticking your pencil in my back so I'd turn around? And then copying my paper? Could you truly not do any better than that?"

Her eyes widened in feigned shock. "I'm hurt, Finley. That you would accuse me of such a thing. Maybe you can go cry on Beckett's shoulder. You know, the one that belongs to Taylor."

I stared her down. I'd been the cheerleading cocaptain, so I could do intimidation *and* a perfect back handspring. "I want you to back off Erin. Bullying is so out of style."

"Who are you to come in here to *my* school and tell me what to do? You walk onto this campus like you rule the place. The little heiress crooked her finger and chased after Beckett Rush until he started paying her some attention." Her singsong voice pressed on my temples. "And that wasn't good enough. Then you got jealous."

"I want you to tell Mrs. Campbell the truth."

"Truth is so subjective. I know my truth. You know yours. Who's to say who's right? Oh, I know. My father. The principal."

"What do you gain from this? Does it make you feel better about yourself?"

"Yes, actually. It does. Have a nice day now." She hoisted her backpack over her shoulder. "And don't get in any more trouble. I'd hate for you to get sent home." She walked away, leaving me in the dust of her snark and venom.

With ten minutes left until the first bell, I headed in the direction of the library, my face aflame from the confrontation. After giving a quiet hello to the librarian, I slipped past the row of fiction and sat down at one of the computers.

First I e-mailed my mom and dad and told them how wonderful everything was going and how nice the people of Ireland truly were. Apparently Beatrice Plummer was their national letdown.

Not wanting to go back into that hallway and stalling for time, I did a quick search under Cathleen Sweeney's name.

I scanned through an entire page of useless results. But it was page two that had my full attention.

Abbeyglen Public Library archives.

Sitting up straighter, I clicked on the link, and it took me to an index of the library, a collection of scanned copies of the Abbeyglen newspaper.

What did we have here?

Typing in a few more keywords, I waited for the database to do its search. Two minutes later I found Mrs. Sweeney's marriage announcement.

I scribbled down the date on my notebook, then continued my perusal.

Scrolling through the listing, I stopped at another mention of her last name.

An obituary. Three years later.

For Charles Sweeney. The man Mr. Murphy had said died of loneliness when his wife left him.

I leaned up closer to the monitor and reread the next find, three months after Mr. Sweeney's death.

Another obituary.

John David Sweeney, son of Charles and Cathleen Sweeney, died April 23. He'd only been two.

My gosh. The loss. No wonder Mrs. Sweeney was so cranky.

"Reading anything good?"

I snapped my head toward the familiar voice and clicked on a different page. "Hi, Sister Maria."

She logged onto a computer beside me and smiled. "Doing some homework?"

"Something like that." I glanced at her computer and saw a familiar screen. "What about you?"

She wiggled her mouse. "Changing my Facebook status."

I squinted to get a better look. "From married to it's complicated?"

"Just waiting to see how long it takes Father Tom to notice."

"But you're married to God."

"And that's not complicated?" She laughed, then noticed the rushed scribblings on my paper. "Research?"

I hesitated to tell her. But one look from the woman and it was like downing a bottle of truth serum. "I was investigating Cathleen Sweeney. She's had a really rough life, I think."

"What did you find?" Sister Maria sat back in her chair and gave me her full attention.

I quickly caught her up. "Time's running out. Mrs. Sweeney's going downhill fast. It's like she's willing it to happen."

"And this is your problem now?"

"I have to help her. She can't die without her sister's forgiveness." I told her about the letters in the drawer. "I haven't read them, but I know they're probably pleas to Fiona Doyle."

Sister Maria considered this. "Perhaps."

"Did you know Charles Sweeney?"

"Knew of him, yes."

"How did he die?"

"Ask his widow."

"She won't talk about him."

"I don't recall what happened. You should talk to the MacNamara sisters."

"They come highly recommended." I smiled. "Erin says they're the town gossips."

"I prefer town historians," the nun said. "Past McGann's pub, over the bridge, second house on the left. They've been there for eighty-five years." She typed something on her computer. "So tell me, Finley. Why do you care?"

"Because . . ." I wasn't even sure I could explain it. "I don't want her to die without having her say. Judging from all the letters, it looks like Mrs. Sweeney has spent years reaching out to her sister. And to die without being heard? Without forgiveness or peace?" I pointed to the notes. "I think she's lived most of her life tormented. Took her sister's fiancé. Shunned by the town. And then lost a child." I knew a little bit about that type of loss, having watched my own mother grieve.

"I'm pretty sure no one asked her to steal her sister's intended."

"Mistakes happen. We all get in situations where we do things we regret. But she's more than those mistakes." My voice elevated in the small lab. "Mrs. Sweeney wants to be remembered for something besides the wrong she did and the people she hurt."

Sister Maria's smile was slow as it tugged up her cheeks. She reached for my hand and gave it a squeeze. "God would want her to know she isn't defined by her mistakes." Her cornflower-blue eyes bored into mine. "He would want her to know he loves her and forgives her. And she doesn't have to be who she once was. She just needs to reach out to him."

"Maybe she wants to," I whispered. "Maybe she has."

The nun nodded. "Then she needs to believe he heard her and is on the job. And listen with her heart." Sister Maria shut down her Facebook page and logged off. "Instead of her head."

"I was referring to Cathleen Sweeney," I said as she walked away.

"Me too, dear." She strolled off with a grin. "Me too."

Chapter Twenty

hy am I going with you again?"

"Because I don't want to visit the MacNamara sisters by myself," I said as Erin counted out her money and handed it to Anne Daly, the proprietress of the Daly Read, a narrow scrap of a bookstore sandwiched between the carnation-pink flower shop and McQuarry's pub. Sean said if a man had one too many at the pub, he could stumble over to the flower shop and bring his wife home some please-forgive-me posies.

"Here's your change, dear." Mrs. Daly placed the coins in Erin's outstretched hand, then tucked her hardback book safely in a cream-colored bag. "Had to special order that one."

"I don't know why." Erin pulled her book from the bag and ran her hand over the unremarkable white cover. "It hasn't been out long, but it's bound to be a best seller. Should be sitting up front, standing tall and proud in its own display."

Mrs. Daly smiled. "I must admit, I did get the same shiver when I touched it as when I first held *Twilight*."

"What's it called?" I asked.

Erin lifted it up for my inspection. "*Hair Cell Micromechanics*."

"I should probably make room on the shelf for its sequel," Mrs. Daly said. "Fine afternoon to you both. As always, Miss Erin, we thank you for your . . . eccentric purchases."

Erin led the way outside, where we hopped on our bicycles.

"Did you hear the way she said *eccentric*?" Erin placed her book gently in her basket. "Like I'm as crazy as the MacNamara sisters. Like I'm destined to grow up with a house of creepy petri dishes and hairy hordes of cats."

"None of that is true." Well. Maybe half.

We pedaled past McGann's Pub, the wind lifting our hair like streamers as our wheels carried us over the bridge. Erin turned at the second driveway in a row of sloping homes, lined up like colorful birds on an electric line. The MacNamara place was old, and I immediately knew it would smell damp and musty inside. It was a two-story thing and looked to have been formed of white plaster, with green trim around each crooked window. Droopy curtain panels hung from half of these windows, barely hanging upright, as if they had given up the fight years ago.

I wasn't sure what I'd find inside, but I feared it was one of those horror movie houses that let teenagers in, but never spit them back out.

Erin had to knock seven times before the door finally opened. It creaked just a few inches wide, enough to see one green eye staring back at us through the crack. "Are you friend or foe?"

With a sigh Erin turned to me. "Are you sure you're up for this?"

"Friends," I called over her shoulder.

"Then go round back," came the gnarled voice. "Only salesmen and robbers come through the front door."

Okay then. The side of the house was decorated with broken flowerpots filled with silk roses, their leaves faded and frayed by the elements.

"What is that?" I pointed to the red tailgate sticking out of a leaning outbuilding.

"The sisters' BMW." Erin climbed the concrete steps to the back door. "They buy a new one every year."

"And drive it?"

"On Sundays."

It only took three knocks this time for the door to open once again. Same droopy-lidded eye peered back at us. "Are you Sean O'Callaghan's daughter, then?"

"Yes, ma'am," Erin said. "And I've brought a friend. We'd like to talk to you if we could."

"A visit?"

Erin nodded. "Yes, ma'am."

The door sprang wide open, revealing a grinning old woman no taller than my shoulder. "I'll put the kettle on. Sister will show you to the parlor." She cupped her hand over her mouth and bellowed into it like a megaphone. "Hilde!"

A carbon copy woman popped out, as if conjured by our host's indelicate tone alone. "Do we have guests, Lavena?" The two were clearly twins, matching from the top of their dyed short black hair to their denim dresses and brown sensible shoes.

"Are you blind, Sister?" Lavena asked as we traipsed through her kitchen and meandered toward the parlor. "Are they not standing right here? Did I not say I would get the tea?"

"You're so snippy today." Hilde's voice dropped in a stage whisper. "'Tis no different than any other day. Come sit a spell, ladies."

The parlor was decorated in the style of *Alice in Wonderland* meets Jane Austen. Sun-bleached paisley wallpaper covered the walls, plastic covered the Victorian couch. Cats covered the plastic.

They were everywhere. Orange cats. Calico. Persian.

"Beautiful, aren't they?" Hilde picked up a Siamese and plopped it in her lap as she sat. "Such good companions. Feel free to pet them. They won't scratch." The plastic beneath her thin arm was shredded to strips. "'Tis a pleasure to have such fine company today. What shall we talk about?" She tapped a red fingernail to her lip. "The terrible prices of beef that new butcher has brought us? The scandalous way Mrs. Clarke hangs her knickers on the line in the front yard? The fact that *Mr.* Clarke was seen—"

"Actually," Erin interrupted, "we came to ask you a few questions about—"

"Where that new librarian has been spending her evenings?"

Erin blinked twice. "No." She slid me a glance and covered up a giggle with a poor excuse for a cough. "Before we get to it, Finley, maybe you'd like to show them your picture?"

I reached into my bag and, after some digging, pulled out the journal. "Have you seen this cross?"

Hilde reached into her blouse and pulled up glasses tethered to a gold chain. "Let's have a look." She took it from my outstretched hand, and one of her cats jumped up to sniff and inspect. "Looks like Ailfred McCarthy's. Yes, that's the one."

"Let me see that." Lavena limped into the room, took the journal, and held it to her face. "You're as blind as a bat. Anybody with eyes can see it's Fergus Fitzpatrick's."

"Is that right? And how is that when his stone got knocked over in the storm of sixty-three?"

"Well, it's sure not Ailfred's," Lavena said, as if her sister had suggested that two plus two was five. "He died in 1856, at the age of eighty-one, leaving behind one wife and three girlfriends." She handed me back the journal. "Mrs. McCarthy bought him the plainest marker she could find. Then spit on it the rest of her days."

"We don't know whose it is," Hilde said.

"No, we don't." Lavena marched back to the kitchen.

Another dead end. But at least it had been an entertaining one.

"My friend Finley here has been spending quite a bit of time with Cathleen Sweeney," Erin said.

"Oh." Hilde's drawn-on eyebrows lifted toward her forehead. "Cathleen Sweeney. She's trouble, that one."

"You don't know what you're talking about." Lavena returned, carrying a tray of cookies. Two cats curved around her ankles. "Cathleen Sweeney was a friend of mine, and you best be watching yourself before you say something mean."

"Friend?" Hilde snorted. "Borrowing a pencil from her in school when you were six does not make you friends."

"What can you tell us about her husband?" I asked. "What happened between them?"

"He died of a broken heart, he did," Hilde said. "Everyone knows that. Cathleen stole him from his first true love with her trickery, then after the ring was on her finger, her true colors came out, sure they did. Then he realized what a terrible person he'd married. But it was too late. Cathleen had the baby, then left poor Mr. Sweeney. Wouldn't even let the man see his own son. Now what kind of woman is that, I ask you?"

"A smart one," her sister snapped. "That man was bad through and through. You could see it in his beady eyes. Didn't he have eyes like a snake? Sure he did. The two would be about town together, and Charles wouldn't let Cathleen out of his sight."

Hilde ran her hand down the back of a cat bigger than her lap. "Cathleen was a cold woman. A snob. Married that fancy man, then wouldn't talk to any of us anymore, like we weren't good enough." She clicked her tongue as she regarded me and Erin. "She didn't have a single friend."

"Because she wasn't allowed any!" Lavena sat down in the chair beside her sister and glared right through her. "She couldn't go anywhere without him, couldn't talk to anyone. He was a possessive man." Turning toward us, Lavena paused for dramatic effect. "One time the baby came down sick. She never left that house without her husband, but he was at work. She walked into the chemist's, with a little hat perched on her head. It had a tiny veil that covered part of her face, very fashionable."

"Charles's money bought it."

"Quiet with you, Sister!" Lavena barked. A kettle whistled from the kitchen, but the two ignored it. "Where was I? Cathleen, Charles, chemist, me daft sister being wrong, oh yes. As I was saying, she walked to the chemist's, and I was working that day behind the counter. I saw her slink in, that veil covering her face, that sick baby on her hip. She stands there and waits for her medicine, and you could tell she was in a terrible hurry."

"Because she was afraid she'd have to speak to someone," Hilde said. "Never wanted to make eye contact with the likes of us."

A black cat stood near my feet and stared up at me, eyeing my legs for landing space. I reached down and scratched its ear and listened to its solid purr.

Lavena ran her red nails through her close-cropped curls. "So there Cathleen was, waiting her turn for that medicine, and her baby started crying something awful. She bounced him and cooed but nothing would do. He cried and cried. Then he reached out and grabbed her hat right off her head."

"And snakes came out?"

Lavena ignored her sister, her eyes trained right on me. "And that's when I saw the bruises. On her cheek. Round her eye. That man did it to her, he did. And *that's* why Cathleen Sweeney wasn't allowed to associate with the towns folk. Because she'd married a horrible, jealous man."

"And so she left him?" I asked.

"Och, of course she did. Moved herself across the river," Lavena said. "What a scandal that was. We never saw her then. Her husband knew herself would keep quiet, so he told everyone who would hear how heartbroken he was, how he walked the floor every night, waiting for his missus to return home. He made more loans at that bank than ever."

"He deserved his success," Hilde said.

Lavena shrugged a bony shoulder. "Then . . . he died."

"And everyone blamed Mrs. Sweeney," I said.

"Sure they did." Lavena picked a wad of cat hair off her denim sleeve. "He had a heart attack. Dropped dead in his office whilst giving Jimmie McBride the money for his chickens."

Hilde shook her head. "Jimmie named his first chicken Charles."

"Everyone said he died of heartbreak," Lavena said. "But I knew better. And then three months later, that boy of theirs passed away from the fever. So if anyone had the heartbreak . . . it was Cathleen Sweeney."

Chapter Twenty-One

*God has written me quite a story in Ireland. Every
day here, there's something new to discover . . .*

—Travel Journal of Will Sinclair, Abbeyglen, Ireland

hat do you think you're doing?"

At ten o'clock Saturday morning, Beckett got
out of his truck just as a rickety taxi pulled up to the
O'Callaghans' house.

A gray-haired old man stepped out of the cab and tipped his
cap. "Good morning."

Beckett thundered toward me. "I asked you what you're doing?"

I glanced at the aging cabbie, who'd apparently left his dentures at home. "Going on a hot date."

Beckett crossed his arms, the dark prince staring down his next
victim.

"Fine. I'm going to Galway. To see Mrs. Sweeney's sister." What
was Beckett doing here? He should've been working.

"And how did you get the address?"

"By prowling through her drawer."

"Why haven't you been on the set in the last few days?"

"Because I told you I quit."

"And I said I didn't accept that."

"My ride is waiting. I have to go. You can yell at me later."

He ran a hand through his blond hair and huffed. "I'll take you."

"No." I took a step toward the tiny car, but Beckett put himself in my path.

"They're filming Taylor's scenes today, and I have nothing better to do, so. Unless you're *afraid* to ride in the truck with me—like you're afraid to be my assistant?"

I just looked at the boy. "After the last twenty-four hours I've had, I am fresh out of any Southern grace, so I suggest you step out of my way."

His left cheek dimpled. "That bad, huh?"

"Your sympathy overwhelms me."

"Are you thinking of having Mr. Donahue drive you back to America, then?"

"I have new information on Mrs. Sweeney, and I'm going to see her sister in Galway."

"Right now."

"Exactly." The woman was getting worse at an alarming rate. How much time did we have? "Please be so kind as to get out of my way. The meter's running."

"I'll take you."

"I'd rather walk."

"Mr. Donahue." Beckett smiled at the old man. "We don't need you today, sir, but thanks for coming out." He pressed some cash into the old man's hand.

"No! I need you!" I made a dive for the back door handle, but Beckett grabbed it first.

"Have a good day now," Beckett said.

Mr. Donahue scratched his head and looked between us.

"Don't you drive away without me, Mr. Donahue."

Beckett clapped the man by the shoulder. "Why don't you go inside the inn and tell Mrs. O'Callaghan you want a piece of pie?"

Mr. Donahue's bushy brows shot north. "Pie?"

"And all the coffee you can put in that flask you keep under your seat."

The cabbie tipped his cap again. "Good day to you." And before I could stop him, Mr. Donahue shut off his car and hobbled toward the house in search of a morning snack.

I closed my eyes and waited for my blood to cool. "I am calling his superior."

"That would be his wife. She's deaf in one ear, so make sure you speak loudly."

Of course.

"Why did you do that?" My voice was flat with defeat.

"Because Mr. Donahue is too old to be behind the wheel and drives in the middle of the road. He's had three wrecks in the last month. Two with a tree and one with a squirrel."

I hated not having a car. I felt so stranded. And mad. And helpless.

In all these things, I am more than victorious . . .

Beckett walked to his truck and opened the passenger door. Bob shot from the porch and bounded into the back, his tail thumping against the bed like a drum. "Get in." Beckett jerked his chin toward the cab before giving into a long-suffering sigh. "Please."

I struck a pose that was an artistic combination of attitude and defiance.

He had the nerve to grin. "You *are* afraid to be alone with me."

"Well, apparently my charm is so overpowering, you can't seem to keep your hands to yourself whenever I'm near. But no, I'm not afraid of you." And I had to talk to Mrs. Sweeney's sister.

"Wasting daylight."

Stomping toward the truck, I shot daggers at Beckett. "Don't try any funny business."

"Wouldn't dream of it." He took my hand and helped me inside.

The radio played as we drove down the winding roads to Galway. Gray clouds mingled above us in the sky, and rain threatened to spill. I watched the green meadows on either side of the truck and wondered if my eyes would ever adapt to such vibrant color.

He turned on the heater. "You going to ignore me the whole way?"

"Probably."

With a pirate's smile, Beckett stretched his right arm across the back of the seat. His fingers grazed my shoulder, and I inched away just as my stomach gave a light growl. After waking up, I'd practiced for three hours, not bothering to stop to eat breakfast. The date for the audition was closing in, and I felt it with every passing second.

"The least you could do is offer a little conversation." Beckett dodged a pothole, keeping his eyes on the road.

"You want me to talk?"

"It would be the polite thing to do."

"Okay. Let's talk."

"Any topic will be fine."

"I'm going to sit here and silently think of one. Might take a while."

"We could talk about the weather." This morning his accent was almost as strong as Nora's coffee. "Or we could discuss politics. But that's never a friendly subject. There's the economy." He took his focus off the road and leveled his gaze on me. "Or you could just tell me what happened that has you so fired up."

"Beatrice happened. She basically framed me for cheating in English. And do you know why?"

"Just her way of showing love?"

"Because she thinks I'm a threat to you and your girlfriend Taylor." I watched his face for any reaction, and of course there was none. The boy was a trained actor, letting me see only what he wanted me to. "Beatrice is afraid if there's no you and Taylor, there will be fewer parts for her." It was so dumb, just saying it out loud made me mad all over again.

The wipers squeaked against the cracked windshield, and I turned around to check on Bob.

"He's fine," Beckett said. "He loves the rain."

Bob ran from one side of the truck to the other, head thrown back, snapping at raindrops with his oversize teeth.

"Nothing about you makes sense," I said. "Not even your dog."

"Maybe Bob and I are just misunderstood."

"Or deranged."

"Want me to have Beatrice fired?"

Yes. "No." What I wanted most was answers. But I guess his silence on the Taylor subject was my answer. They were together, messed up though it was, and my lips could never touch Beckett's again.

The rest of the hour crept by in silence. Beckett watched the road, and I stared out the window, committing the sights to heart. What would it have been like to just keep driving? To have pushed Beckett out, taken the wheel, and just kept going?

After a few wrong turns, Beckett finally pulled onto a gravel road. Rock walls lined the field around us, which was filled with grass as high as my knees.

"This is it." Beckett passed me the directions, and I tucked them in my purse. "It's that white house there."

The two-story home sat in the middle of a field. A fence contained the horses that ran in the backyard. Red shutters sent out a cheery greeting, giving me hope that the woman within was just as inviting.

The truck rambled down the driveway before lurching to a stop. Beckett hopped out and came around to open my door.

"Thank you." I delivered my appreciation to his chin as I ignored his outstretched hand. "I'll be back in a little bit."

"You're not going in there by yourself. Sean and Nora would kill me."

"A tempting idea," I mumbled. "Fine, then, come on. But don't get in my way."

His smile was infuriating. "Wouldn't dream of it."

Not bothering to wait for Beckett, I bounded up the steps and knocked on the door.

No answer.

I set my fist to the door again. "Hello?" I called.

I heard clomping and movement in the house, and a full thirty seconds later the door opened and a small woman appeared. "Yes?"

"Mrs. Doyle? I'm Finley Sinclair—"

"Are you here about the pig?"

"No." I cast a glance over my shoulder. "Though I brought one with me."

"Eh?" Her bobbed hair gently curled around her ears, and her clothes were as fashionable as Mrs. Sweeney's pajamas were not. "Who did you say you were?"

"I'm a friend of one of your family members."

She smiled, revealing nice, even teeth. "And which one would that be?"

"Your sister."

Her face fell like I'd sucker punched her. "I don't have a sister."

"Cathleen Sweeney?"

"She's dead to me." Mrs. Doyle started to shut the door, but I stopped it with my hand.

"Please, you have to listen to me. Cathleen is sick."

"In the head!"

"No." Well, maybe a little. "She's dying. Bone cancer. She doesn't have much time." The words fell to the ground like angry little bombs. Mrs. Doyle's face tightened, but she remained expressionless, her eyes only mildly annoyed.

"I suppose she sent you to me."

"No." I steadied my voice, though I was desperate for her to see the urgency. "She has no idea I'm here. Please, Mrs. Doyle. Don't let her die with this between you."

"Did she tell you what she did?"

I shook my head.

"She took my fiancé, she did. The man I was supposed to marry. She up and married him herself. Charles Sweeney had sworn to love me all the days of my life, and he just left me for her." Red splotches climbed up her pale neck. "You have her tell you the rest of the story. She got what was coming to her."

"A man who abused her?"

"I'll not listen to that. Charles was a dapper, kind man. Wouldn't have hurt a fly. And then she lured him into her web and bled him dry. Maybe he did turn to the bottle, but she forced him. There was a curse on that marriage, and it came to no good. Cathleen stopped being me family the day she said 'I do' to that man." Mrs. Doyle pulled the screen door closed. "Good day to you." And she slammed herself inside.

I stared at the Gaelic welcome sign in my face. "That went well." I turned to Beckett. "Nice lady. Her heart's just brimming with mercy."

"Her heart's brimming with pain."

I guess I knew a little something about that. "I have to fix this."

Beckett cocked his head, his eyes soft on mine. "Why, Finley?"

How could I explain? "Because Mrs. Sweeney can't die thinking her soul is condemned. She can't go without knowing she's been forgiven." I shook my head, uncertain of my own motives. "It's important. That's all I know."

He nodded. "'Tis enough."

"Enough for what?"

He walked down the steps, then faced me again. "Enough for me to help you."

I dogged his heels, following him to the truck. "I didn't ask you to."

"I know." He held open my door with a lopsided grin. "That's just the kind, generous type of guy I am."

"And what do I have to do in return?"

Beckett smiled. "I just so happen to have an opening for an assistant."

❧❦

"Cathleen's had a rough day."

The afternoon nurse spoke in a hushed, bless-her-heart tone, as if Mrs. Sweeney were as fragile as glass. I felt the anger build in my chest. Didn't she know Mrs. Sweeney didn't like sympathy?

I just nodded and headed down hall C, where I found Mrs. Sweeney in bed, eyes closed and her face taut with discomfort.

I wanted to ask her if she was okay, if there was anything I could do to make it all go away, but I'd have been no better than the nurse. Beckett had dropped me off on our way back into Abbeyglen, and my mind was filled with so many thoughts, so many worries, I just wanted to pull them out and put them into proper order like the shoes in my closet.

Sitting in the chair beside her bed, I reached into my bag for the Stephen King book. It was a grisly thing, but Mrs. Sweeney must've liked it. Not that she'd have told me. But her snoring had cut down considerably.

"I thought I'd read a few chapters today." I took out my bookmark and set it on the table. "Unless you'd rather do something else."

She shook her head and shivered beneath her blankets.

I reached for the thick comforter at the end of her bed and spread it over her, tucking it around her shoulders, talking as I went. "You will not believe what Beatrice has done now. She totally set me up to get in trouble for cheating." I fluffed Mrs. Sweeney's pillow, adjusted the incline of her bed, and got her some fresh water. "Erin said she's going to create a plague just for Beatrice." The chair's legs scuffed the floor as I sat down and pulled it toward her bed. "Mrs. Sweeney, I want you to know I don't care what happened with your sister and her fiancé all those years ago. I know you weren't a bad person. Not on purpose."

"'Course I was," came her wheezy voice. "Don't be so naïve. Took away me sister's fella. 'Tis just as it sounds, so."

"I know about your son."

Five long seconds ticked by before she spoke. "Ah, John." She breathed the name like a prayer, a plea, a regret.

"Can you tell me what happened?"

Her lips thinned as she shook her head. "'Tis not a happy tale."

"You have me reading a book about a girl who tries to kill an entire town. Anything else at this point would be a pick-me-up."

She inhaled slow and deep, as if calling up the memories with her breath. Her sleepy eyes peeled open, and I could tell from the glaze they'd upped her morphine, taking away some of the pain. And her usual filter.

"Me father was a gambler, so he was," Mrs. Sweeney finally said, her words slightly slurred. "He'd bet on anything—horses, politics . . . the weather. Caught up with him. He was on the verge of losing the house. It would've killed me mother, since the property had been in her family for generations." She licked her parched lips before I helped her sip from her water. "Times were hard. Me father got a loan that had a high interest rate."

"One of his daughters?"

She nodded against her pillow. "Our name meant something back then. Charles Sweeney had money, but he didn't have the respectability. So he bought it."

"You?"

"Me baby sister. She was the pretty one. Fancied him immediately. Charles was a charmer, he was. But I saw through him, I did."

"Was he abusive?" I couldn't very well tell her I had talked to the MacNamara sisters, but maybe she'd just think I was a very good guesser.

Mrs. Sweeney coughed into her fist. "Not with his hands. Oh, but he was too smart for that. He left bruises where you couldn't see . . . at first."

"So how did you end up with him?"

The three lines between her eyebrows deepened. "I'm tired, girl. Leave me alone now."

But I couldn't. Not yet. "You took your sister's place, didn't you?"

"The story is I wanted him for meself."

"No, you didn't," I said softly. "You were protecting your sister. And she doesn't know."

Her coughs wracked her thin frame, and I helped her take another drink of water. "Leave me now. I'm old and sick. And you're just nosy."

"How did he die?"

"The town said I killed him."

"Did you?"

"If wishes were bullets . . ."

A feeling came over me, so powerful it could've lit that darkened room. "I . . . I want to pray for you."

"Save it."

I reached for her hand anyway, hanging on when she attempted to pull away. "I'm kind of rusty, so this won't exactly be poetic."

"I just want it to be quick."

I closed my eyes and waited for a feeling of godly peace to steal over me before I began.

It did not.

"Lord, you know Mrs. Sweeney's hurts. She's carried them around a long time, and she needs to let them go. Open the door so she can make peace with her sister. Help both of them see truth and find their way back to each other. And to you. God, let me be Mrs. Sweeney's hands and feet. Use me to help her however I can." I cut her a glance. "Even though she can be mean. And she makes fun of my voices when I read."

"Wrap it up anytime."

"Amen."

She said nothing, but when I gave her hand a squeeze, she didn't pull away. Or yell for the nurse. And that in itself was some small miracle.

"Leave me now."

I stood up, filled with a tattered sense of purpose. "I'll be back Monday."

"I'll count the seconds."

"We'll talk more. I like this heart-to-heart stuff."

"We're through talking about this. Leave it be."

"You don't want me to do that."

"I've lived with this for over fifty years. Don't be adding to my grief."

"I'm going to fix this, Mrs. Sweeney."

She lifted one thin, fragile brow. "Do us a favor."

I leaned closer. "Yes, ma'am?"

"Fix your own blooming life instead."

Chapter Twenty-Two

~~~~~~~~~

Your Facebook pics of Abbeyglen are gorgeous.
Maybe you could smile in some of them for your
favorite sister-in-law? Love you, girl!
—Lucy

Sent to my iPhone

~~~~~~~~~

I spent the hour before dinner running up and down the O'Callaghans' road. The steep incline of the driveway provided extra resistance for my legs, and I envisioned my thighs becoming leaner with every step. A string of worries floated through my mind, and it just made me run harder. At least my troubles were fuel for burning calories. With staying away from craft services and riding my bike, I'd lost at least a jeans' size. It gave me such a thrill of accomplishment. So many things seemed out of control in my world. Finally, something I could manage.

When I slipped through the back door and into the kitchen, the family was already gathered. Nora and Sean stood at the stove discussing the messy occupants of the Rosebud room while Liam sat next to his sister, who held her phone to her ear.

Nora stopped stirring as I walked past. "Out for a run?"

"Yeah. It's supposed to rain tomorrow, so I thought I'd squeeze one in."

"Didn't you run this morning?" she asked.

I knew Mom had informed her about my "issues" back home. "My counselor told me it was a good way to counteract anxiety or the blues," I said for her ears only.

"Ah." Her pause was uncertain. "Well, you'd come to me if you were feeling overwhelmed, wouldn't you?"

"Of course."

The door between the guest dining room and kitchen swung open, and I knew without turning around who'd just walked in.

"Beckett!" Liam leaped from his seat.

"Hey, dude." Beckett held up his hand, and he and Liam did some tribal masculine handshake.

"Liam," I said. "Don't you know the proper way to greet an actor is with an air-kiss?"

Beckett walked to the table. "Not for my man here." His voice dipped as he stood beside me. "But you're welcome to greet me that way anytime."

"Just in time for dinner." Sean peered into the stove. "Finley, would you get Beckett something to drink, please?"

Beckett caught my less-than-pleasant expression. "Water will be fine. Not too much ice. Add a slice of lemon." He reached for my hand and electric currents blazed up my arm. "And don't spit in it."

"That's a lot to remember. You'll understand if I forget at least one of those commands." His thumb slid across my arm as he laughed and let me go.

Erin put the phone beside her plate, then propped her chin in her hand. "Samuel Connolly is avoiding me."

Beckett smiled at Erin. "Do you realize you just spoke a full sentence in front of me?"

"I guess dropping the potatoes in your lap was a bonding experience."

"Glad some good could come of it."

I returned with Beckett's water, minus the lemon, and set it beside his plate. "Surely Samuel's not ignoring you."

"No, he is." She shot Beckett a sheepish glance, then scrolled through her texts.

"Out with it," Beckett said. "Let's hear this tale."

Erin took a fortifying breath. "Two weeks ago we were talking on the phone, texting, messaging each other on Facebook. But now he won't even answer his mobile."

"Maybe he's just busy." I sat down beside her, inhaling the aroma of baked chicken.

"Or maybe he knows I intend to ask him to the dance."

"Or maybe," Liam said, "maybe he was attacked by a zombie and he has mush for brains and his limbs are rotting off as we speak."

Erin blinked twice. "I guess as long as he'd be my date, I wouldn't care."

Sean meandered to the table, wearing a "Real Men Make Flaky Pie Crusts" apron. "This boy would be crazy not to go with you, Erin." He pushed up his sleeves. "Do I need to have a chat with him? Show him me old weapon collection?"

"Not helping, Dad. I just don't understand what changed. We were talking every day and suddenly . . . nothing. I wonder what I've done."

Associated with me, for one thing. I'd have bet my phone Beatrice was behind this.

"No big plans with the cast?" Nora set a platter of chicken on the table.

Beckett flashed her his million-dollar smile. "They're out celebrating a birthday. But when you told me you were fixing your famous chicken again, I knew this was where the party was."

Seriously? Could he not turn off the charm for one second? He was practically flirting with someone's *mother*.

"I'm just glad someone appreciates my cooking." Nora stood behind me and gave my shoulders a squeeze. "This one eats like a bird anymore, and Liam wants nothing but hot dogs and crisps."

Dinner was a slow affair, with Sean and Beckett swapping stories of their world travels. Nora tried to cheer up Erin about her dance date potential, but nothing perked her up except the promise of dessert. Liam wove himself into every conversation, somehow finding a way to insert girls or Legos into every topic.

I cut up my chicken into small pieces and ate what I could. As soon as the creamy taste of butter passed my tongue, I gave myself permission to leave more than half on my plate. I was all about eating, but I refused to clog my arteries with fattening dairy products. Ireland was not the easiest place to maintain a diet.

My remaining chicken pieces got shoved under my mashed potatoes. Though my stomach told me it wasn't quite full, it would have to do. I refilled my water and drank two more glasses instead.

"Time for dessert." Nora stood up and went to the fridge. "Sean made a lovely tart."

"Let's take it into the living room," Erin said.

Sean stood up. "I'll grab the coffee."

I rose with the intention of helping Nora serve, but Beckett beat me to it. With nothing else to do, I joined Liam on the couch.

He reached for the remote and turned on the TV. The room filled with the sound of a BBC station.

. . . Taliban sent a video message to the British prime minister threatening another attack unless the suspected terrorist is released from prison. Mullah Kakir is accused of plotting the London subway bombing. He was also suspected of having ties to the bombing of the school in Afghanistan that took the lives of twenty-five children and American reporter—

"Change it." Beckett snapped up the remote and hastily switched the channel as my brother's face smiled back at me on the TV. "Let's watch something else, eh?"

"Turn it back," I said. "Why did you change it?"

"How much more of that can you listen to?" He handed Liam the remote, then turned to me, his eyes searching. "There's nothing new to hear."

I shook my head as the unwanted tears pressed against my eyes. "Will's name." I sniffed and blinked away the moisture. "I wanted to hear his name."

"Dessert time!" Nora and Sean came bearing plates of their homemade tart.

"I'm going to take a walk." The room closed in on me, and I struggled to catch my breath.

"But you just ran," Nora said.

"I'll be back. I need some air." I grabbed my jacket off the back of my chair at the table and all but raced outside.

The night sky still had hours until complete darkness, and I walked in the dimming light, past the backyard fence, beyond the grove of trees, and into the meadow. I breathed the air, reveling in the lack of humidity like back home. I'd traded the smothering heat of Charleston for the chill of Abbeyglen.

God, when will the chill in my heart go away? I have a feeling even a hot Charleston summer couldn't melt it down.

I cut through the grass and walked until I found the castle ruin Erin had told me about. Little more than a stone cylinder now, it must've been a tower once upon a time. Pulling my jacket tighter around me, I stepped inside and ran my hand over the rocky wall. The vines wove in and out of cracks, defying gravity as they clung. How many years had this stood here?

At the sound of leaves crunching, I turned. And there was Beckett.

"Finley."

Just one word. That was all he said. But I heard all the pity within it, and it made me want to rip down the tower stone by stone with my bare hands.

"I want to be alone."

He crossed his arms and leaned against a deteriorating wall. "I'm not going anywhere."

I swiped my eyes, pulling back fingers painted with watery mascara, and turned so he wouldn't see. "There's such evil in the world, isn't there?"

"Yes. But goodness too."

"Those men who killed Will and the children—they tore so many families apart. Families who will never be the same."

"Ah, Flossie." His arms came around me from behind and pulled me against his chest. His chin rested on my head as he held me tight.

"I have to find that cross in the picture. Everything's wrong wihout it."

"Fin, you know when we find it . . . your brother's not going to be there."

I closed my eyes against the pain. "I know."

"And he's not going to meet you in New York City. Whether you nail your audition or not, Will's not coming back."

The bottom dropped from the well of my tears, and I couldn't hold it in any longer. With a coughing gasp, I gave into the sorrow that now filtered into my every breath.

Beckett spun me around and hugged me to him. His strong arms held tight with a mix of tenderness and strength as he whispered comforting words I could barely hear for my own crying.

Seconds, minutes, what seemed like hours passed before I could lift my head and brush the last of my tears away. Shame rolled through me. I had just blubbered all over one of the most famous boys in world, practically using his shirt for a Kleenex.

I stepped away and filled my lungs with a cleansing, chilled breath. "I had a tree house." A bird flew overhead, as if returning to its loved ones before bedtime. "Will would call up to me like I was Rapunzel. He was so much older, but he always made the time. Both my brothers were good to me, but Will and I were different. He treated me like I was special."

Beckett gave a crooked smile. "You are."

I wanted to laugh at Beckett's words, but I didn't have the energy. "It's weird to be where Will was. Walking his same steps, seeing the exact same things he did. I know what he thought about all of them—but that cross. It had to be in his journal for a reason."

"Then we'll find it."

His gaze was so heavy on mine, I couldn't look away. It held me in place, making me powerless to even blink. "Why are you here, Beckett?"

His voice was rough as the stones. "Something told me there was a damsel in need of saving." He captured my hand and held it against his chest. His heart beat a steady tempo beneath my palm. "Maybe I'm just watching out for my assistant. Or maybe God put it on my mind to follow you."

Nice to know the Lord spoke to one of us. "You know, I read my brother's journal and I wish I had his absolute faith, his view of the world. He thought everything was beautiful."

"Isn't it?" Beckett stepped back. "Look around."

"But then people go away." I drew back my hand and hugged my arms against the dipping temperature. "Brothers die. Children disappear. War rages. It's hard to watch the news and not question life . . . God . . . the point of it all." I cleared my throat against a lump. "I watched the video footage of the explosion that killed my brother. The whole world did. How do you explain what I saw?"

"You doubt there's a God?"

"No." Thoughts tumbled in my head, and none of them seemed to make enough sense to even speak aloud. "But I don't see him like I did as a little kid. He's no longer the God of happy stories that came with stale Oreos and watered-down punch. I guess . . . I don't know who he is."

"Umm . . . His law is love, and his gospel is peace?"

I blinked my watery eyes. "Did you seriously just quote a Christmas carol?"

"I'm kind of new to this." Beckett laughed, then scuffed the ground with the toe of his shoe. "So last year we did this movie in Italy." He stuffed his hands in his pockets and studied a weed at his feet. "I was sightseeing on my own and walked into this beautiful old building. It was a church. I've never told a soul this, but . . . something seemed to just reach out to me there. I came back the next day. And the next after that. I borrowed one of the camera guy's Bibles and started reading it. I still don't have a lot of it figured out, but somehow I know it's real. And I'm not through searching. I don't have the answers to your questions. I just know God said to trust, and that's what I'm trying to do."

"That's not good enough for me anymore." I couldn't believe I was debating faith. With a Hollywood prince. "I want answers. I want to understand this world again."

Beckett walked to me and reached his hand over my head. He plucked a wildflower growing on a vine in the cracks, a violet bloom that hadn't received the message that summer was gone. "Maybe you should stop going by what you feel." He opened my hand and pressed the flower in my grip. "And start going by what you know is truth."

Chapter Twenty-Three

From: Finley_Sinclair@SinclairEnterprises.com
Subject: Bambino

Alex, congrats on the baby news. Things are great here. No, I'm not getting Beckett Rush's autograph. I spend so much time practicing, I barely know the boy exists.

I heard the O'Callaghan family rustling around downstairs on Sunday afternoon, getting ready for lunch. My stomach reminded me I had skipped breakfast to practice, then spent thirty minutes reading Will's journal after that.

The sharp corners of the picture glued to the page lifted at the edges as if straining to break free. While the images were blurry, the colors were not. Above the ocean, rows of houses lined up together in sharp blues, greens, and yellows. They looked like confections, as if you could run your finger over them and draw back sugary icing. Beneath the photo Will had scrawled a verse, one I recognized from Psalms.

Lord, You light my lamp; my God illuminates my darkness.

As I read the rest of the words, I heard Will's deep voice as if he were sitting next to me.

Lahinch is only about ten miles from Abbeyglen. On the Liscannor Bay, it's a popular spot for surfers and golfers or just a guy in search of some good pub food. Went into McDougal's Pub where I was told I could find the finest cup of tea and the crispiest cod. While it rains a lot, nothing can dim the shades of this town. Color is all around. I want to keep my eyes on the good. And not the dark clouds.

Words from an eighteen-year-old boy. Most guys his age were waxing poetic about girls and cars. But most guys didn't grow up to be breakout reporters for CNN by the age of twenty-three.

"Finley?" Erin called from the steps seconds before she appeared. "Beckett's here for you."

"Why?" My host sister's face was still drawn with gloom.

"Said you guys were going to Lahinch."

Oh. I hadn't really thought he'd been serious. Or that he'd even remember.

"Any word from Samuel?" I asked.

She nodded her red head. "He sent me a short text to say he couldn't go to the dance with me."

"Did he give you a reason why?"

"No."

"Ask another boy. Show Samuel he can't get you down."

"I did. I e-mailed Patrick Sullivan just an hour ago. It's the strangest thing." Erin sat down on the edge of my bed, still in her skirt from church. "He said yes, and I got all excited. But then thirty minutes later he texted me back and said something had come up." Erin looked at me, eyes wide. "What's wrong with me?"

The question of every girl.

"Nothing." The bed squeaked as I plopped down beside her. "Those boys should be paying you for the opportunity to be your date."

"At this rate, I'm the one who's going to have to cough up the money. I just don't understand what I've done to make them turn me down. Patrick and I have been friends since we were in nappies. Our mothers sing in the choir together. He's never had a girlfriend in his life, so it's not like going with me to the dance would be some big threat to his reputation."

"Erin, I don't think this has anything to do with you. I think it all points to Beatrice."

"That girl is a . . . *Bufo marinus*."

"Did you just cuss in scientific terms?"

"She's a toad."

"Beatrice hates me, and she's punishing you." And I didn't know what to do about it. "But we'll fix it."

"I told her I was going to St. Flanagan's with a boy."

"And you will." I nudged a slouching Erin with my shoulder. "You'll have a date."

"I guess I should pray about this. Then just let it go. Let God have it."

"Right." Assuming God wasn't on his extended lunch break with her like he was with me.

"Girls!" Nora called from below.

"Go to Lahinch with me and Beckett."

"No." Erin stood and straightened her shoulders with resolve.

"I think I'm going to console myself by praying for a date. Is that sacrilegious?"

"God said love endures all things."

Erin found her smile again as we walked down the stairs.

My eyes narrowed as I watched the boy in the living room talking to Sean and Nora. Dark hair straightened with a Chi. A flamboyant pink shirt and gray slacks. Shiny black shoes with a sweater tied over his back and a tilted fedora on his head.

I hoisted my purse onto my shoulder. "Did your Vegas act get cancelled?"

A dimple popped in his cheek. "The hair color washes out."

I surveyed the outfit he'd chosen for his disguise. "The color is the least of your worries. Tell me you're not carrying a purse too."

He slapped his back pocket. "I had to draw a line somewhere." Beckett held out my coat and helped me into it. "You look beautiful though."

My heart soared like a bird before crash landing as I realized these were just practiced words he'd probably told every female he'd ever encountered.

With good-byes to the O'Callaghans, we walked outside to Beckett's truck. He swung open the passenger-side door and took my hand. His fingers tightened on mine as his hard gaze swept over me and beyond my shoulder. Turning around, I saw the focus of his ire.

A black stretch limo.

"One of your girlfriends?" I asked as the vehicle pulled up beside the truck.

"My manager."

As Montgomery Rush climbed out of the backseat, Beckett

planted a hand on the truck, as if anchoring himself for whatever wind tried to blow him over.

"Good morning. Hotel is booked tonight, so I'm staying here." His father peeled off his sunglasses. "Those Calhouns will get my bags, right?"

"O'Callaghan," Beckett said. "And no, they won't. This isn't the Four Seasons."

Montgomery Rush looked at the three-story house and grimaced. "Did you catch the tabs? Your Tuesday night brawl with some paparazzi made the headlines. It would've been the top story, but you can't ever trump a celebrity divorce scandal."

Beckett didn't move a muscle, but I could feel the tension bouncing off him like static.

"The E! channel wants the exclusive interview. I told them you could call tonight or tomorrow, so check your schedule and let me know."

"I'm not doing that interview and you know it."

"Your publicist has already committed."

"Uncommit me."

The two stared one another down like gunslingers in a western. As the silence lingered, I expected a tumbleweed to come rolling by while a buzzard cawed overhead.

Mr. Rush eyed his son's disguise. "When you get back from wherever it is you're going, boy, you and I are going to have a little talk. Right after you hand me those signed contracts."

"I didn't sign them."

His father's left eye twitched. "In this business, we're not guaranteed the next deal. Today's hot is tomorrow's has-been. I don't want you to lose out on these opportunities."

"What if I want to pursue a different opportunity?"

"There's time for that. Later. When the vampire market is dead. So, this afternoon. You and me." He glanced toward me as if just now noticing he and Beckett were not alone. "Unless you want to deal with this now."

"Taking a drive," Beckett said tonelessly.

"You can't put this off forever."

Beckett muttered something under his breath and walked around to his side of the truck. He pulled his long legs inside, then shut the door with a resounding slam.

The engine revved to life, sounding louder than ever, and with jerky motions Beckett made quick work of getting us down the driveway.

"So your dad—"

"Not gonna talk about it."

"It's only fair. I snot cried all over you last night."

"I don't want to mess up my mascara." He flipped on the radio and a man sang a song about a love gone wrong.

I sneaked a glanced at Beckett. "If you just told me—"

"Let it go, Florence."

"Fine. See if I ever tell you anything again. You are such a girl."

"And I've got the outfit to prove it."

⇌

The meandering, narrow drive played out before us like a symphony, and at one point I had to pull out my phone and hum a new piece of melody. Beckett didn't even comment. He was used to it by now.

I couldn't help but be touched when he stopped at two cemeteries on the way, but we didn't find my Celtic cross. Though at least ten of them were dead ringers.

Thirty miles later we arrived in Lahinch, and I walked beside Beckett taking pictures of all I saw. With my brother's photo in my mind's eye, the quaint port-side village matched up exactly with what I had expected. Houses of rainbow colors. Gulls flying overhead. The smell of saltwater in the air. And ominous clouds above us that threatened to unleash watery torrents any moment.

"Slow down," I called as Beckett walked on ahead.

"I don't want to waste the day."

"Afraid your hair will turn blond at the stroke of noon?"

He stopped, his posture rigid, his mouth a thin line. He was still upset over his fight with his dad. I knew what that was like. I'd argued with my parents every day the year Will died.

We passed a group of teenage girls toting cameras. The tall leggy blonde looked at Beckett, then did a double take. I heard their whispers as we strolled by.

"Is that—"

"No."

"It looked like him."

"Go see."

I glanced back. "They're coming our way."

Beckett wrapped his arm around me and drew me to his side. "Do something about it, and I'll buy your lunch."

"I think it *is* him!" The girls giggled behind us.

I leaned my head on Beckett's shoulder and, with a burst of courage, threaded my fingers through his. "Johnny." My Charleston accent was just as exaggerated as it was loud. "Don't worry about that rash you have. Our love will see us through."

His arm squeezed a little tighter. "Frances, dearest," he drawled, "when we get back home, I will give you that wedding ring you've begged me for. It's only right after you gave me those triplets at the ripe age of sixteen."

"I'm an unwed mother?" I hissed.

"I'm a diseased baby daddy."

This made me laugh. "I think you just got the title for your next movie."

The girls twittered with whispers behind us and slowed their pace.

"You know I won't marry you, Johnny." My voice boomed enough for the whole town to hear. "Not until you come off the road, give up your all-boy flute band, and finally get that middle school diploma."

Beckett leaned his face near mine and shot me a quick glare before composing his features into the appearance of a love-struck guy. "I'll come off the road, Frances. Just as soon as you give up your dreams of the rodeo. Every time you get gored by a bull, you rip me heart right out of me—" Beckett turned his head and exhaled. "Okay, they're gone."

I dropped my hand from his and tried to step out of his hold, but his arm remained glued around my shoulder. "You can let go now."

His grin was as decadent as melted chocolate. "Danger's lurking around every corner. I need you to protect me." He angled his head down as a crowd walked past us and filed into a restaurant. "Ready for lunch?" Above us swung a sign for Mickey Burdick's. "Best fish and chips in town—at least according to them."

"No. I'm really not hungry. I had a big breakfast." Why had I said that? The lie had tripped so easily off my tongue.

"You sure you don't want to eat?" Beckett asked.

I looked to the restaurant, inhaled the fried batter. "Yes."

I'd get a sandwich at the house. I'd grab some fruit. Some potatoes from last night.

He led us on the paved road past a blue surf shop toward the water. We stopped at the rails that overlooked the sea where an incline of heavy gray rocks introduced the shoreline. The dark clouds dueled with the sliver of visible sun, but the light seemed too weak to hold off the gloomy sky. Two boys on skateboards zipped by us, while I just stared out at the water, still tucked into Beckett's side.

I should've moved.

But I didn't. I was just helping with his disguise.

Wasn't I?

I closed my eyes and listened. Waited for the moment the sounds would become a song in my head—the crescendo of the birds, the tempo of the waves, the *fermata*—the pause—of the wind nipping at my face.

"It's beautiful, isn't it?" His voice was reverent, as if he were watching God paint the scene himself.

In the distance the lapping water met the green fields. Beyond the village shops, houses lined up. They were cozy places where people lived with their families, and I wondered if any of those people were aware of how quickly life could change. How their loved ones could be taken in an instant.

Down below, a man in a wet suit paddled his white surfboard away from the shore.

"It's freezing," I said. "People surf in this weather?"

"All year long." I caught the envious note in his voice.

"Have you ever surfed here?"

"Yeah." The man paddled farther out, the waves coming to meet him. "It's a feeling of freedom like no other. I don't get to surf nearly as much as I'd like."

"Don't you and your dad ever take vacations?"

"You can't make money if you're not at work."

"Beckett, about your dad—"

"Watch the surfer."

I followed Beckett's pointing finger and saw the attempt try to get on his board, only to fall right back down. He tried five more times. "What's the point?" I asked as the rain started to sprinkle on us. "It's like winter out here today."

"The point is," Beckett said, turning his eyes on me, "that guy doesn't care about the rules. He doesn't care about the temperature or all the other reasons why he shouldn't surf. He just wants to be on the water and do what he loves. To be out there where no one can tell him what to do or what meeting he has next. Just the wind in his hair and the salt on his lips." His voice was more passionate than in any line he'd ever delivered.

"And that's what you want?"

He reached out, and my pulse doubled as his thumb slid across my bottom lip. "You know what I want, Finley?"

I couldn't look away. Couldn't speak. I just shook my head.

"This." Beckett lowered his head and sealed his mouth to mine.

The kiss dragged me under like the undertow of the Atlantic. I tasted sea, anger, rain, and something I couldn't begin to define. His lips gently sought and soothed as his hands pried away my damp hair and framed my face like I was delicate enough to be swept away.

And that's exactly what I was.

"Stop." I pushed at his chest. Tried to gain some distance. "I can't do this. You're with Taylor."

"Finley—"

"I'm not going to be another one of your easy conquests. I don't take this stuff lightly."

"And I do?" He balled his hand into a fist and pressed it against his temple. "Don't answer that." He turned to the railing and stared at the surfer, now standing on top of his board and riding the waves. "If you still think that about me, then you don't know me at all."

"Then tell me, Beckett. Give me one reason not to believe all the hype about you."

"I think we're done here." The surfer fell into the water and Beckett walked away. "I have a meeting with me father."

Bitterness coiled in my stomach as another thread of control unraveled.

I took one last look at Lahinch.

And wondered about the light my brother couldn't forget.

And the one I struggled to find.

Chapter Twenty-Four

Watching the town get ready for the St. Flanagan's
Day Festival was almost as much fun as the
actual event. The girls get totally stressed
about it. I have no idea why.

—Travel Journal of Will Sinclair, Abbeyglen, Ireland

*Y*ou're deliberately sabotaging any chance Erin has of getting a
date for St. Flanagan's Day."

Wars had been started with the kind of hatred Bea directed
at me Monday after school as I stood toe to toe in her space.

"I thought she had this *amazing* date already lined up." Beatrice
said each word as if it was embarrassingly beneath her to talk to me.

"Maybe she changed her mind." Girls marched up and down
the hall as they escaped Sacred Heart for the day. Some lingered
nearby to listen to a conversation that was more interesting than
anything waiting for them at home. "What are you saying to these
guys to get them to turn her down? They're her friends."

"I don't have any idea what you're talking about. Surely between the two of you, you can manage to scrounge up a date for Erin."

"Erin is kind and has a heart of gold. She would never hurt you. Why do you want to do this to her? Do you even care how much it hurts her feelings? No matter what you believe of me, it is the lowest of lows to attack her for no reason." It made me sick to even look at Beatrice. "You are seriously messed up."

"Like you?"

"What's that supposed to mean?"

At the appearance of that feline smile, I suddenly knew how girl fights got started. "There's so much interesting information out there on the Web, isn't there? Like details of your exploits. Your wild nights in the clubs."

"That was a long time ago." Not long enough. "Everyone knows about that."

"You're playing with the big leagues now. I warned you if you messed with me, you'd be sorry."

"What do you want from me? An apology?"

She tossed her dark hair and laughed. "We are so past that now. I wouldn't take your apology if you served it to me on a silver platter. But I see the worry in your eyes. And you *should* be worried. Because what's the use of having information . . . if you don't use it?"

Anger trembled in my limbs as Beatrice took three steps away, then stopped and turned back around. "You might check your phone. I sent you a link of your *crush*. Not that you delude yourself into thinking you're anything but disposable to Beckett, but I knew you'd want to stay up-to-date, so."

I waited until she was out of sight, then I whipped out my phone and pulled up my e-mail. In three clicks I followed her link to a page on the *Entertainment Tonight* site.

Beckett Rush spends Saturday night in the arms of three Irish beauties partying the night away.

I zoomed in on the picture beneath the heading and saw Beckett in the middle of a girl sandwich on the dance floor. Their hands were all over him, and his lips were pressed against a girl's cheek. Reading the rest of the article, I frowned.

Then read it again.

"That snake." I could not believe him. "That low-down, dirty, lying snake."

Running outside, I hopped on my bicycle and pedaled as fast as my legs would go.

Because it was time to report back to work.

And time to give Beckett Rush a piece of my mind.

❧

"Open up." I pounded on Beckett's trailer door, not caring who was watching. "Open this door!" This was getting me nowhere. I yanked on the handle and it pulled easily in my hands. I all but leaped inside.

"You . . ." I edited myself and picked words that wouldn't make Sister Maria blush. "You dishonest, manipulative, user of a weakling."

Holding a thick history book, Beckett sat in a chair in full costume and sipped a mug of coffee. "Do shut the door. I suddenly feel a draft."

I pulled the door so hard the trailer rattled, then advanced on Beckett again. "How can you just lie like that?"

His face was as neutral as Sweden. "You're going to have to be more specific. So many possibilities."

I drew my phone from my pocket, punched a few buttons, and shoved it toward him. "Does this look familiar?"

He studied the website for only a second. "Looks like I had a good time."

Irrational laughter bubbled to the surface. "So this is you? In the picture?"

He blew on his coffee. "Looks like it."

"Wow, I didn't know you had so many talents. Not only are you America's favorite vampire, but you can also be in two places at once."

Something flickered in his eyes. "I need to get back to work."

"Why not let someone else do it and digitally enhance it with your face?" My lips curved into a rueful smile. "How long has this been going on?"

He slapped his book shut. "You're not even making sense."

"You couldn't have been in Limerick at this club Saturday night. You ate dinner with us. You followed me to the castle ruins."

"Then maybe I went out."

I shook my head. "You stayed up for three hours playing video games with Liam. Sean told me." He had been singing Beckett's praises yet again, just like Nora and Erin.

"Maybe after that—"

"You're lying. Why can't you just tell me—"

"Because I have nothing to do with it." Beckett jumped to his feet and towered over me. "You couldn't possibly understand my life, Finley. I tried to tell you it didn't belong to me, and I meant it. I have a whole team of people who organize every minute, every detail." He gave a soulless laugh. "I'm not even there for half of it. And I'm certainly not allowed to refute it."

"You didn't get in a pub fight last week, did you?"

"Last fight I had I was still in braces."

"Last year's scandal with the trashed hotel rooms and outland-ish demands to the director?"

Beckett sat back down and cradled his head in his hands. "Never touched so much as a bag of hotel peanuts."

"Are you dating Taylor Risdale?" I had to know the truth. This boy had kissed me, held my hand, made promises with those movie star eyes.

He tilted his head back onto the chair, his gaze tired and weary as he took a moment to study the ceiling. "The first movie opened in limited release, and it was dying. Reviews were awful. Everyone had so much on the line. So they decided to create reports of a rela-tionship between me and Taylor. It happens all the time."

"Who decided?"

"Does it matter?"

"I think it probably does to you."

Beckett rubbed the bridge of his nose and sighed. "My manager."

"Your dad."

"One and the same."

"Beckett." I was suddenly filled with the desire to call my par-ents and tell them how much they meant to me. How lucky I was to have them in my life. People who cared about me and helped me. Instead of turning me into some puppet for their own gain. "I'm so sorry."

"I don't want you to be sorry." He stood again and went to the kitchen, bracing his arms on either side of the sink. "You should understand that better than anyone."

Pity could be such a cruel tormentor. "Why do you let it go on?"

"It just spun out of control. It started with one story, then half a dozen, then me da' started fabricating things way beyond a few dates between me and Taylor. He created this whole different persona . . . and you want to know the really terrible thing?" Beckett looked right through me. "It worked. The movie spread like wildfire and everyone was saved. And now we've all got producers and directors knocking down our doors."

"And fans."

He nodded. "Ticket-buying fans."

"But you've sold yourself in the process."

Beckett closed the distance between us, and his hands curved around my upper arms. "I've never been anything but myself with you. You . . . are real. You're honest. You're . . . you."

The reverent look in his eyes made me want to confess every sin and tell him I wasn't who he thought I was. I was the girl who got up at 3:00 a.m. to practice. The one who had to have her underwear folded in fourths, who didn't like her food to touch on her plate. Who had nightmares about her audition. Who sometimes Googled Will's name just to see if there were any new pictures.

"Just tell your dad how you feel."

"It's not that easy." He ran his hands up and down my arms, and warmth flooded my veins.

"You don't want to sign those contracts he's been throwing at you, do you?"

"I just . . . need some time. To figure out who I am and what I want to be. See that history book there?" He jerked his chin toward the table. "I've been taking a few online classes. Me da' doesn't even know."

"Do you want to be an actor?"

His shoulders lifted in a shrug. "I don't know what I want to do. It may sound stupid, but I've been praying about it."

"It's not stupid." It didn't seem to work for me, but I'd heard it did wonders for others. "Talk to your dad, Beckett."

He shook his blond head. "I have the entire cast relying on me to do the next two movies. I can't just walk away from this." He reached for my hand, his eyes on me. "And I can't seem to walk away from you."

My heart flapped dangerously in my chest.

Beckett Rush, Mr. Cover Boy of *People*, liked little Finley Sinclair from South Carolina? It was the most impossible thing ever.

"I'm not like those other girls," I said. "I don't look like them or act like them."

"You're better." He took a step closer, his hand reaching out to touch my cheek, his lips a whisper away . . . then only a breath. "You're so much better."

The trailer door flapped open, and Beckett and I broke apart. My face flamed red as Montgomery Rush stepped inside, his eyes missing nothing. "You're wanted on the set. We do still have a movie to make."

Beckett watched me. "I'll be right there."

"Don't keep us waiting, Beckett." His dad stepped outside. "You have a lot of people depending on you."

Had I just become one of them?

Chapter Twenty-Five

- Hours of practice: 3
- Hours of sleep: 5
- Hours listening to Mom gush on about Alex and Lucy being preggo: too many

With more than an hour left, I waved good-bye to the girls at our usual picnic table in the courtyard, tossing my uneaten sandwich in the trash. I hopped on my bicycle, my violin in my basket, and turned toward the familiar path of the nursing home. The sun warmed my skin through my light jacket, and after days of dreary rain, I found myself grateful for the change. I would never grumble about the tropical Charleston weather again.

I knocked twice on Mrs. Sweeney's door, then walked on in. The room was dark, and a vague sadness hung in the air like a cloud ready to spill rain. Nurse Belinda gave me a small wave and a grim smile.

"One last pill, Cathleen. You can do it. Sit up for me."

"Too tired."

"I know. You've had a rough day. But this will help the pain."

I stood, frozen by helplessness, and just watched the nurse ease Mrs. Sweeney up enough to safely swallow the pill. Belinda held a cup of water to Mrs. Sweeney's dry lips, then lay her back down. The breath whooshed from Mrs. Sweeney as if she'd just expended all the energy she had left for the day.

"Finley's here to see you. Looks like she brought her violin." Belinda's voice came out songlike, and I knew it must've grated all over Mrs. Sweeney. "Are you up for a visitor, then?"

No response. Mrs. Sweeney lay there, eyes shut, brow furrowed, a thin sheen of sweat clinging to her temples.

"Maybe you should come back tomorrow," Belinda said.

Because Mrs. Sweeney was dying. And there was nothing anyone could do about it. "Okay."

I turned to leave, grateful to be excused, only to stop when I heard that weak voice.

"Stay." Mrs. Sweeney coughed for a few seconds before repeating herself, like she knew I needed to hear it twice to believe it. "The girl can stay."

"Are you sure?" Belinda tucked the blankets around her thin patient.

Mrs. Sweeney just nodded her gray head.

"Don't let Cathleen talk your ear off." Belinda gave me a wink, then disappeared.

I settled into my usual chair and just sat there. Wondering what to say. What to do. "Would you like me to read to you?"

She shook her head. The room was charged with a new heaviness. It made me want to hop right back on my bicycle and pedal home.

Uncomfortable with this new territory, I picked up the brush and lightly pulled it through her hair. "I'm sorry you're feeling bad today." That was lame.

God, help me. What do I say to her? Sorry you're dying, and I really don't want to be around you when it happens? Or when it gets bad? Or when you're not well enough to say something snippy?

"I talked to my mom yesterday," I said, watching Mrs. Sweeney's breath come in uneven puffs. "She's worried because I haven't called much. But I think Skyping every few days is more than enough, don't you?" Her chest rose and fell as she dozed, but I continued to tend to her hair. And somehow, between the easy rhythm of the routine task and the weight in the room, my thoughts took a different direction. "I have been lax about calling my mom," I said, knowing I was talking to myself. "But I'm afraid those all-knowing eyes of hers will look at me and see I'm not keeping it together very well here. And I'm afraid to tell her that I think I'm going to mess up my audition. What if they don't like my song for Will? I need them to. And I need to find that darn grave. I just . . . I'm just trying to find closure. I've tried so hard, and I'm not getting it. Beckett thinks I'm too hard on myself, but what does he know? He's living two lives and can't decide which one he wants. Like I need to follow *his* advice. But sometimes . . . sometimes I think this hole inside me will never be filled."

I plopped back down in the chair, feeling a little better for unloading.

And a little worse.

Bowing my head right there, I whispered a prayer. "God, help me. Help Mrs. Sweeney. We both need you. I want you to heal her. Take away her pain. Make it go away so she can live longer, so she can have more picnics. I pray that she would totally turn her heart over to you. And forgive herself. And please help me finish my song.

And ace that audition. It's everything." With eyes squeezed shut, I sniffed against the tears that threatened to spill.

A hand fell on my shoulder and gave a faint pat. Looking up, I found Mrs. Sweeney watching me through heavy eyelids. "Let it go," she whispered.

My nose was a drippy mess. "How much did you hear?"

"Enough." She waved her hand toward her water cup, and I moved to get it. Holding her head up like Belinda did, I put the straw to Mrs. Sweeney's lips as she took a few labored sips before returning to her pillow.

I stared at the blue striped pattern of her sheets. "My life must sound silly to you."

Mrs. Sweeney closed her eyes, and just when I thought she'd gone back to sleep her voice arrowed into the dark room. "Bitterness. It will eat you up. I was angry that me father sold me off like cattle. Angry that me own sister wouldn't forgive me and see that her life was better off without Charles. Angry that I was stuck with the likes of a vile husband." She pressed her lips together and shook her head. "And furious that God had taken me child, my only joy in this world."

"Sometimes God isn't fair, is he?" I knew I was supposed to be the salt and light there, but I just couldn't pretend I was that confident in my faith.

"All those years wasted." I had to lean closer to hear Mrs. Sweeney's words. "Gone."

"You never married again?" I asked.

She gave a slight shake of her head.

"But you could've started over. Had more children. Been happy."

"Too easy to be miserable. And make others just as unhappy. Didn't I wear it like a grand fur coat? I just . . . locked meself in this prison of gloom and anger. And where did it get me?" A cough racked her body. "Don't make the mistakes I did. Don't hang on to old hurts. You can spend your years blaming God, blaming other people, but in the end it was a choice. And I'll die knowing I made the wrong one. Could've fixed it. And I didn't."

"It's not too late to talk to your sister."

"This is about you now. Not me."

"But—"

She shook her head again. "Go on. Leave me. I'll hear your song another day."

Her complexion. Her voice. Her dwindling strength and bloodshot eyes.

Mrs. Sweeney was fading fast.

Time was running out.

❦

I found Beckett in his trailer, talking to a woman I recognized as a costume technician.

"Hello, Finley." His smile made me want to write sonnets. "Marta here is just fixing my shirt."

"Did your ruffles lose their fluff?"

"Lost a button," Marta said. "But I think it will hold now."

"Thanks, Marta," Beckett said. "You were telling me how your husband was getting on?"

"Better now that he's employed," she said as she put away needle and thread. "Thanks for talking to the studio and setting up that interview."

"Glad I could help."

Marta straightened. "There's been a tear in Taylor's purple

gown. Must go see to it, then locate shoes for . . ." She didn't even finish her sentence before she bustled out of the trailer, carrying on a one-way conversation with herself.

Leaving Beckett and me alone.

He tugged on the string of my hoodie. "Hey." His forehead wrinkled in a frown. "Everything okay?"

"Of course."

"That didn't sound the least bit believable. What's wrong?"

Everything. "I'm fine."

"Talk to me, Finley."

The way he was looking at me now? I could stare at that face forever. "Mrs. Sweeney had a rough day."

"And so you did as well?"

"She's gotten much worse in the last few days. Belinda said bone cancer can do that, move fast. I just . . . feel like I need to do something."

"Such as?"

I could hardly concentrate for his fingers playing with the ends of my hair. "I . . ." What had we been talking about? "Um, I don't know."

"Would it make you feel better to visit with her sister again?"

"I wish she'd just see Mrs. Sweeney. All the woman wants is for her sister to say 'I forgive you.' I keep thinking, what if my brother and I had ended things on bad terms before he left for Afghanistan? But we didn't. A few days before he left, he took me out to eat, we went to a movie." I could see it so clearly in my head. I'd worn a white sweater, some new jeans, and shiny red flats. He told me to stop growing up. And then he died.

And I'd grown up overnight.

"What movie did you see?" Beckett asked, as if it mattered.

"One with Brad Pitt."

"I've heard of the guy."

"It's one of my favorite memories. The best night. But what if Will had been angry? Or had believed something awful about me? It would kill me that he died thinking those things."

"Like Mrs. Sweeney and her sister." Beckett slowly pulled me to him and rested his chin on my head. "Tomorrow we'll go see Fiona Doyle."

I wondered at this new closeness of ours. What were we? "On the off chance she speaks to us, you know she won't speak to Mrs. Sweeney."

"I once sat by a feisty girl on a plane who refused to have her picture taken with me or get my autograph. She would have the courage to try again."

"This girl didn't fall in sobs at your feet? She sounds really smart."

He smiled. "So's the guy she's dating."

I took a step back as his words crashed into me like a meteorite. "Is that what you are?"

"I could be."

Me. And Beckett Rush. My brain could hardly process it. "But you're . . ."

"Interested in you as more than a friend." He stared down into my confused face. "You make me want to—"

"Wear normal button-downs?"

"—be myself. To tell me da' I've enrolled in college. To tell *People* I'm not dating Taylor."

"Then do it."

A shadow fell across his face. "I have a lot of people counting on these movies. It's not that easy." He reached for me as I moved out of his hold. "But being with you is."

"I can't be with someone in secret, like we're sneaking around." To date him meant to live his double life, and I couldn't do that.

"Do you really want to be with me—in public? To have your name dragged through the mud? I don't want your reputation trashed."

"It already is. A little more won't hurt."

"You say that now. But just wait until you see your name on *OK!* magazine with some trumped-up headline of how I'm cheating on you with three other girls or we're both on drugs and our families want us to go for treatment."

Treatment. I guess that was one thing I had on this movie star.

"Finley, trust me. It's better if we keep this to ourselves for a while."

The door to the trailer flung open behind me, and as I watched Beckett tense, I didn't even have to turn around to know who was there.

"Hey, Da'."

"You and me." Mr. Rush jerked his thumb outside. "We need to talk. Now."

"I'm busy."

His dad held up the dreaded contracts. "You didn't sign these."

"No."

"Why?"

Beckett shrugged. "We'll talk about this later."

"You'll do these movies, son."

"Going to forge my signature?" Beckett asked. "Like you did the last one?"

"It wasn't illegal. You were underage."

"Well, now I'm nineteen." Beckett glared at his father. "And I'm calling my own shots."

"There's a line of young men just waiting to take your place."

"My roles as an actor?" Beckett asked quietly. "Or my role as Montgomery Rush's talent?"

Mr. Rush regarded his son through narrowed eyes. "If you don't do this next vampire movie, someone else will take your place. Is that what you want?"

"I don't know." Beckett shook his blond head and walked away. "I just don't know."

Chapter Twenty-Six

O n Saturday, I walked into the dressing room next to Erin's at Hargood's House of Formal Wear, changed out of my jeans, and pulled up Beckett's last text one more time.

You. Me. Date. 4 p.m.

"Let me see the dresses when you get them on," Nora called from outside. "This is your last chance to have them altered before next Saturday."

Sliding up my white dress, I reached around for the zipper and gave it a pull. Staring in the mirror, I looked at the empire waist, how it gathered in an hourglass shape, and I didn't like what I saw.

In all these things, I am more than victorious . . .

I told myself to focus on the positive. My counselor used to always say negative thoughts were just lies from the devil. Right now it was like he had a bullhorn to my ear. He was also telling me my South Carolina tan was long gone.

I dragged my eyes to the rest of the dress, admiring the way the calf-length skirt billowed when I turned, making me feel like a princess. Maybe one who'd danced in grand balls in the castle that used to sit on the O'Callaghans' land.

Or one who dated a boy named Beckett Rush.

"Time to model!" Nora had a group of quilters due to check in at the inn today, and I knew she was anxious to get back home.

Erin and I both peeled open our doors at the same time. She hesitantly stepped out and went before the full-length mirror as her mother snapped a picture with her phone.

"Mam!"

"Your father will want to see." Her eyes crinkled at the corners. "You look gorgeous, Erin. Just beautiful." Then Nora turned to me.

As I stood to the side.

Clutching the top of my sagging dress.

"Doesn't it fit?" Nora asked.

"It's fine." I tugged on it and watched the cap sleeves drop at my shoulders.

"Well then, I'll go and get the seamstress. We can't have it falling off of you for the dance."

"Wait—"

But Nora was already gone, running out into the store to get some help.

"You've lost weight." Erin studied me in the mirror. "I thought maybe you had, but now I can really see it."

Part of me was thrilled with her declaration.

Part of me wondered at the look on Erin's face.

"It's just a few pounds. That's what I wanted."

That was all I wanted.

". . . and we think the measurements must've been wrong. Or there has been an error in the alterations." Nora bustled back to the dressing room with a harried-looking employee who wore a tape measure around her neck.

"Step up here, please." The woman waved me to the mirror.

"It's fine. I can fix it back home. Wear a shawl." It sounded dumb even to me, and when the woman and Nora both shook their heads, I knew it was useless to resist. I took to the small platform and let the woman put her tape measure all over me, my cheeks flushing in the mirror.

The woman took one last measurement at my waist, then consulted her job ticket. "It is the exact size I have written down. We did not make a mistake."

"You've lost more than a pound or two," Nora said. "And you've been working much too hard."

"I don't feel like I have. I . . . I guess . . . I've been running a lot. And I usually put on some weight in the summer, then it falls off when I get back into school. It happens every year. Usually it comes off with cheerleading, but now that I'm here and not doing that, I'm riding my bicycle everywhere and running in the mornings. It's only natural some weight would fall off." The words flowed out, one after another.

Nora hesitated, processing my meandering explanation before finally giving a curt nod. "You have been getting a lot of exercise. But you've also not been eating properly, so. Do you eat the lunches I pack?"

"Yes. Of course."

"I've been under a lot of pressure lately. I'm sure my appetite will return." As soon as I aced the audition, walked every step of my brother's, got Beatrice off my back, reunited Mrs. Sweeney and her sister, *and* figured out what Beckett really wanted from me. They didn't understand. My parents, Nora, Erin—they should try spending five minutes in my shoes.

"It's quite a bit to take in, but we can fix it," the seamstress said. "We can have it back to you by next week. It will cost extra."

"That's fine," I said. "I'll pay it."

"I'm going to check on your shoes," Nora said. "I'll be out front."

"You never eat lunch with us anymore." Erin looked at me as if I'd somehow disappointed her, as if I were suddenly not quite who she believed me to be.

"I have to see Mrs. Sweeney during lunch so I can get to the set after school. You know that."

I expected her to agree with me. But she didn't.

"Is there something you want to tell me?" she asked instead.

My life started spiraling out of control the day my brother died, and I keep trying to stuff everything back in its place, but nothing is staying put. "No. Can't think of anything."

"I'd be glad to pray for you. Or just listen if you need someone to talk to."

"I'm fine. Truly." My laugh came out a little too loud. "We Americans aren't used to walking anywhere. Or riding a bicycle. I've never been healthier."

"It's just . . . at dinner. I see you pushing things around on your plate. Giving Liam your chicken or passing him your dessert."

"I'm stressed, that's all. But it will soon be over. The movie's going to wrap up in a few weeks." Oh my gosh. Shooting would be done in no time. Then what would become of Beckett and me? Would he just forget me? Never contact me again? What if I really was just his summer fling? An autumn distraction? "So . . . I'll be fine. Right now I have a lot on my mind."

"Okay." Erin didn't sound quite so convinced. "But if you want to—" She stopped midsentence and craned past me toward the store front. "There's Patrick Sullivan. He's here. Getting his tie." Her cheeks broke out in scarlet splotches. "I can't go out there."

"The guy in the green T-shirt?"

She nodded mutely.

"With the ripped jeans?"

"Yes."

"I'll be right back."

"Wait! No!"

Clutching my gaping top, I stormed toward Patrick and his friend, following them as they made their way to the men's section.

"Excuse me, Patrick, is it?"

He turned around. "Yeah?"

"I'm a friend of Erin O'Callaghan's." I saw him pale. "You remember her, right? The girl you agreed to go to the dance with, then suddenly cancelled when Beatrice Plummer got ahold of you?"

"I don't know what you're talking about. I just . . . couldn't take Erin."

"Yeah, because you're a weak-kneed jerk who hurt my friend." His Adam's apple bobbed, but he didn't protest. "I want to know what Beatrice said to you to get you to bail on Erin."

He looked at his friend, then back to me. "Nothing."

I took a step forward. "I'm not afraid to make a scene here."

"Okay, fine!" His cheeks flushed pink. "She told me she could get me a date with Taylor Risdale if I didn't go to the dance."

"And did she?"

He suddenly found his shoes very interesting. "Sort of. I got to sit at Taylor's table one night at the pub. With Bea, her friends, and about ten other guys."

I cast furious eyes at his friend. "Were you one of them?"

"Yes. But it was worth it. I mean, have you seen Taylor Risdale?"

"Worth it? Patrick, you broke Erin's heart and ruined your friendship for half an hour and some beef stew with an actress who wouldn't even remember your name if an Academy Award depended on it."

Patrick raised his head and looked at me with hound dog eyes. "Basically. But I did get her autograph."

"Not really the date you thought it would be though, was it?"

"No."

"You're being used."

"I'm okay with that."

"You could still go with Erin anyway. Two can play at that game, right?" But before I even got my whole sentence out, Patrick and his friend both shook their heads.

"I'm staying out of this," Patrick said. "I'm done. I'm a happy man."

"Me too," said his friend. "Worth every second. I had Taylor sign me chest. I'm gonna get it tattooed."

"Attractive." I was so done with this conversation. "Is there any guy at your school Beatrice hasn't talked to?"

"Maybe Joshua Smith," Patrick said. "He just transferred here three days ago. Other than that, all fifth and sixth years were promised dates with Taylor."

"To stay away from Erin. Your friend." My voice dripped with disgust.

"This movie's the biggest thing to ever hit Abbeyglen," Patrick said. "It's not anything personal against Erin. We just had to take advantage of the opportunity."

They were numbskulls. All of them.

Except for maybe this Joshua Smith.

Someone I had to talk to.

Before Beatrice got there first.

Chapter Twenty-Seven

- Breakfast: Diet Coke
- Lunch: tuna, rice cakes
- Time spent running: 30 minutes
- Time spent practicing: 1 hour

So where is it you're taking me?" I asked later that evening as Beckett drove the truck down the highway. Bob sat between us, and from his thumping tail and dreamy eyes trained on me, I could tell he liked the arrangement.

"Going to Galway. To see Mrs. Sweeney's sister."

"This is our date?"

"No, the dinner afterward is." He glanced my way and grinned. "I knew you wouldn't be much of a date until we got this settled."

"So this is all about you?"

He reached across Bob and held my hand. "Totally selfish motives."

But it wasn't. Beckett had proven to be quite the opposite of what the world painted him. Or what his father made them believe he was.

"Have you spoken to your dad?" I asked.

"No, he'll stay in L.A. until he thinks I've calmed down and can be reasoned with again. I'm not taking his calls at the moment."

"You know you have to talk to him sometime."

"But not now." He turned on the windshield wipers, and they squeaked in a synchronized rhythm against the rain. "I have a lot to figure out."

"Wanna tell me about it?"

His hand found mine again, and he held on like he was searching for strength, grounding himself with the comfort of whatever we had. Tonight he wasn't wearing any disguise. It was just Beckett—his own blond hair, wavy and a little long, no hat. A gray cable-knit sweater, like one I'd seen in a downtown store. Jeans that said he was a no-frills kind of guy. No fancy pockets for him. No sunglasses. Just his piercing gray eyes looking at mine.

"I might want to take a break from acting." The words came out slowly, as if he were testing them, trying to decide how it sounded.

"And do what?"

"Go to school perhaps."

"Any college campus that accepts you will have to go on lockdown for all the screaming girls."

He shrugged it off. "Those are details to figure out later. I just want to be normal for a while."

"And leave the false teeth at home?"

"Exactly. I missed out on a childhood. All I've known is work."

"I don't know that your life will ever be normal."

"Maybe not, but it doesn't have to be so orchestrated that I don't even recognize myself. I'm tired of being lied to. Of not knowing the person I'm talking to. Never knowing if people are telling me what I want to hear or if they have some hidden agenda. All I want is to be with people who are real. Who have it together. Who don't get caught up in all this Hollywood phony crap." He lifted my fingers over Bob's sleeping head and kissed the back of my hand. "Like you. I love how you have everything figured out. You know what you want to be, where you're going, who you are. You see something, you go after it and make it happen. Being around you makes me want to let go of all the lies and just be myself."

This called for a topic change.

"Are you going to leave with the crew when the movie wraps up soon?"

"I thought I'd stay on a few more weeks."

"And then?"

He gave me a smile meant to reassure. "Then maybe a few more." The truck splashed into a puddle as he made a left turn. "I deserve a vacation. I've been thinking of taking six months off. Get back to my roots. Hang out with you. The O'Callaghans. People who know me for me. People I trust."

I should've been happy about this. Six months would have had him staying until the spring, when I left. But something about it snipped at my unraveling nerves.

Six months would also give him time to figure out that I was just a plain nobody. Time to fall out of love with the real world.

And time to realize I was not who I pretended to be either.

"Here we are now," he said. "The lovely Mrs. Doyle's house."

The home looked the same, yet the urgency was so much more elevated than the last time we were there. My assignment with Mrs. Sweeney was almost complete. I only needed two more hours; I had to get this settled.

Beckett held an umbrella over us as we walked up the gravel drive to the front door and knocked. The smell of his cologne, normally bliss to my senses, danced on my gag reflexes and teased my empty stomach. Knowing dinner would be involved, I had skipped breakfast and eaten only some tuna and rice cakes for lunch, using that time to practice instead. But I'd make up for it at the restaurant. Maybe even go crazy and have some bread.

The door opened and a familiar face peeked out. "Yes?" Recognition dawned on Mrs. Doyle's face. "What are you thinking, coming all the way out here in the rain?"

"We'd like to talk to you," I said. "Please. It's important."

"I've nothing to say."

"We've come a long way. This girl's only trying to help." Beckett turned up the voltage on his megawatt smile. "Please, missus."

She huffed and stared at our drippy umbrella. "Be quick about it." She held open the door. "You're liable to catch your death out there."

Shaking off the rain, we followed Mrs. Doyle into her living room.

"Sit down." She swatted a small Yorkie off her couch. "I'll get us some tea."

"You can stop looking so arrogant," I whispered to Beckett as I took a seat beside him. "You haven't won her over yet."

He looked down at me, eyes smiling. Then pressed his lips to my cheek.

And my bleak heart became a little more his.

Some time later Mrs. Doyle returned, carrying a tray she set on a cherry coffee table, and doctored up our teacups. "Well, get on with your news, so."

Beckett held the dainty china in his movie hero's hands. "We just wanted to let you know Cathleen Sweeney isn't expected to make it much longer."

Mrs. Doyle's spoon paused in her cup. "So . . . Cathleen . . . she's that bad, is she?"

"She sleeps a lot," I said. "She's in pain. She talks about the past some. Mentions you, of course."

Mrs. Doyle sliced into a loaf of what looked like pumpkin bread, her hands slightly shaking. "And who did you say you were to her?"

"I go to Sacred Heart in Abbeyglen. I was assigned to visit Mrs. Sweeney for a project. She was my adopted grandmother, so to speak. She, um . . . there have been quite a few talks about her regrets. She told me about her marriage, her guilt, her anger . . . her bitterness."

"*Her* bitterness?"

"Mrs. Doyle," I said. "Your sister married Mr. Sweeney to protect you."

She placed a piece of bread on each of the three plates and slid them our way. "I loved that man. I never understood how she could just take something so precious from her own sister."

"She was protecting you."

"She wanted him for herself."

"He abused her," Beckett said. "That wasn't just village gossip. It was not a happy courtship or marriage. She was trying to spare you from that. She left him to save her own life."

Mrs. Doyle sat still as a museum statue. "I . . . I don't know."

"It was in her letters to you." I picked at a corner of the pumpkin bread. Half hour of running. A slab of butter added another fifteen minutes. "Didn't you read any of them?"

"And why would I?" Mrs. Doyle's voice lifted half an octave.

"Didn't you want to know why she did what she did?" I asked.

"I saw it with me own eyes. Saw her flirt and finesse her way into his heart."

"Your father was broke." So weird to be giving a stranger such personal information about her own family. "And Charles Sweeney had a wretched reputation. He had banks to build, but the town didn't trust him. So . . ."

"No." Mrs. Doyle shook her white head. "No, me father would not have taken money in exchange for our marriage."

"That's exactly what happened," Beckett said. "Money exchanged hands. You were wooed by Mr. Sweeney first. His first pick between you and your sister."

White-faced, Fiona Doyle sat back in her chair, her hand clutching a napkin, as if the revelation was almost too much to bear. "I'm to believe me sister did this for me?"

"Cathleen asked around. Did some digging on the newcomer Mr. Sweeney," I said. "Found out he had an ex-fiancée in Dublin. A woman he had treated miserably until she left him at the altar, causing a big scandal to herself and her family."

"Then she begged your father to drop the arrangement," Beckett said. "But your father wouldn't hear of it. He was in too deep and Charles Sweeney was too dangerous to cross. So she convinced him to let her take your place."

Mrs. Doyle's eyes brimmed with tears and her lips quivered. "If that's true, why didn't she just tell me?"

"She wasn't allowed to when Charles Sweeney was alive. He threatened her with your father's farm and who knows what else. And then after he died, she tried to contact you."

Taking off her rimless glasses, Mrs. Doyle gave a sigh and welcomed the dog into her lap. "I was so embarrassed that Charles tossed me over for Cathleen. Everywhere I went in town, people would look at me with such pity. The old ladies would point and whisper, 'There's that Fiona Higgins. She couldn't hang on to one so fine as Charles Sweeney.' I got my fill of it; I simply left. Father gave me money and I went to work in an office in Limerick and never looked back."

"And you married?" I asked.

"Oh yes." A ghost of a smile crossed her lips. "Two years later I met a man. He was a county doctor and stopped by to check on Mrs. Travis, the old woman who rented me a room. I saw after her in exchange for a place to stay and an evening meal. We were married until his death last year." She gestured with her chin toward the mantel. "Those are our three kids. Ten grandchildren."

"You had a whole beautiful life." It was so unfair. "Your sister lost her awful husband, lost her one child, and never remarried. She spent the rest of her life writing to you and—"

"Finley." Beckett's hand on my arm stilled me. "Mrs. Doyle, your sister's dying wish is that she would have your forgiveness. We think it would be a grand gesture if you'd come and visit her at the nursing home. Forgive each other."

"Why on earth would she need to forgive me? Your story is quite . . . fantastical. I don't know what to believe. Still so much hurt after all these years." Mrs. Doyle sniffled into her crumpled napkin. "As for my visiting, I'm afraid that isn't possible. Me children don't live nearby. I, meself, do not drive."

"Easily solved," Beckett said. "I'll send someone to pick you up. You need only call."

She watched him with clear reservation. "I don't know."

"Are you a woman of faith, Mrs. Doyle?" Beckett asked.

"I've been a devout Catholic all my life."

"Then think of it as blessing someone else." Beckett regarded her with eyes as watchful as Steele Markov's. "Or just doing the right thing." He stood up and pulled me with him. "Thank you, missus. We'll leave you to your evening now."

She led us to the door, her face unreadable when she closed it behind us.

"How could she have any doubts now?" I asked as soon as Beckett started the truck.

"Nothing about the lives of those two women has been right. She has years of heartbreak to sort through. She'll come around though." The rain fell in sheets on the windshield, and the cold slipped inside and settled between us.

And though it was all so crazy, I wanted to believe him.

Because somewhere along the way Mrs. Sweeney had become important.

And she couldn't go without knowing there were people in the world who loved her.

Like me.

→ᶠ

I was seconds away from throwing Beckett's phone out the window.

"You're a popular guy," I said as he ended his seventh call since we'd left Mrs. Doyle's.

"Sorry. Business." He sent me a sheepish grin as he drove. "And I realized I forgot something on the set. Do you mind if we stop by there before going to dinner?"

With the way he was looking at me, I'd have agreed to anything. "No problem."

The familiar outline of Abbeyglen greeted us, and I felt a stab of disappointment. I had hoped our date would've involved Galway, some soul spinning music, and just enough dancing to have carried my heart away. But Beckett wanted to eat at one of his favorite pubs downtown.

I was too upset to eat anyway. How could Mrs. Doyle sit there and listen to all we'd said and not immediately race out to see her sister?

The truck came to a lurching stop, and Beckett climbed out and walked to my side with an unhurried stride.

"You want me to go in with you?" I asked as the door opened. The castle stood before us, almost hidden in the dark shadows. I could imagine it being a vampire's lair.

"I don't want to leave you out here alone." His hand clasped around mine as he helped me down. "Something might get you."

I was afraid something already had. It was six feet of enigmatic boy with a lethal grin and hypnotic eyes.

Holding the umbrella over me, Beckett pressed his hand to my back and guided me through the wet grass to the entrance of the castle.

"They forgot to leave the porch light on." I smiled as Beckett stepped in front of me, his hands working on the latch of the door the set builders had created, as time had long ago done away with the original.

The door creaked on its large hinges as it swung open. Beckett took my hand, his fingers surrounding mine, and pulled me inside.

Darkness consumed us as we stepped into the entryway, and I blinked against the wave of dizziness that tugged at my head. Surely it was just my eyes adjusting to the dark.

"Just around this corner are the lights. Not much farther." His grip tightened on mine. "I've got you."

I shuffled my feet slowly across the uneven floor, wary of tripping and landing flat on my face. "What did you say you needed here?"

He pulled me closer to him, and I inhaled the warm scent of his shirt. "This."

Rounding the corner, dim lights appeared. My sight returned. And my breath suspended on a gasp.

In the center of the great hall, amid modern cameras and equipment, stood flickering candles covering the space and turning it into a magical dream. From the candelabras to the pillars on iron stands reaching from the floor, the tapers shimmied to their own rhythms as they formed a circle around a table with two seats just waiting for late-night visitors.

"Oh," I sighed. "My."

Beckett gave a quiet laugh, his hand still tight on mine. "You probably had your heart set on Galway."

"No." I shook my head and blinked away the tears. "No, it's perfect." Then my arms went around him, holding him close. There were simply no words. "How did you do this?"

His breath tickled my ear as he laughed. "All the phone calls. I had a lot of help."

I pulled away. "You did this—for me?"

"Not all the world is dark, Finley." He pressed his lips to my forehead and gave me a half smile. "I know you must be starving. I'm pretty sure I heard your stomach rumble a time or two." He led me to the table, then with a swooping bow, pulled out my seat. "Me lady."

At this rate, I would never recover from his spell.

"We have a fine dinner tonight. I think it will meet with your approval."

On the ivory-covered table sat six silver serving dishes, with a polish so shiny, I could see my own reflection. Beckett lifted the lid off of each one as he listed their contents. "Roast. Green beans in a butter sauce. Here we have some bread, courtesy of Mr. O'Callaghan. And a salad with slivered almonds and those little dried cranberry things." Grinning over the last item, Beckett presented it for my inspection, but I didn't have to look inside to know what I'd find. He had somehow discovered my favorite meal from back home. It was my comfort food, my mom's favorite things to cook for me. A menu I'd dined on many times since my brother's death.

"Is that strawberry pie?" I asked.

"'Tis." Beckett swooped his finger through a curl of whipped cream. "You have no idea how hard it was to pull this one off. The Irish don't adore a strawberry pie like you Americans. Took a small miracle."

"I love it." I wanted to laugh. Cry. A hundred emotions pounded in my mind. "How did you know?"

"I talked to Nora, who talked to—"

"My mom."

"Yes. And, by the way, she says you haven't called in a few days. But you can take care of that later, because right now, we eat."

He handed me a china plate, white and rimmed in a thin band of gold. "Beckett, this is incredible. I don't know how to thank you."

"Thank me by eating." He served up two slices of roast on my plate, then scooped out the side items. "Don't want anything to touch on your plate, right?"

I should've been enchanted, but I was too busy watching the sheer amount of food growing on my plate. "I can't eat all this."

"Eat what you want." He dished out some salad for himself, his eyes watching me. "We'll take the leftovers back for Bob. Then maybe he'll forgive us for leaving him alone in the truck." Beckett kept the conversation light, regaling me with animated stories of his first TV experiences before moving to L.A. With his lilt and laugh, I could've listened until the sun came up.

"Why are you frowning at your bread?" The light flickered across the contours of Beckett's frowning face. "Is it not good?"

"It's great." I tore my roll in fourths, then set it aside to cut my roast into bites fit for a three-year-old. "I'm just worked up over Mrs. Doyle, I guess." If I ate this meal, the emptiness in my stomach would go away.

And I was growing rather accustomed to empty.

"You've done all you can do." Beckett slipped a bite of meat between his lips. "Now we just have to have faith that she'll come to her senses."

"But I'm running out of time."

Beckett put down his fork, letting it clink onto his plate. "You're not responsible for their mistakes."

"I know."

"Do you?"

He didn't understand.

"You know what I like about you?" Beckett reached for my untouched plate and set it aside with his own.

"My good looks and brilliant mind?"

He leaned toward me and smiled. "Your heart." Beckett's mouth hovered near mine, making my pulse kick up in tempo. "I love your heart, Finley Sinclair. But you take on the weight of the world in that head of yours." His fingers pushed back my hair and grazed the skin on my cheek. "And it's time to let it go and focus on something good."

Chapter Twenty-Eight

Boys were all merry, and the girls they were hearty
And danced all around in couples and groups,
'Til an accident happened, young Terrence McCarthy
Put his right leg through Miss Finnerty's hoops.

—"Lanigan's Ball," Irish pub song

*Y*ou look lovely, Finley." Erin clipped a sequined rosette in my hair, and we both studied ourselves in her dresser mirror. There was something about an updo, a little extra eye shadow, and donning a dress that lifted the spirits and made me believe anything could happen on such a whimsical night.

"You look like a total princess," I said, wishing for the millionth time that I had her impossible waist. And she got it so effortlessly. Didn't have to watch what she ate, exercised twice a week, and consumed her dad's French toast like I did my carrot sticks.

"I'm glad the dress shop was able to fix your dress on time. It fits you like a glove."

Fanning myself against a nervous heat, I smiled at her in the mirror, careful not to get pale pink lipstick on my teeth. "A simple small nip and tuck."

"Just think, you'll see your parents in a little over a week. You'll have such a grand time in New York."

Last night I had another nightmare that I screwed up this audition. I still didn't have an ending to the song, and the committee kicked me out. "I think I'll go on down." I picked up my clutch, my dress swishing around me as I walked. "You're going to wow your date, Erin. I promise."

The room suddenly warmed an extra ten degrees and spots floated across my line of vision. I reached out and steadied myself with the doorframe.

"Finley? Are you okay?"

Slowly I inhaled, praying against my clammy skin. "Yes. I'm fine. Just . . . had too much caffeine today, I guess." And not enough to eat. There hadn't been time.

Erin dusted her frown with powder. "I'm concerned about you. You've been . . . different."

"Just stress—it's getting so close to the audition. Still have lots to do. And I'm worried about Mrs. Sweeney." She had spent most of the week sleeping round the clock. It was hard to witness her decline.

"I guess." Erin hesitated, wringing her newly manicured hands. "But it seems that you're kind of distant. And kind of . . . I don't know, extra quiet. Especially at dinner. I'm worried about you is all. I've been reading lately, and . . . sometimes when you've suffered a trauma, you overcompensate in other areas to help you cope."

"Translation, Dr. Erin?" My tone was light, yet Erin's face was anything but.

"I just . . . wonder if you've noticed how little you eat. It's getting worse. Could that be why you feel poorly tonight?"

"I'm fine. Maybe a little under the weather."

"You can tell me anything, you know."

"I don't have a problem with eating. Is that what you mean?" I laughed. "That's ridiculous."

"You're under a lot of pressure. It would be understandable. The human brain—"

"Our dates are probably waiting. We can talk about this later." Or never.

Fighting a headache, I walked down the stairs, one hand on the hem of my dress and one hand on the rail.

Nora stood at the bottom, snapping pictures with her camera. "Like a model, you are. Don't you think, Beckett?"

Beckett Rush, star of film and fang, stood beside my host mother, his eyes shining on me like they did when he looked on the cliffs or the sea at Lahinch. "She's amazing." Taking my hand, he kissed the top of it like he was straight out of the 1800s. Clearly his movie was going to his head. "Beautiful inside and out," Beckett said.

Nora took a few more pictures of us together, me in my dress and Beckett in his immaculately tailored suit the color of wheat. "I wish we could go," Nora said. "But Liam's come down with a nasty cold, so no fun for us." Liam chose that moment to call from upstairs. "Better go see what my patient needs now."

"I would tell you you look fetching," I said to Beckett, watching Nora stomp up the steps. "But I guess tonight doesn't compare to all the red carpet events you've seen." All the glamorous girls on his arm.

"I've never been to a village dance. Or prom." His smile did nothing to help my light-headedness. "This is a special night for me too. I get to be a regular guy."

"Except you're not. You're Beckett Rush. You know there's going to be a small mob. The media will have pictures posted by midnight."

He warmed one of my hands in both of his. "I'm sure someone in my camp will spin it, so."

"Like your dad."

Beckett gave a dismissive shrug. "He doesn't know what I'm doing tonight."

The doorbell rang, and I heard Sean make his way from the kitchen to answer it.

"I think my date is here," I said.

Beckett looked over my head. "And mine is coming down the stairs."

Erin floated toward us, a vision in white. Her hair sat atop her head in an intricate twist, thanks to our afternoon at the salon. Her dangling earrings sparkled in the light and matched the sequins on her heels. One day I wanted to have her elegance, her chic.

"Hi, Beckett," she said, her cheeks a bright pink. "Thanks, um. Thanks for . . . going with me."

"Hey, it's me." He gave her a big-brother grin meant to put her at ease. "The guy who's been eating dinner with you for weeks. You've seen me with tartar sauce on my chin and milk on my lip. Don't be nervous, okay?"

My heart melted a little bit more as Beckett went into a story about a time he split his pants at a premiere.

"Your date, Finley." Sean stared down the new arrival. "You boys are aware of my vast army experience?"

Nora came back down with the camera. "Sean, you bake pastries and fluff pillows now. Leave the fellas alone."

"Glad you could join us." Beckett held out his hand and my date shook it. "I'm Beckett Rush."

"Joshua Smith." He took anxious eyes off Sean. "Wow, who'd have thought after just a few weeks living here, I'd meet a famous actor *and* get a date for the dance?"

⇥⇤

I heard the music from a half-mile away.

Sitting beside Beckett as he drove, I was pressed up against him and the knobby gearshift until I could hardly draw a breath. On my other side Erin and Joshua laughed at the four of us, crammed in Beckett's truck like circus clowns.

As glad as I was for an excuse to be so near Beckett, my mind kept replaying Erin's words, her face. But she was wrong. There was nothing wrong with me. Nothing that wouldn't go away when I found the source of my brother's last picture, finished my audition piece, and had my acceptance letter in hand from the Conservatory.

But what if Erin told Nora? What if Nora told my mom?

"Here we go." Beckett parked in between a compact car and another truck on the side of the road, cut the engine, then opened the door. "Saint Flanagan would be glad you're here, sure he would," Beckett said as he held out both hands and helped me out. "And so am I, Finley Sinclair." Handing me my shawl, Beckett leaned toward me. "Is something bothering you tonight?"

"Just a headache." I forced a smile and pushed back the fear that my sky was falling. "Save me a dance?"

"I'll be fighting off the lads just to get to you."

I patted his lapel. "Promise me you won't bite anyone."

We stopped by a trailer selling food, and the smell was as strong as the music was loud. I read the limited menu and twisted the necklace at my throat. Not a salad to be had.

"I'll have the lamb stew and a Coke," Beckett said. "Finley?"

I don't know. I don't know.

I am hungry, but it's all bad for me. Why can't they just have some fruit? "Diet Coke and . . . fish and chips, I guess."

"There you are!" Orla waved with one hand and dragged an unfamiliar teen boy with the other. "Aedan McCourt, these are me friends. Friends, this is Aedan."

The guy was only as tall as Orla's nose, his teeth crooked as country fence posts, but Orla seemed captivated by him all the same.

"I had no idea you were taking a date," Erin said. "You haven't said a word about it."

"It was kind of last minute." Orla looped her arm around Aedan's. "His date cancelled just hours ago."

Aedan frowned. "She's terribly sick. Miserable with food poisoning."

Orla grinned. "Isn't it awesome?"

A large event tent sat in front of the school, and at least half the town stood under it. The other half spilled outside and onto the grounds, where fairy lights were strung from tree to tree. As we four carried our food, it was a wonderland we entered, complete with a soundtrack that sang to my frayed nerves as the strains of a fiddle and dueling guitars wove around me.

Beckett opened the door flap and held it for us to step inside.

As long as I lived I would never forget the look on Beatrice Plummer's face as Erin walked into the dance on Beckett's arm. The whole room seemed to stop. All the girls under the age of twenty let out a collective squeal and five of them rushed him.

Beckett handled it all with his usual finesse. He signed a few autographs, promised a couple of dances, but then politely told the crowd that he was all Erin's tonight. And to think at one time I thought he was a world-class jerk.

We sat at a folding table and watched the band.

"That's your friend Donal Murphy, isn't it?" I pointed toward the stage, trying to get my mind off my queasy stomach.

"He comes back every year." Erin grinned as she clapped to the tune. "I think he and Saint Flanagan were mates in the fourteen-hundreds."

"Well, Beckett." Beatrice stood behind his chair, her tall, lanky date hovering behind her. "What a surprise to see you here. Without Taylor."

Beckett's face tightened, but within a second his easy smile returned. "I've never been to a village dance. When I asked Erin if I could join her, I couldn't believe my luck that she said yes."

Beatrice's eyelashes fluttered like angry ant legs. "Really. Is that so?"

"It is." Beckett rested his arm around Erin's chair. "But who wouldn't want to go with Erin? Five minutes after meeting her, I knew she was one of the kindest people I'd ever encountered. So refreshing to find someone with such a genuine heart, don't you think?" Beckett's grin never wavered, but his eyes held a warning for Beatrice. "We've gotten so close over the last few months, it's like we're family. And you know how protective of me family I am." He laughed and gave Erin a small squeeze. "Anyone who hurt her would have to answer to me for sure. Not that anyone *ever* would. That would be crazy, sure it would."

"Totally crazy," I said, enjoying the color crawling up Beatrice's neck and the smile glowing on Erin's face.

"Count me in for the Erin O'Callaghan fan club too." Joshua

Smith reached for a fry on his plate. "Did you know she can recite the entire periodic table?"

"Have a lovely evening, Beatrice." Beckett turned his back, dismissing her for the night.

Orla watched Beatrice stomp away. "She's got war on her mind."

"I can handle her." Beckett gave me a small smile. "And I can handle me father when she and Taylor run right to him."

"Thank you," Erin called over the music. "That was truly nice of all of you."

"I meant it." Beckett ladled his spoon into his stew. "I'm grateful for everything you and your parents have done for me. Beatrice needs to know she can't mess with you."

"She'll be back," I said. "I know that look, and she's not done yet."

"Nothing to worry about." Beckett eyed my untouched plate. "Not hungry?"

I didn't even have to look up to know Erin was watching me with the intensity of an international spy. "No, it's fine. I've been too busy talking and taking it all in."

"Dance with me soon?"

"I don't know." I cut my battered fish into small pieces, stacking a few on top of one another and shoving some under my fries. "With the way all the girls are looking at you, I might never get my chance." I glanced behind us. "Heck, even that big boy in the blue suit over there is watching you like candy."

"It's possible I might've offered him a slow dance." Beckett eyed the high schooler who stuffed his mouth with a heaping bite of kraut. "I sometimes get a little free with me promises."

An hour later I'd taken in so much Diet Coke, my stomach was gurgling. But it didn't fill the burning from hours without a proper meal, a feeling that gave me a strange charge. And it didn't relieve the weight in my head. A few bites of fish, three fries. Still probably a five-hundred calorie day. Erin wouldn't approve. But it was just for today. Tomorrow I'd start over and eat right.

God, I can control this. I can.

"Time to show me your dancing skills." Orla grabbed her date by the hand. "We'll see you all in a few hours." She leaned down to whisper in my ear. "I've had a few of those energy drinks. Hope the guitar players can keep up."

Lured by Donal Murphy's fine fiddling skills, I let Joshua lead me out into the mad crush of dancers. I had no idea what the proper form was, but my hesitance was soon overridden by Joshua's unusual windmill arms and his head jerking like an angry ostrich.

A group formed around us as Beckett, Erin, Joshua, and I all danced. And I should've been enjoying it. I was a cheerleader for years. This was my thing. I loved dancing, the movement of body and rhythm.

But instead I was worried.

And winded.

Breathing like I'd just run a marathon instead of skipping around to four measly songs, I began to make my way back to the table.

"Hey, I believe you owe me." Beckett intercepted me as the band shifted to a slow song. I was so tired. Just a little break was all I needed.

But this was Beckett Rush. How often in a lifetime did a guy like this ask a girl like me to dance?

Beckett took my hand, led me back to the floor, and reeled me close to his chest as we danced on the outer edge of the crowd.

"Any luck on my brother's cross?"

"Not yet. But I'll find it. I've had a few leads, but so far none have been the one."

"And you'll keep searching? We can't give up. My audition is next week and the last few measures of the song are still not finished and I know that cross—"

"Finley, I'll not be giving up." He held me tighter, and I squinted against the lights that were suddenly too bright. Pressing my head to Beckett's chest, I thought to listen to the beat of his heart, but instead found myself closing my eyes against the seasick feeling that washed over me. How much longer was this song going to last?

"Ready to spin?" Beckett asked.

The spots returned before my eyes and I blinked to chase them away. My head fizzed with dizzy air. "No, I don't think—"

But it was too late. Smiling, he spun me out and my fingers slipped from his before he could pull me back in.

"Finley?" Beckett's voice came from far away, and I wanted to respond, but my lips wouldn't move, and my limbs morphed into jelly.

The ground tilted beneath me, and I catapulted straight down. Reaching out blindly, I crashed to the floor.

Where my scene faded to black.

Chapter Twenty-Nine

*Abbeyglen has a way of slowing a person down.
Usually when I need it most.*

—Travel Journal of Will Sinclair

"Finley."

When I opened my eyes, I saw two things—Beckett leaning over me, his eyes wide and his frown heavy. And every citizen of Abbeyglen hovering behind him in a gigantic circle.

"Oh no," I whispered.

"Are you okay?" He glared at a few standing too close. "Step back. Give her some breathing room." He looked back to me. "You just crumbled. It happened so fast, I couldn't even catch you."

"Like something out of a movie," Orla said.

I peeled myself off the floor, aware of a throbbing knee and obliterated pride. "I'm pretty sure I want to die."

Beckett helped me to my feet. "You're really pale.

"It must be bad if *you* find me pasty."

Beckett pulled me closer and studied my face with a look that was far from romantic. "Are you all right?"

I laughed. "Yeah, of course. I'm such a klutz. I haven't had a pair of heels on in a long time."

"Finley, you didn't just fall," Erin said. "You passed out."

Beckett took a steadying breath. "Longest moment of my life."

I fought a groan as Principal Plummer, dressed in a linen suit the color of spring peaches, walked our way, the old mayor limping beside him.

"We need to call a doctor," the mayor said.

"No!" They couldn't.

"Should I call my mother?" Erin's face pinched in worry.

"Definitely so," Mr. Plummer said. "Young lady, you were out for a good ten seconds."

"No. Please." My heart beat a wild tempo. Why hadn't I eaten today? I was so stupid. I'd just let it go. I'd wanted to be sure I fit in the dress. And it just . . . made me feel better not to.

Until now.

Lord, help me. If my mom finds out, I'm dead. She'll make me come home.

"It's the lights." I startled as the music struck up again. "And the crowd. I just got dizzy from it all."

But Beckett and Mr. Plummer both looked doubtful. "Let's go sit down and get you some water."

The principal frowned at one dangerously intertwined teenage couple, then gave me his full attention as Beckett helped me to our table. "Are you sure you're quite all right?" Mr. Plummer asked. "You took a good spill, sure you did."

"Yes." Humiliation. Could you die from that? "I'm fine. Truly. No need to call anyone."

"But your knee," Erin said.

"It's just a little sore. Seriously, it'll be good as new in a few minutes."

"No." Erin pointed. "I mean *look* at your knee. It's bleeding right through your dress."

Sure enough, a crimson stain had seeped through my dress right at my knee. My gorgeous dress. Ruined.

And so was this evening.

The principal scanned the perimeter, then gestured to someone behind me. "Plasters!" Mr. Plummer called for a bandage, handing over his keys. "In the school, please. Be quick about it."

The mayor tut-tutted. "We'll get you something for that."

Erin put her arm around me. "Go ahead and sit down for now. Get the weight off your leg."

I just wanted to go home. Fatigue and exhaustion waltzed with embarrassment as I grabbed a napkin off the table, pulled my hem above my knees, and stuck the napkin to my oozing wound. I must have looked so glamorous to Beckett. "It's fine. I don't need anything." Did the entire village have to look this way? Hadn't anyone ever tripped?

Five ridiculously long minutes later someone returned bearing a handful of Band-Aids.

"What took you so long, Beatrice?" asked Mr. Plummer.

Of course it would be her. Because this night needed a cherry on top.

"Sorry. There's so much stuff in the nurse's office, I had trouble finding the plasters and had to open a lot of cabinets and drawers. Here you go, Finley." Beatrice watched me with a movie villainess grin as she handed them to me. "Different sizes. Wasn't sure what you needed, so I just . . . grabbed a few things."

"Very helpful," Mr. Plummer said. "Thank you, dear."

Helpful? I wondered if this would be a good time to remind the *dear* one's father about her setting me up for cheating. Or how she'd nearly sabotaged Erin's chances for a date.

"Your hands are shaking." Beckett took a medium bandage from me and kneeled on the floor. He leveled those famous eyes at the small crowd around us until people drifted away.

"Just let me know if you need anything else." Beatrice gave one last smirk, then swiveled on her fancy heels and walked away.

Beckett's fingers were cold on my skin as he blotted at my knee with a napkin, the crisp white cotton coming away red and gross. "You took quite a fall. I'm really sorry."

"It wasn't your fault." I watched him gently apply the Band-Aid.

"We need to call your host mother." Mr. Plummer reached for his phone.

"No!" He couldn't. *Please, God, no.* "I don't want to worry her. I feel fine now," I lied. "I'll just sit here the rest of the night. Drink some Diet Coke. Take it easy." I implored him with my eyes. "Tonight's a big deal, and I don't want to mess up anyone's evening. Please." I shot Mr. Plummer a pleading look.

He reluctantly put the phone back in his suit pocket. "If you become the least bit light-headed, you are to let someone know. I still think I should call the O'Callaghans."

"I'll keep an eye on her, sir," Erin said.

"As will I." Beckett watched me with a frown.

"Fine. But I'll be checking on you later." He walked away with the mayor, making a beeline for a large gentleman dancing on a table, and my shoulders sagged in relief.

"Why didn't you tell me you were feeling this badly at the house?" Erin turned to Beckett. "She had a little spell earlier."

Beckett gazed up at me as I righted my stained skirt. "You've felt like this all night?"

"It's nothing. Just a little under the weather. No big deal." I wanted to go home. I wanted to go to bed, pull the covers over my head, wake up on a brand-new day. One where I did things right.

"Why didn't you say something?" Beckett asked.

"I'm okay." How many times did I have to say that? "Let's go back out and dance. That's what we're here for." My voice sounded a bit too snappish, so I countered it with a smile and held out my hand to Beckett. "Besides, I didn't get my whole dance."

"No way," he said. "Erin, you and Joshua go on. I'm going to sit here with Finley."

Joshua offered his arm to Erin. "I do a mean pop and lock. Want to see?"

Erin hesitated. "Finley, I don't know . . . Can I talk to you for a second?"

"Go." I waved toward the dance floor. "I'm fine. Orla, you go too."

Beckett and I watched Joshua lead a worried Erin to the center of the crowd, with Orla and her date beside them. I knew they were talking about me.

"Erin will be watching you all night," Beckett said.

The ice in my glass clinked as I took a sip of Diet Coke. "She has no reason to be concerned. She's just so kindhearted." And I hoped her kindness extended to refraining from telling her mom about my little episode. Though I knew I couldn't count on that. Panic coursed through my nerves as I thought of all the possibilities for fallout.

Beckett pulled his chair closer until his legs touched mine. "You'd tell me if something was going on, right?"

His eyes looked at me so directly, I feared he could see straight into my mind, where my every lie, every truth scrolled by. "Yes. I'm sorry I ruined your night."

"Except for nearly having a heart attack, I've had fun." Beckett rubbed my hands in his, as if trying to transfer some of his heat. "Now I can say I've been to a village dance. Check it off the list."

I pushed past the weariness and the fog in my head and tried to focus on his eyes on mine, his gentle hand covering my fingers, his comforting nearness. Tomorrow I'd eat more. Erin was right. I couldn't keep doing this. "I didn't know there was a list."

"Look at your arms. You've got goose bumps all over you." Before I could protest, he peeled off his jacket and draped it over my shoulders. I was instantly surrounded by his warmth and the smell that was only Beckett Rush. I wanted to remain in this safe cocoon, but when I got home, there would be Erin to answer to.

"I just came up with a list," he said. "Things I've missed out on."

"Like what?" I watched a couple clear the table beside us.

"School. Senior trips. Holidays." He ran his finger over my hand. "Fin, you swear you'd talk to me if there was more to this, right? You've just been . . . different lately."

Him too? "Of course I'm behaving differently. I'm going to lose my mind before this audition."

"I know you're working really hard on it, but—"

I moved in closer, hoping to distract him. "What else is on that list?"

"List?"

"The things you haven't gotten to do."

He blinked at the topic change, but let it go. Then smiled. "Kissing a girl under the stars."

"Too bad we're inside."

He looked up, pointed to a web of fairy lights above us. "Looks like they found us anyway."

I rested my forehead against his chin, wishing I could stay there forever. "People are looking."

"In my life, someone's always looking."

I smiled, despite the sad note in his voice. "Sometimes it's worth doing anyway."

His grin returned. "You are worth it, Flossie. You are definitely worth it." And as the band played, my friends danced, and my knee burned, Beckett Rush covered my lips with his, and I felt my head spin once again.

Chapter Thirty

From: LisaRivers@SeaScapeCounseling.org
Subject: Checking in
We haven't talked in a while, and your mother
thought you could use an ear. I called your
number, but it went straight to voice mail.

iss Sinclair, you're wanted in the counselor's office."
Mrs. Campbell folded up the note from a student aid
and handed it to me on Monday morning. I read the
summons, a message scribbled in blue ink on recycled paper with
old vocab tests printed on the back.

As I stood up and walked out of the English class, I was positive if I turned around I would find all twenty-five girls in the room
staring at me. Whispering about me. *That's the girl who passed out
at the dance. That's the one who dates Beckett Rush? What on earth
does he see in her?*

By the time I got to the counselor's office, it was a wonder my
knees could hold me.

Yesterday was so strained and tedious, dragging on forever. Beckett had to film, and I went to church with the O'Callaghans. Erin was quiet, pensive, and not her usual bubbly self. I knew she was thinking about Saturday night, whether to tell her mom or not. I kept watching Nora, expecting her to pull me aside and talk to me, to ask me a million questions about passing out. I waited upstairs in my room most of the day, playing Will's song over and over until I broke a string and had to put the violin away.

In all these things, I am more than victorious . . .

I said rushed prayers under my breath and knocked on the counselor's door.

"Come in."

Walking inside, my stomach dropped to the floor. There sat Mrs. Mawby, the counselor, in front of her file-stacked desk. Nora O'Callaghan occupied a chair next to her.

And there was my mother's Skyped-in face on the computer screen behind them both. Watching us all.

"Shut the door behind you, Finley." Mrs. Mawby gestured to a maroon cloth chair. "Take a seat please."

It was worse than I thought.

"Hey, Mom." My smile felt plastic and brittle on my face.

"Hello, sweetie. Mrs. Mawby thought we should all have a chat."

The counselor cleared her throat. "About your health."

No.

No, no, no.

I looked to my mother at once. "I'm fine. Nothing's wrong. I promise."

"It's my understanding you fainted Saturday night," Mrs. Mawby said.

I cast a sheepish glance at Nora. "Erin told you?"

She shook her head. "No. Mrs. Mawby just called me."

"Why didn't you tell us?" My mother's voice sounded tired, as if this were a song she'd heard on repeat every day for the last two years.

"Finley, a concerned friend came in to talk to me today." Mrs. Mawby crossed her legs and propped an elbow on her messy desk. "She witnessed your spell at the festival and is quite worried, so."

The walls of the small office seemed to shift, as if moving at once to the center, closing me in. "And who is this *friend* of mine?"

"Beatrice Plummer."

"That's your informant?" Nora asked. "The same girl who got Finley accused of cheating? And who bullies my daughter? I thought this information was from a reliable source."

My mother cut right to it. "Finley, did you pass out?"

My head moved in an awkward nod. "Yes."

"Has this happened before?" Nora asked. "Since you got here?"

"No, ma'am."

"Actually Beatrice overheard Erin mention you had a dizzy spell at home before the festivities." Thin red glasses slid down Mrs. Mawby's nose, and she peered over them with big, owlish eyes that blinked too much. "True?"

"I . . . sometimes I get stressed and I think my blood sugar drops." Like when I skipped meals.

"And what had you eaten Saturday?" Mom asked.

"Not enough," I said casually, as if it was just a silly thing I let slip by. "We were so busy with getting our hair fixed, and I'm still working on my audition piece. But I ate at the dance. I did."

"A full meal?" Nora asked. "She's been eating like a wee bird almost since she arrived. I thought nothing of it at first, but now . . ."

"I had fish, some fries. The fries were good." I sounded ridiculous. They were staring at me like I was someone they didn't know what to do with. Like I had some big bad secret in my closet, and they wanted me to be the one to drag it out.

God, what is wrong with me? Why am I here—in this situation? Why can't everyone leave me alone and let me deal with problems my way?

"Miss Sinclair." Mrs. Mawby drew out my name, a nasally sound that was in need of tuning. "No matter Beatrice's intentions, I do believe she has stumbled upon something that we need to have a care with. Mrs. O'Callaghan, the school nurse, and I were all informed of your . . . previous difficulties."

"My depression? My year of therapy? Wouldn't you have been sad?" My voice snapped like twigs in a flame. "My brother died. Murdered."

"That's enough," my mother warned.

Mrs. Mawby continued. "I had hoped that if you had felt any of those same feelings coming on, heard any of those old negative thoughts, you would stop in so we could talk."

I had an audition in a week. Did they honestly expect me to care about any of this? I had too much to do before then. Couldn't we deal with this later?

"Beatrice is out to get me. She *told* me that. She specifically said I needed to watch my back. She's angry—that I became friends with Beckett Rush, that I'm his assistant, and that I'm the new girl who instantly made friends and she wasn't one of them. She's jealous and bitter and mean." Tears clogged my throat, but I kept going. "Nora, she arranged it so every boy Erin might even think about asking to the dance would turn her down. She had a whole plan. And all because she wanted to get back at me."

"That part is true," Nora said. "She's always been a challenge to Erin, and I was never so glad when my daughter got out of her circle."

"But I think we've established you did indeed faint at the dance," my mother said. "And you felt ill earlier that day."

In all these things, I am more than victorious . . .

"I'm not sick. Why can't you trust me?"

"Finley," my mother said. "This isn't a matter of trust. It's a matter of your health, your life. You've been very . . . fragile since Will died. Your father and I debated letting you go to Abbeyglen, but we'd seen such improvement. What if your grief is just showing itself in a different way?"

"I have this under control. Please," I pleaded. "Have faith in me. I've overcome so much to be here, to be able to do this program. On day one of being at this school, I got assigned a project involving a dying woman. Me! After the last two years I've had? And then Beatrice came after me with a vengeance. I bombed my first audition for the Conservatory. And now . . . this." I pushed my hair from my face. "This has not been easy for me, but I'm trying. I am. Just give me credit for that. And trust me to know if I feel all dark and broody like I did when you sent me to that therapist. I'm fine."

"Sometimes she'll go out for a run morning *and* night," Nora said.

"I'm stressed." I grabbed a tissue from Mrs. Mawby's desk and blotted at my eyes. "And that's what I do to unwind. My counselor told me to do that. Would you rather I binge eat or drink or do drugs? I thought it was healthy. I have a *lot* going on. Doesn't anyone get that?" The way they were looking at me. I couldn't stand it. Like I was already tried and condemned. Like my mother didn't know what to do for her sick daughter. Well, I wasn't sick. I could change this today if I wanted to.

"I think you have too much going on," my mother said. "You don't even look like you're sleeping."

"Och, she practices in all hours of the night, she does," Nora said. "The sound barely reaches us, but she can't be getting any rest. And the closer it gets to time for her to leave for New York, the more she plays." Nora patted my hand. "We're just worried and—"

"Mom, you know how serious I am about my music. My chance at this school is everything."

"What I know is that you do everything to the extreme. Always have. From your music, even to your season of rebellion after your brother's death. Your counselor talked to us about your perfectionist—"

"Just stop." I covered my ears and shook my head. Everything was so messed up, this tangled ball of string that I couldn't fix, couldn't unwind. "My audition is in nine days. Then you can look at me yourself and know that it's just been stress. And when I play that final note for the committee, I know I'll be myself again. I know it." I would let Will go. My future would be set.

Mother rubbed her hand over her bare lips. "Finley, I love you. After all we've been through, I just want you to be able to talk to me. To tell me what you're feeling."

"And I have."

She let out a breath, and her bangs fluttered against her forehead. "I want you to take it easy. That audition isn't worth getting so upset."

"Trust. Me." Angry tears melted down my cheeks. "You told me before I came to Ireland that you were giving me my freedom, that you were trusting me to take care of myself. Now let me do that."

"And this is nothing more than audition anxiety?"

"Yes." My voice begged with her to let this go. "Yes."

"Maybe it is nothing," Mom said. "I hope and pray it is. But all I have to go on is what these ladies are telling me. And the fact that you passed out Saturday is frightening. I want to see you in person, hug you, and know that you are safe and okay."

And if you're not, I'll bring you home. She didn't say it, but it was there. An unspoken promise.

My mom didn't believe me. None of them did.

"And you will. Next week." I shook my head as the panic spiraled with the force of a tornado. "I have to get back to class."

"Give us a hug." Nora stood up and held out her arms. "We care about you. I want Abbeyglen to be a peaceful place for you. I want to see you happy."

"And I will be." Please let her *believe* me. "Soon."

"But I couldn't live with myself if we didn't make sure we were doing everything to help you, love. You've become like my own daughter."

Guilt. Grief. Humiliation. It choked me until I was coughing. "I have to go." I flung open the door and stumbled into the hall on rubbery legs.

God, they're so wrong. Like I needed one more thing to deal with. Where are you? Why don't you hear me? Why don't you speak to me?

Finding the first water fountain, I leaned over it and let the cool water fall over my lips and slide down my throat.

I'd had it. I was done with God's silence.

Running down the hall, not caring who I passed or that I had tracks of mascara streaking down my face, not even concerned that I was expected back in class, I got to the music room and ripped open the door.

I sat at the piano, pressed my feet to the pedals, placed my shaking fingers on the chipped keys.

And played.

Tears fell unchecked as Will's song flooded the room. I put every bit of anger, every ounce of fear into the notes, closing my eyes and letting the melody saturate and wrap around my heart like a bandage.

And then I got to the end.

And stopped.

The song just died. Why couldn't I simply write a few measures and be done? Why hadn't anything worked?

What if there was no end?

What if it was bottomless as my grief? That it just . . . never stopped.

"God, you've taken so much from me," I said into the deafening silence. "Why? And every time I turn to you, I just feel more alone. Where are you when I call? Where were you when my brother died? Why won't you talk to me?"

"Because you're not truly listening."

I turned, dashing my tears, my cheeks blushing scarlet. "Sister Maria."

She walked down the aisle like a mighty avenger and sat beside me on the piano bench. "Bad day?" She reached into her pocket and handed me a tissue.

I just nodded. And burst into tears again. "I can't do this. I don't know how to . . . just live a normal day."

"So your normal got changed. You will survive this."

"You don't understand."

"Then tell me."

How? "I've done some stupid things. And I thought I had it under control. That's all I've ever wanted, just to fix things. To make it all okay. To make this black feeling go away once and for all. But it hasn't. And I don't think it ever will."

"You're still convinced God doesn't hear you?"

"Would my life be such a mess if he did?"

"If you're doing it all your way, yes." Sister Maria propped her elbow on some keys and gave me a small smile. "Didn't a fellow named Peter once walk on water? We're all asked to do this throughout our lives. It just looks different for each one of us." Her bony fingers gripped my wrist. "Right now, this is *your* time. And Jesus has been waiting . . . hands out, saying, 'Eyes on me. I've got you.'"

"Like it's that easy. Like I haven't been trying."

"To truly try means to accept God's love, his healing, to accept the world can be ugly, but your heart doesn't have to be. It takes courage, Finley the warrior. You haven't held on to your anger and bitterness in search of healing, but as a banner of your hurt. Because it's real and visible and strong," she said. "But so is God's love and so are those arms he's holding out for you."

"I read my Bible and I see nothing. And when I pray, I feel . . . nothing. I'm so sick of that. That . . . emptiness."

"And yet it becomes like an addiction, doesn't it?" Sister Maria's crystal-blue eyes seared into mine. "Because it's something you've come to know and trust. Closing your heart to God and the rest of the world won't fill those raw places. It just makes more room for Satan to settle in your heart. Makes his lies easier to believe—that you're not worthy, that God doesn't truly care. That he didn't care about your brother, your family, or you. Finley, you can't hear the Lord's voice over all that distraction, even over the sounds of your own pretty music."

It sounded too simple. "You're a nun. You're supposed to tell me God cares, that he's been there all the time."

"When it's Satan, he leaves his calling card—destruction.

That's how you know it's him. And that's certainly what you're dealing with. Is that what your brother would want, then?"

"No," I said. "He was so at peace with God. So full of faith and hope . . . and then he was gone." I sniffed and blew my nose in the tissue. "Sometimes I think what his final moments must've been like and I can hardly stand it."

"Jesus was there. Waiting. With those same arms out. He loves your brother more than even you do. And he grieves with you. God's been speaking—in this beauty of Ireland, in the majesty of the cliffs, in the healing rhythm of the waves, in the words of Mrs. Sweeney. In your brother's journal." Sister Maria gave my hand a squeeze, and her skin felt as soft as a baby's. "He says, 'I'm here. Waiting. When you're ready to trust what you know . . . and not what you feel.'"

What had Beckett said that night at the tower ruin? Trust truth? These two made it sound so simple.

"You can't walk on water holding all that weight," Sister Maria said. "It just makes you sink right down. Let it go, my dear. Your anger isn't keeping Will's memory alive."

"This is all I've known for the last two years."

"Look at Mrs. Sweeney. She's had a wasting disease most of her living days. Fear held her back." Sister Maria shook her head. "All those lost years. Does it make sense to you—all she gave up?"

"No." No, it did not.

"You and Mrs. Sweeney—you both think you're controlling things. But really, you control nothing. Mrs. Sweeney wasn't brave enough to surrender, and neither was her sister. *Choose you this day, life or death.* Be a victory story. Don't be just another life claimed by that bomb, left in the ashes beneath the rubble of that school. I believe you've changed Mrs. Sweeney's life." Sister Maria hugged my limp body to her. "Now, let God change yours."

Chapter Thirty-One

- Hours of practice: not enough

- Hours worrying: too many

I avoided Erin and anyone else who dared to talk to me for the rest of the day. Tomorrow would be better. But today? Today was bad.

My breath came in shallow puffs, and my hands were slick with sweat on my bicycle handles as I pedaled to the set. Helping Beckett was the last thing I felt like doing right now. I just wanted to be alone in my room with my violin.

In a daze, I parked my bicycle. I saw some of the crew working outside the castle and walked to Beckett's trailer. With feet made of lead, I hoisted myself over the broken step and let myself inside. My chest jerked with a new round of tears as I reached into the refrigerator and grabbed a Diet Coke. I pressed the can to my cheek and allowed the coolness to seep into my skin before opening it, letting the familiar burn trickle down my throat.

The door swung open again, and I turned in relief. "Beckett, I've had the worst—"

"What are you doing here?" Montgomery Rush stepped inside, the door hanging open behind him. "Where's me son?" He took in my disheveled state but made no comment on it.

"I . . . I don't know." My nose dripped like a faucet. "He's probably in the castle with everyone else." It was then that I got a look at the tabloid in his hand. Not even two full days since St. Flanagan's Day, and a picture of Beckett with Erin decorated the cover.

Mr. Rush caught the direction of my stare. "Having trouble seeing the headline? It says 'Vampire Star Crashes Festival with Drunk Castmates.'"

Like I needed another reason to hurl all over the floor. "How can you do that to your son?"

"What I do *saves* me son. Domestic ticket sales on last month's release will go up ten percent this week." He tapped the paper. "All because of this."

"But it's so . . ."

"Sensational? Sleazy? Look, it's exactly what you Americans want to read. You eat it up."

"But that's not Beckett."

"He shouldn't have been at that festival in the first place, and he's lucky me assistant managed to salvage the story in the nick of time. Taylor and that cousin of hers tried to talk to me, and I wouldn't take the time to listen. But they were right—ever since Beckett came here, ever since he started hanging out with you, he's been unmanageable. Do you realize how important his image is? Taylor's part of that. Not you."

"He's your son . . . not just another deal."

"What he is, is a professional."

"Really?" My temper flared, and I was so worn down, I didn't even care. "That's not how the world sees him. Thanks to you."

"What do you know about this business? You're a liability to Beckett and all we've worked so hard for." He pointed a finger at me. "In fact, if you cared about him, you'd stop seeing him. It's not good press."

"Why? Because it paints him as a calm, normal guy?"

"You're not Hollywood enough for him." He took an assessing glance, and I knew I was found unworthy, too ugly, too plain.

"Do you even realize how unhappy Beckett is?" I asked.

"*What* is going on here?"

Heads turned as Beckett stepped into his trailer. Taylor and Beatrice followed in behind him.

"Your *friend* here was just telling me how *unhappy* you are," Mr. Rush said.

"He does all this to please you."

"Finley, be quiet." Beckett crossed the space and pulled me to his side.

"I think I know me son."

"Really?" I felt Beckett's fingers press into my arm, but I kept going, my tongue possessed by fury. "Did you know he takes online college classes? That he wants a normal life?"

"That is *enough*," Beckett growled.

"But you do. You—"

"Do you have something to tell your da'?" Mr. Rush rolled the tabloid in his hands and slapped it against his palm.

"Now would not be the time," Beckett ground out.

"Then when?" I asked. Didn't they get it? "Life is too short for this. What if you don't have tomorrow?"

"Did you learn that little platitude in the mental hospital?" Beatrice moved from behind Mr. Rush, a brilliant smirk on her ivory face.

I just stared. And shook my head.

"SeaScape Counseling," she said. "You were there, weren't you?"

Beckett exhaled as if it was torturous to even look at Beatrice. "What are you talking about, Bea?"

"Your new girlfriend," Taylor butt in. "She took a little vacation last year at a treatment facility." She tilted her head as if struggling to recall the facts.

I felt naked, exposed. And utterly alone. "How . . . how do you know about that?"

"I have my ways."

My voice rose with every word. "Like Beatrice digging in the nurse's files when she so kindly went to get a bandage for me?"

"You're a famous name in America." Beatrice's eyes glimmered with victory. "It wasn't that hard to find online."

"Actually, it would be *impossible*." I wanted the floor to swallow me alive. To pull me down, cover me up, and spit me out somewhere in Middle Earth. "The only ones who know are my parents, Nora O'Callaghan, and the school."

"Oh." Beatrice sent Beckett a pouty, sympathetic look. "Didn't Beckett know?"

I turned to him, expecting him to take up for me, to put Beatrice in her place. But he stood beside me, arms crossed, his face as hard as stone. "I think everyone needs to leave. *Now.*"

"We're not through with this," Montgomery said to Beckett as he stepped outside.

"Get out," Beckett repeated, glaring down the girls as they attempted to linger.

"We need to regroup." Taylor looked between me and her fake boyfriend. "Soon."

"We'll fix this, Taylor," I heard Mr. Rush say.

"Leave." Beckett shut the door with a slam that had me blanching. I watched him scrub his hands over his face before slowly turning around.

"Beckett, I'm sorry, but your dad—"

"I don't want to talk about that." He gestured to the chairs. "Sit down."

His tone tilted my world, and I knew something was very wrong. Something beyond Beckett's father, beyond Beatrice. "Are you breaking up with me?"

He sat beside me, stared at his hands. "Erin and I have been talking . . ."

"What Beatrice said, if you'd let me explain, I—"

"I don't care what she said." He lifted his head. "I don't care where you've been, what you've done. All I care about is now."

"I didn't stay at any clinic. I saw a counselor there. Grief therapy. Anxiety." The words bled out, and I didn't stop until Beckett put his hand on mine.

"Finley, something's wrong."

I blinked back tears.

God, God, God.

Sentences failed me. All I could manage was his name.

"I should have seen it," Beckett said.

"What?" I was afraid he wasn't going to tell me. Even more afraid he was.

"I think . . . I think you have the beginning of a problem."

I couldn't help the laugh that escaped. "Is this just pick-on-Finley day? Does the whole world think I'm crazy?"

"I don't think you're crazy." His thumb slid over my knuckles. "I think you're on the verge of . . . having an eating disorder."

My hand turned to ice in his. "Passing out was a one-time thing."

"I can't pretend I don't recognize the symptoms. I'm an actor. You think I don't see this all the time? I should've clued into it sooner."

I jerked my hand from his and stood. "I'm not anorexic. Is that what you're thinking? Do I look it to you?"

"It's not about—"

"I'm a long way from eighty-five pounds."

"Erin and I both think you're just right there at that point of no return. And I'm worried."

I could hear my pulse pounding an angry beat in my ears. "So you and Erin have been talking about me. Anyone else? Taylor? Beatrice?"

"Of course not." He rose to his feet and stood in front of me. "But I think we need to talk to Nora."

"Too late. Already talked to her today. Know what the consensus was? I'm stressed. Because I am. In case you haven't noticed, I have a lot on my mind. My whole future will be decided by next week."

"And then what?" Beckett's eyes dared me to look away. "Then what, Finley?"

"Then . . . everything will be fine."

"Will it?" He stepped away to pace in the small confines of the trailer. "Will you be over your brother then? Will you have your peace about the music? Or will you move onto something else to obsess about?"

"Like you?" I reached for my Diet Coke for something to do

with my hands. "Is that what you're afraid of—that I'll focus all my attention on you? That I'll have time on my hands to think I'm your *real* girlfriend?"

"That's not fair, and you know it."

"But I'm not your real girlfriend. I'm the girl you're seeing in secret. The one your dad wants to write out of your script. Permanently."

"You're more than that. You've become my closest friend, the person I want to spend my time with. If anyone has my heart, it's you."

"But that's not good for your image, is it? So you continue to let your dad feed all these stories to the press. My face with yours wouldn't sell tickets. But Taylor's does."

"We're talking about you. And the fact that you need help."

There was a knot in my chest where oxygen should've been. "I don't need your help or anyone else's."

Beckett stopped in front of me, held my shoulders in his hands. "I've seen this. Do you hear what I'm saying to you? I know how it starts, and I know how it ends. I've seen the way you run like hell itself is chasing you. The way you have to control everything you touch, be so perfect." He swallowed and his Adam's apple bobbed. "I saw you slip your food into your napkin that night we were here."

"The roast was bad."

"No." He shook his head, his eyes calling me a liar. "That's not true."

A sob worked its way up my throat and I tried to breathe it away. "I'm tired, Beckett. I just want to go home and—"

"And pretend like this is going away? Play that violin until your bow snaps in two?"

"Yes! So what if I do? And then hopefully at some point the

ending will write itself. Because we didn't find my brother's cross, so the song is still wrong. It's wrong!" And my audition would be wrong.

"What's messed up right now is you. Eating disorders are—"

"Just shut up!" I wanted him to stop talking about it. Like it was a brand I had to wear. "What about you? Like you're perfect? I'm not the only screwup here, am I? Why don't you come clean with your dad?"

His brow slowly lifted. "I think you've already done that for me."

"Tell him you hate acting. Tell him you want to go to school. Is that really so hard? Maybe it's just easier looking at someone else's problems."

"This is different."

"Is it?" I got right in his beautiful face. "Don't stand there in judgment of me when you're living a lie too. You think everyone's fake, a phony. Well, you're the king of it. You don't even have the guts to live your own life. You're just Montgomery Rush's puppet."

Beckett stared at me so hard, I took an involuntary step back.

I expected him to yell and roar, but instead, in the silence of that moment, he closed his eyes, as if he was summoning up every ounce of his strength not to toss me out of the trailer with his bare hands.

"Finley." His voice was deadly calm when he finally spoke. "I let you in more than I've ever let anyone into my life. I thought we had something. No matter what it appeared, it was real to me. Every second. I've been honest about that."

"It's not enough," I said, surprised by my own words. Because this boy had a piece of me, and he'd been my brightest spot in Abbeyglen. "I won't date someone who lets the world think he's somebody else."

"And you're not doing the exact same thing, then?"

I looked at his stubbled face, his blond hair falling over his forehead, those full lips I'd kissed. The eyes that had shown me nothing but kindness. Until today. "I can't do this anymore."

"Finley—"

"No, Beckett. It's over. We're over."

He pointed right at me. "You want to break up with me, you do it for the right reason. Don't walk away from me just because I'm the first one to say you could be anorexic. Have the guts to face this."

I shook my head. "This is about you. I'll never be Taylor. I'll never be good enough. If I were, you'd tell your dad, you'd tell the world that she's not your girlfriend."

"I have people depending on these movies. Hundreds of people. We have to handle it just right."

"You sound like your father." My arrow hit the mark, and I grabbed my purse. I was done here.

"You need help," he said as I put my hand on the door. "You know I have to talk to Sean and Nora."

"You can't fix me, Beckett. No one can. Apparently even God himself can't. I'm asking you not to go to the O'Callaghans. For me. It's all I want from you."

"I can't do that. No matter what you think, I care about you."

"The audition. Just give me 'til then. Then it won't matter what you say or who you tell." Because I had absolutely nothing left.

He gave a weary sigh, then nodded once. "You have 'til then."

Chapter Thirty-Two

Just a short time in Ireland, yet I know I am
forever changed . . .

—Travel Journal of Will Sinclair, Abbeyglen, Ireland

"What're you doing here? So early."

I walked into Mrs. Sweeney's room at Rosemore at seven Friday morning, with my violin case in my hand and the whole world on my shoulders. Normally I would've been running, which was exactly what my body craved. But today I was here.

"I thought I'd stop by and see you."

"Getting your last hour in." Her slurred voice was so weak and slow, she didn't sound like herself. Or look like herself. An oxygen tube was strapped in her nose and an IV plugged into her papery hand.

"How did you know I had one more hour to go?" She didn't answer, but she didn't have to. Nothing got by Mrs. Sweeney. I settled into the chair beside an untouched breakfast of some meal replacement. Lately when I came, that was all she had. Something she could swallow now that she barely had the energy to chew. Or the stomach to keep it down. The canned drink looked vile, and she'd told me as much.

"I finished my audition piece last night."

She licked her lips. "Happy?"

Not in years. "It'll do. Would you like me to read to you?"

She shook her head against the white pillowcase.

"I have a new Stephen King. Guaranteed to make you smile. And give me nightmares."

"No," she whispered as her eyes drifted shut.

We sat there in the hush of her room as the hands of the clock moved much too quickly. Outside in the hall, a nurse pushed a cart with medicine and aids delivered trays of breakfast for those starting their morning. Or counting their remaining hours.

My own breakfast was oatmeal, which had seemed to grow and multiply in the bowl. I'd swallowed some of it down, telling myself that the steel-cut oats the O'Callaghans served were crazy healthy and whole grain and all of that nutritious stuff. Though that had been hours ago, my stomach still felt like it had blown up twice its size. My uniform stretched across my body too tightly. And my lack of sleep the past four nights weighed me down to the point I must've looked like a total slug.

The night before, Erin had watched my every bite, just like she had every meal that week. I'd eaten half a chicken breast.

And shoved the other half in my napkin when no one was looking. I broke it into pieces and later flushed it down the toilet.

And then I sat down on the lid and cried.

Maybe I was that girl.

The one who was losing the battle with the emptiness.

It had started out so simple. To lose a few pounds. And then the weight started flying off when I began riding my bicycle, and it had become something I could count on, control. I liked it. I did.

"Mrs. Sweeney . . ." My eyes glazed over with renewed sadness as I brought my thoughts back to my dying friend. "I'm sorry about your sister. Beckett and I tried talking to her again."

She nodded. "He told me."

"Oh." Just the thought of him made me hurt. "You've seen him?"

Eyes still closed, she moved a finger toward her dresser where a giant bouquet of roses sat. "From Beckett?"

She didn't respond, but I could see the card from there. And his name.

"He and I kind of got into a fight," I said. "We said some . . . stupid things. He thinks—" Could I even say it? "Well, he thinks I don't take care of myself very well. But it's so hard to live up to this ideal girl he has in his head. Most guys want supermodel, Hollywood, full of drama. Beckett wants someone who doesn't mind his double life. And he's mad because he thought I was something and I'm not. I couldn't be any further from his idea of this girl who has it together." Why was I blathering on like this? I couldn't seem to shut up. "And my parents think I have issues too. But I could turn it around right now if I wanted to."

But then why was I still ravaged by guilt for eating dinner? And why did breakfast make me want to go to the bathroom and throw it all up?

"I don't know what's wrong with me," I said.

Her hand moved a few inches toward me on the bed, and when I looked up, Mrs. Sweeney's glassy eyes were on mine.

I reached out and lightly covered my fingers with hers. "I'm sorry about your sister, Mrs. Sweeney. I thought I could fix it. I seem to think I can fix everything, but I can't. And I messed up. But you apologized to her over and over. You tried to explain it, and if she didn't have the grace to forgive you and *thank* you, then she is the one in the wrong. I hope you can . . ." *Die with some sort of peace. Not take bitterness with you when you go.* "I hope you can trust that what you did for her was an amazing sacrifice. I can't imagine what you gave up, what you endured. And all to save your father and to keep your sister from that horrible man."

Her hand clutched mine, and I just kept talking. "God wants you to know that you are forgiven. You don't need to ask one more time because your slate was wiped clean decades ago. And he loves you. He's always loved you. When that husband treated you bad, when he couldn't show you love, God had your heart right in his hand." I didn't know where the words came from, but they poured out of me like I was Sister Maria. "You are beautiful and worthy. And you're going to be reunited with your son, and you'll never be in pain again. Do you believe that, Mrs. Sweeney?"

Tears trickled from both her eyes. She pressed on my hand again.

A hundred thousand words spun in my head like snowflakes in a winter storm, but none seemed right for what was in my heart, for what this woman needed to hear. "Your sister will see the truth." *Though maybe not this side of heaven.* "And she'll regret all the years she didn't get to have you in her life." I leaned down and pressed a kiss to Mrs. Sweeney's cool forehead. "Because she missed out on knowing what a wonderful person you are."

"Play." She pointed to my violin. "Play."

"Are you sure you're up for it?"

She nodded.

So I did.

I picked up the bow, set it to my violin, and let Will's song pour out. In each movement, I saw him on the cliffs, watching the waves at Lahinch, looking over the edge of the forge on the island, losing his heart to the music of Galway. I played my guts out, praying the music would heal one girl and one woman from their heavy sprits, their hollowed hearts.

I struck the final A-flat, drawing it out, letting it echo in the room, above the beep of Mrs. Sweeney's IV. Above the beating of my heart.

Mrs. Sweeney sniffed, then mumbled something.

"What?" I leaned closer to her.

"I know . . . that melody, that loneliness you play." She took a labored breath, her frail chest rising beneath her gown. "The ending's still wrong."

"It's the best I could do," I whispered.

"Needs hope." Eyes closed, tears slipped down her alabaster cheeks. "For me . . . please." Her hand reached for mine. "Find your hope."

Chapter Thirty-Three

STEELE MARKOV

This hunger, it gnaws at me. And if I let it go—what would remain?

Fangs in the Night, scene 8, page 49
Fierce Brothers Studios

Saturday morning.

Nobody had said another word about "the incident" to me. The family tiptoed around, and I knew they were waiting for tomorrow, when I would be my parents' problem again, at least temporarily. I hoped.

I'd just run the flatiron through my hair for the last time when I got a text.

Meet me at the bottom of the stairs.

Beckett.

I hadn't talked to him in exactly one hundred and twelve hours, and he hadn't been coming to the dinner table and eating with the family. Yet he never left my mind.

The phone dinged again.

Ignore me, and I'll come up and get you.

Though that sent a cautious thrill down my spine, I slipped a headband over my hair, letting the minutes stretch out as I made my bed, tidied up my desk, and finally slid into my flats and went downstairs, one hesitant step at a time.

Beckett stood in the living room, talking to Sean. Conversation stopped when he saw me.

"Good morning to you," Beckett said evenly.

"Good morning." What if he was right about me?

"Well, I'd best check on my banana cake." Sean walked back into the kitchen, whistling a tune, oblivious to the awkwardness rushing through the room.

"How have you been?" I asked.

Beckett's eyes studied my face. "You're not sleeping."

I inhaled, focusing on drawing air through my lungs. Trying to keep my heart from falling from my chest. "I've been practicing a lot. Composing. I thought I had the ending for the song, but . . . turns out I didn't."

"I need you to come with me."

I blinked at his abrupt tone. "I don't believe that's a good idea."

"This isn't about"—he lowered his voice—"*that.*"

"I still don't—"

"I found it." He held up a copy of my brother's cross. "I found it."

His words were a miraculous chorus. I stood there and let them repeat in my head. "How is that possible?"

"I checked nearly every gravestone within fifty miles of here. Even hired some people back in the States to research online. But I found it yesterday. I don't know why I didn't think of this place to begin with." He waved the photo. "Clonmacnoise."

"Is it close?"

"It's about a two-hour drive." He squashed a hat down over his head, another partial disguise for the day. "We can get there and get you back so you can pack for New York."

"I don't know." How could I be in the same truck with Beckett when I missed him? And when I was furious with him? "I have a lot to do today."

"You've been waiting for this for weeks. Don't miss it just because of your stupid pride."

"Such pretty words," I said. "I'm getting all flustered just standing here."

"Get your coat."

"I'm still mad at you."

"Duly noted."

❧

Two hours and ten minutes later, turning off a curling narrow road in the middle of nowhere, we reached the parking lot at Clonmacnoise.

"And what exactly is this place again?" We were so busy in the truck not discussing how screwed up he thought I was, I'd forgotten to ask.

"An old monastery. It goes back more than four hundred years. Monks from all over Europe came to pray and study here."

He was strangely quiet, and I wondered why he was even doing this.

Because he was a guy of his word.

We wove through a small museum that explained some of the history, but, sensing my urgency, Beckett pressed his hand to my back and led me through a crowd of people through the various rooms and, finally, outside.

Leaving the darkness of the exhibit, I squinted against the sun as we stepped onto the grass.

There before us was a sight that stole the breath from my body.

Celtic crosses. Hundreds of them. Ivory, gray, white, in all shapes and sizes. If peace was a place, the map would lead a person right here.

"Oh," I said. "Wow."

Beckett slipped his sunglasses over his eyes and looked at the dramatic spread before us. "I know. It's stunning."

"It's . . ." I took a few steps, hardly able to take it all in. "Holy. It's holy and reverent."

Many people walked about, but few spoke. It reminded me of the silence of Arlington Cemetery, a place my parents had taken us one summer. Yet these grounds were much older. The sun shined brighter over the white crosses, the sky that stretched over us seemed bluer. The River Shannon flowed in the background, a contrast of life against the emblems of death.

But it wasn't what I saw.

It was what I felt.

A presence. *A power.* Like invisible arms wrapping me in a hushed embrace.

"That's an old cathedral. St. Ciaran's," Beckett said. A ruin stood in the center, just walls, and we walked toward it. "Look at the way the sky looks so blue through what's left of the window openings."

It wasn't just the ruin, it was everything. The riot of headstones and crosses. Their stark white shapes against the vivid green grass beneath them and the cloudless sky above. I had to walk the grounds, touch the stones. My fingers ran over inscriptions, the shapes and designs, the rough grain, the textures so cool to the touch.

God, you are here.

As sure as I breathe, I know you are.

In a cemetery of all things. Markers of death all around me.

Blackbirds flew and called overhead before landing on one of the towers. Soon many more followed, their *caw*s an abrupt intrusion to the stillness of the morning.

"They're always around." Beckett pointed to a group in a tree. "They flock here by the hundreds."

"It's like they hover on the perimeter. Like the dark is always there." Waiting.

"But dark doesn't win." He watched me. "It doesn't here. And it didn't for your brother. And it won't for you, Finley."

My laugh was small, awkward. "You sound so sure."

"Come on." He took my hand and pulled me through the graves.

The sun warmed my skin as my feet trod over the uneven terrain. "They all look so similar," I said. "Are you sure it's the one?"

"I know it is." After passing by three more rows, he stopped. "There. Check the picture."

And he was right. The very stone my brother captured in the photo.

It stood there a little crooked, with a lean to the left. In the center was a circle, linking to the stem and arms of the weathered cross. Celtic knots filled the bottom, mostly faded and one-dimensional from time. Behind the cross were three more that looked almost identical to it. But this one was different.

Because it was the one that had caught my brother's eye. And was significant enough to be glued to the last page of his journal.

I eased to the ground and wiped away some of the dust from the engraving at the base. "Eamon McDonagh."

Beckett stooped down beside me, his knee touching mine. "Can't make out the date, but it doesn't look to be as ancient as some of the others. Maybe a couple hundred years old."

I struggled to decipher the faint Celtic font. "Can you read that?" The writing was so faded and timeworn, I feared the words on the cross would be lost. And so would my brother's message.

Beckett scooted closer and took off his sunglasses. "'Nay, in all these things' . . ." He paused and squinted. "'We are more than conquerors through him that loved us.'"

My hand automatically reached out and pressed against the letters. "Romans 8:37." Tears pooled in my eyes. "It's my verse."

"What do you mean?"

I swallowed hard and tried to breathe in some courage. Goose bumps danced on my arms, and I knew I was in one of those moments God had designed just for me. "When my parents got me that last counselor, I had to pick a verse, my battle cry. Every time I felt down or just needed help, I was to say my verse out loud. That was mine."

Beckett pulled out his phone and touched the screen. His brow furrowed as he scrolled until he found what he was looking for. "You're right." He held it up, and I saw the verse in bold black letters. "Do you know the rest of it?" he asked.

"I don't think so." I shrugged. "When you're dealing with evil and darkness, you tend to keep it short and sweet."

Beckett's hand found my arm. "Finley, read it."

"I really don't think—"

"Just read it."

I took the phone and sighed.

"Out loud. Like it's your battle cry."

Humiliation warred with curiosity as I focused on the next few verses. "'For I am persuaded' . . ." I cleared my throat and tried to listen to my own voice. "'That neither death, nor life, nor angels, nor principalities, nor powers, nor things present, nor things to come, nor height, nor depth, nor any other creature, shall be able to separate us from the love of God, which is in Christ Jesus our Lord.'"

My heart filled, the emptiness disappearing drop by drop.

And I read it again.

Neither death nor life would have the power to separate me from the love of God.

No height, no depth could separate me from the love of God.

It was just like Sister Maria said. That he'd been there all along, a constant. But I wasn't willing.

Just like this cross had sat there for hundreds of years, the rest of my message was in that verse the whole time. Waiting for me to find it. Waiting for me to believe it. And live it.

"Sister Maria tried to tell me. But I wouldn't listen to her. I haven't been listening to anyone." My fingers caressed the hard lines of the grave. "My mind's so filled with . . . junk. I can't . . . I couldn't hear anything good. Couldn't hear God. I thought . . . I thought he had left me. Just like my brother had." Tears flowed unchecked as I turned to Beckett. "Beckett, I'm sorry. I was wrong about so much."

He reached out his hand and wiped the moisture from my cheek. "No, I'm sorry, Fin."

The thoughts crashed and tumbled, and I didn't know where to start. "I don't know that I have an eating disorder, but . . . something is wrong." I hadn't been able to eat breakfast again that morning, and I knew. I *knew* I needed help. Beckett clasped my hands in his and just listened. "I'm not who everyone thinks I am," I said after a moment passed by. "Lately I . . . I feel better when I'm hungry, when my stomach hurts. When I see the scale dip, I get this rush of total joy. And I've been looking for happiness for two years." It was out. I'd said it. And Beckett still stood beside me, holding my hand. "And . . . I'm scared. I don't know what I'm going to tell my mom. She's had so much sadness lately, I can't stand what this will do to her." But I knew I had to tell her.

"She'll be proud of you for giving her the truth," Beckett said. "That's all anybody wants, some honesty. And you'll go back and fight this. And if I know you, and I think I do"—he ran his thumb across my cheek—"you'll come out of this stronger and better than ever."

"I was meant to see this cross, that inscription. And you found it for me." The wind blew, and my hair flew around my face. "Why would you spend so much energy on this?"

Beckett's mouth slowly curved. "In case you hadn't noticed, I've totally fallen for you, Finley Sinclair." I wanted to press pause on his words, then rewind them over and over. "And because I know what it meant to you. You're looking for closure, and this is one thing you can put to rest." He lifted his face to the sun and gave a small smile, letting my hands fall from his. "My real name is Michael Shaunessy. Me da' changed it when I was three, and Beckett Rush was born. I'm crazy about Shark Week, Dickens novels, and comic books. I don't understand most foreign films, and no matter how much I brag, I don't like Mrs. O'Callaghan's corned beef." His voice fell low and deep as his gaze held mine. "And not too long ago, I hurt a lovely, wounded girl. I haven't been able to stand myself since.

"Tomorrow a story will hit the media, telling the world Taylor and I are over." He took off his hat, showing his face for all to see. "There's a new girl in my life—when she's ready."

With tears in my eyes, I leaned over and kissed him. My lips covered his with all the heart I had left, even those dark and dangerous parts that cried out for repair. As Beckett's hands cradled my face and the sharp breeze pushed against my back, something bloomed inside, like a flower pushing through the ground in the winter chill. There was life for me. And I wanted to live it.

"I've missed you." Beckett kissed my forehead, held his lips against my temple.

"I missed you too. I've been running our fight over in my head. Everything I said was wrong."

"No, you weren't. I realized you said some things that were true as well. I talked to me da' a few days ago." He paused to let a couple walk around us. "I told him I wasn't going to do anymore movies for a while, and I needed a break. Some time to get my head together, figure out what I want to do. And some space to be a normal guy. I want to take Bob fishing. Go to the beach. Maybe train for a triathalon."

"That last part really isn't normal."

"I want to check out some colleges and see if maybe I want to go to school full-time on this hiatus."

"What did your dad say?"

"Too much." Beckett watched some tourists two rows over. "We had a big fight, then he left. I haven't talked to him since."

"I know that's killing you."

"We have to refigure our roles, you know? I need a father right now. Not a manager."

"So no more vampires?"

"Filming wraps up next week, then I'm officially retiring my fangs."

"Girls' hearts will be shattered."

He tipped up my chin, and his steady gaze locked on mine. "I'm only worried about one girl's heart."

Oh. My.

"I'm messed up," I said. "I mean I'm completely jacked up. You get that, right? As in petrified, have no idea what's going to become of me, *jacked* up. My mind is not in a good place, my sense of reality—apparently it's kinda skewed."

Beckett pulled me to him and wrapped me in his arms. "I've dealt with Hollywood actors for years. I think I might be some good support, so I do."

"I'm one big panic attack waiting to happen," I said against his chest. "Do you really want to be around to see that?"

"Yes. I do." He kissed the top of my head. "You can do this, Finley. I know you can heal."

"Wait . . ." I put my ear to the wind and listened to the sounds around me.

The melody entered my heart, and I saw the notes fall into place in the last few bars of Will's song.

I had to hum it, seal it in my spirit.

Beckett smiled. "You getting something there?"

"Yeah." I laughed, really laughed. "I think I finally have it."

"And what is it?"

"Hope," I said. "I'm humming Mrs. Sweeney's hope."

Beckett held my hand in his. "And your own?"

"Maybe." I nodded. "Just maybe."

God, I don't know what lies ahead or what will happen next. But you're going to be there, aren't you? Even when the world tricks me into thinking you're not. Things are going to be different. I'm going to be different. And I'm going to get it right this time.

"So why do you believe your brother put the photo on a blank page?" Beckett asked as we both looked up at Will's cross.

I thought of the picture glued into that final spot in his journal.

"Because it was my story to finish all along."

Chapter Thirty-Four

- Days 'til audition: 2

A re you sure you want to do this?" Beckett threw my carry-on in the back of his truck beside Bob, who waved at me with his cheery tail.

"I have to. I've waited an eternity for this."

He opened my passenger door as the morning mist covered us both. "You could stay here, and I could show you some sexy vampire tricks."

I leaned up on tiptoe and kissed his lightly stubbled cheek. "I don't even want to know what that means."

"Finley, your brother—"

"I know." I slid into the seat and buckled in. "But I'm going to play for him." I had added the last few measures. It was finally perfect.

"And you'll let it go."

Beckett raised a brow at my pause.

"Yes, then I'm sure I'll let it go."

He drove me to the Shannon airport, where he reluctantly let me off at the curb. "I could go with you."

"You could. And that's really sweet of you. But I need to talk to my parents. Alone."

"Promise you'll be back?"

"One way or another." Even if it was just to get my stuff and say my good-byes. My parents were serious about my health. There was a really good chance I wouldn't be finishing this year in the program.

Beckett helped me with my bag, then pulled me in for a kiss. I relaxed into his arms, loving the feel of his strong chest and the security of his embrace.

"Be careful," he said. "Call me if you need me. Night or day." He gave Bob a pat on the head, then walked around to his driver's side. "And, Finley?"

"Yes?"

"You're gonna rock this thing."

I nodded and pulled my jacket tighter around me. "I think I will," I said. "It's right this time."

For the next hour and a half, I waited for my plane in a crowd of screaming babies, a woman yelling into her phone, a man three times the size of me, plus two nuns who looked ninety if they were a day.

In all these things, I am more than victorious . . .

"Flight 1028 to New York now boarding groups two and three."

With nerves jittery from caffeine and adrenaline, I handed the woman my ticket and walked onto the plane. I was really doing this.

Crawling at a snail's pace, I followed the line as we made our way to our seats, stopping to let passengers fill overhead bins and make the transition into their seats.

I finally sat down in 12C, smiling at the woman knitting on my right who occupied the window seat. I pulled out my iPod, wanting to catch a quick listen of Will's song before takeoff. I was just putting in my earbuds when my phone rang.

"Forgot to turn that off." I scrambled into my bag and dug out my phone. "Hello?"

"Finley, it's Belinda. From Rosemore. I wanted to let you know Cathleen took a turn for the worse last night. She's not expected to make it through the day."

My bubble of happiness shattered. "I'm on my way to my audition."

"Honey, I just wanted you to know. If you were here, she wouldn't even know you were in the room."

"Did her sister ever show up?"

"No."

"Mrs. Sweeney's all alone?"

"We're here."

But it wasn't the same. She didn't have someone to brush her hair. Or hold her hand. Or read her Stephen King.

Or play the violin.

"I'll see you when you get back," Belinda said. "No worries. She knew you cared about her, she did. And that's what's important." And the line went dead.

Mrs. Sweeney was alone. Just like she'd been her entire life, with no one to care about her—except the staff.

But I had to get to New York. My entire future depended on this. This was me reclaiming part of my life. Sharing my tribute to Will. I could feel good about the fact that I had put in my time with Mrs. Sweeney. Been one of her only friends.

I held my phone and absently touched the screen as my mind spun.

Before I knew it, I'd pulled up my pictures and my fingers automatically went to a familiar set.

And then I was looking at my brother's face. The last photo he'd sent me, just two days before the explosion. Will stood in the middle of a dusty, barren plot of land surrounded by smiling children holding books. His kids. His school.

It was a picture of life. Of joy.

Of love.

"Excuse me." I gathered my bag, then reached overhead and extracted my carry-on. "Excuse me." Waddling through the aisle, I found the first flight attendant.

"Is there a problem?" the petite blonde asked.

I wanted to do what would honor Will the most, not chase another patch for this heart.

"Miss, is there something wrong?"

"Yes." But I was about to make it right. "I'm supposed to be somewhere else."

⤗⤙

When the taxi dropped me off at the nursing home, I bypassed the nurses' desk and went straight to Mrs. Sweeney's room.

Please let it not be too late, God.

Pushing open the door, I took a breath as I found Mrs. Sweeney right where I left her last, lying in her bed. But this was not the Mrs. Sweeney I knew. She was still as the room, her face pinched in discomfort. Her skin looked pale against the sun that had managed to trickle in through the crack of her curtain.

I sat in my usual chair and picked up her hand. The tears that had become my constant companion of late fell hot and quick. "Mrs. Sweeney," I whispered. "I . . . I have so much to tell you. I didn't go to New York. I wanted to be here, with you. Because my brother's gone. And nothing I do is going to get him back or make up for what happened. But you taught me that—that I need to live for the people who are here and let go of the bitterness and anger. It sucks away your life, and I'm tired of living like that. But being here with you? He would've loved that. He would've loved to have met you." My voice thickened. "I wanted to tell you that even though neither of us wanted to hang out with each other in the beginning, I grew to love it. Our talks, even though I was the one doing most of the talking. Reading your scary books. Just seeing your face. You've changed me." Her hand was cold in mine, and I could feel her every bone. "And I think you're brave. For what you did for your sister. I want to be brave like that. So . . . I'm going home. Back to America." The words came out fractured and hitched as the decision hit my lips in the same instant it settled in my mind. "I need to get my head straight about some things, and I'm going back. I know I can't stay here. But I'm not leaving you. I'm going to be right here the whole time." *The whole time it takes for you to die. To leave this world and leave me.*

But this time, I wasn't going to be angry. And I wasn't going to blame anyone. Because it had been a gift.

"Mrs. Sweeney, where you're going there isn't going to be any more pain or hurt. You are going to be loved and adored and happy. I can see you dancing in heaven now with your son. Smiling, laughing." I took a moment and rested my head on my arm, quietly crying as life slipped away. "Thank you," I whispered. "Thank you for being my friend. And for all you taught me. For all you trusted me with. I will never forget you. Never." I pulled out my phone and pressed buttons until the song played. "I redid this ending. For us." I smiled, thinking how proud Sister Maria would be.

A knock sounded behind me, and turning, I saw a familiar face standing in the door.

"Hello," I said. "Come in."

Fiona Doyle took one look at her sister and began to sob. "I wanted to talk to her. To tell her I was sorry. To thank her . . . and I've lost my chance." Mrs. Doyle held on to the rails of Mrs. Sweeney's bed, her shoulders shaking. "It's too late."

Standing, I took Mrs. Doyle's trembling hand and joined it with Mrs. Sweeney's. "It's never too late."

Three hours later, in the dark of the room, surrounded by Nurse Belinda, Fiona Doyle, and me, Cathleen Sweeney took her last labored breath. And stepped into the arms of Jesus.

Because I believed she was in heaven.

Finally living her life.

When I left the nursing home, I placed one more important call.

"Mom?" The green of Abbeyglen splayed all around me as I stood outside and breathed it in, capturing its beauty with my heart and mind, and making a silent promise that one day I would return.

When I'd completely healed.

When I was whole.

"I didn't get on the plane. No, I'm fine. I mean . . . no, I'm not okay. Mom, I need to come home."

In all these things, I am more than victorious through Him who loves me.

"I'm ready to come home."

Epilogue

Two years later

The fall wind makes a grab for my hair as I run across the campus of the New York Conservatory. My shoes swoosh across the cut grass as the sun warms my face. I hold the string tighter in my hand and stop and watch overhead.

Where my white kite dances and soars above.

"I thought we were studying for midterms."

I turn and find Beckett Rush standing behind me, a backpack slung over one shoulder and laughing eyes trained right on me.

"It's too nice a day. We need a break."

"You sound more like a senior than a freshman." He walks to me, wraps his arms around my waist, and kisses my warm cheek. He gestures to the kite. "Did you learn this in your support group?"

The one I go to once a week. The one I'll be leading beginning next month. "Nope. Did you make a decision about that script?"

"Da' and I are still discussing it."

Since Beckett's only doing one movie a year now in between his studies at NYU, he has to make it count. And so far he has.

Last year he got a Golden Globe Award for his portrayal of a young Charles Dickens in a small indie film. Good roles are starting to come his way.

And so far, no biting required.

"Bring it back in a bit," Beckett says. "Your kite's getting too far out."

But I don't.

Instead I think of it touching heaven, sending a hello to my brother Will. To Mrs. Sweeney.

This Christmas Beckett and I will return to Ireland, to visit some of his mother's relatives and to put flowers on Mrs. Sweeney's grave. Which is right by her son's.

The woman who taught me to let go. Let God in. And mend.

To let love fly like a kite in the clouds, untethered by darkness and hurt.

Four years ago my brother Will died, and my world crumbled into a million tiny fragments.

Two years ago I went to Ireland.

I met an arrogant vampire, an angry old woman, and a mischievous nun.

And I met God.

Who slowly, painfully, divinely pieced me back together.

A huge gale blows across the commons. "Hold on to it, Finley." Beckett reaches for my string.

But it's too late.

I let it go.

Acknowledgments

This book kicked my tail, so my tail and I would like to thank:

Everyone at Thomas Nelson Fiction for all you do for my books and for me.

Editor Natalie Hanemann for making this book better and giving me the time to start over. A few times.

Editor Becky Monds for your encouragement. You have a very kind way of saying "This stinks." I appreciate your valuable input on the book. Though you are seriously misguided in your WWE loyalties.

Editor Jamie Chavez for . . . oh, where to start? I know this book cost you a lot in time, effort, and sleep, and I am forever grateful. Thank you for sticking with me and for all I've learned through our eight books. I also appreciate all your fab Irish connections and for talking me into going myself. (And yes, I'm so challenged I require three editors.)

Ashley Schneider because you funny, girl. You funny.

Kristen Vasgaard for creating one awesome cover. I adore it.

Straight-up legit Irishman Gerry Hampson for your input and critical eye.

Orla Hampson for patiently answering my many e-mails about your Irish life. If you ever have any questions about Arkansas, let me know. The answer will probably be Razorbacks and pork rinds, but one never knows . . .

Andrea Ramsey for your wonderful advice on music and composition. You are one of the most talented people God has created, and I'm so honored to know you.

Erin McFarland, a gifted photographer and blog friend, for your kind words and for being part of the blog family.

Christa Allan for your snark, listening ear, and for being my conference BFF. From one short, lippy teacher to another, I am very grateful for your friendship and laughs.

Natalie Lloyd, brilliant author and sassy friend, for making me laugh and for the God-inspired encouragement. I am so blessed to know you and call you friend.

Cara Putman, Kim Cash Tate, Nicole O'Dell, and Cindy Thomson for the many prayers you've sent up on my behalf. I appreciate you wearing out God's ear for me.

The Southern Belle View gang, consisting of Rachel Hauck, Lisa Wingate, Marybeth Whalen, and Beth Webb Hart, for the prayers (apparently I recruited everyone in the human race to pray for me during the creation of this book) and for all the sweet tea and porch time we share at www.southernbelleview.com. Though I have to come clean—I don't like sugar in my tea. I'm sweet enough already. (Okay, no, I'm not, but that stuff is just nasty.)

Kristin Billerbeck for showing us all humor and Christian

fiction could coexist and for opening the door that led to my career. I will name my next cat after you. My current one is a barfer, and you're more worthy than that.

Lizann Tollett for the encouragement and silent messages (I'm not saying prayer again) to the Lord Jesus you sent up for me and this novel.

My family for leaving food on my doorstep during deadline crunch time when you knew my condition inside the house was akin to rabies.

Erin Valentine, for being my friend and my unpaid editor. Thank you for reading all 500 versions of this book.

Carol Roberts for your bravery, courage, and warrior-mom heart. You totally blessed me with your story and time.

Father, Son, and Holy Ghost for my career, another finished book without doing anyone bodily harm, and the ministry of fiction. You deliver me. Daily.

I had a lot of help from certified real Irish men and women. Any inconsistencies are my own fault in the name of fiction and sleep deprivation.

Reading Group Guide

1. Finley has endured a lot and didn't feel like God was in it with her. Have you ever felt distanced or abandoned from God? How do you explain this? What did Finley attribute it to?

2. Beckett is an example of how things aren't often what they seem. Describe a time either you made an incorrect assumption about someone or you were assumed to be something/someone you're not.

3. Describe Beckett's relationship with his father. What advice would you give Mr. Rush in being a more effective father?

4. Sister Maria tells Finley that Mrs. Sweeney has wasted her life in her bitterness and regrets. Explain what she means.

5. What is Finley's verse that she clings to? Describe a time you've singled out a verse to use in a particular situation. If you've never tried that, what are some verses you could use when going through times of:
    - anger
    - stress
    - doubt

6. Finley is someone who likes to be in control and likes everything to be neat and tidy. Describe where you saw this in the book. How can this be positive? How can this be negative?

7. What would you do if you suspected a friend had an eating disorder?

8. Describe the importance of music to Finley. Why was her audition piece so important? Do you have a talent or hobby in your life that means the world to you?

9. Mean girls are a reality, especially during the teen years. Why do you think Beatrice acted the way she did?

10. *If There You'll Find Me* was made into a movie, who would you cast in the parts?

ew York's social darling just woke up in her nightmare:

Oklahoma.

Problem is, it's right where God wants her.

The only thing scarier than living
on the edge is stepping off it.

A NOVEL OF LOSING FEAR
AND FINDING GOD

*Just Between
You and Me*

JENNY B. JONES

A Carol Award-winning novel

THOMAS NELSON
Since 1798

Alex Sinclair makes Lucy a proposition: pose as his
fiancée in return for the help she desperately needs.

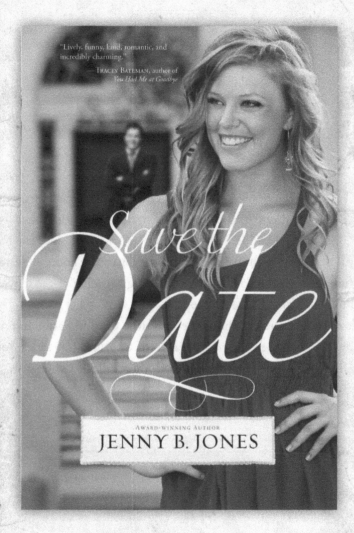

Catch Finley in this spunky romance as
her brother fumbles into love.

About the Author

Author photo by Belinda Robbins

J enny B. Jones writes Christian fiction with equal parts wit, sass, and untamed hilarity. When she's not writing, she's living it up as a high school teacher in Arkansas. Since she has very little free time, she believes in spending her spare hours in meaningful, intellectual pursuit such as watching E!, going to the movies and inhaling large buckets of popcorn, and writing her name in the dust on her furniture. She is the four-time Carol Award-winning author of *Just Between You and Me* and the Charmed Life series. You can find her at jennybjones.com and southernbelleview.com